Rachel Cusk was born in 19   vels:
Saving Agnes, which won th   ward,
T   porary, *The Country Life*, which won the Somerset
M—— Award, *The Lucky Ones*, which was shortlisted for
th   tbread Novel Award, *In the Fold, Arlington Park*,
w   as shortlisted for the Orange Prize, and *The Bradshaw
V   s*. Her non-fiction books are *A Life's Work, The Last
S   d Aftermath*. In 2003 she was chosen as one of Granta's
B   ung Novelists.

F   raise for *The Temporary*:

'C   a knowing and often funny ear for office life [and]
re   ips.' *Sunday Times*

'A   ronic tale that fights shy of easy solutions and deals
w   mmon female predicament that is largely taboo in
c   rary fiction . . . She shows the sadness of existence
w   ge of worldly-wise malice. Juggling metaphors like a
p   t, she writes as if she has been doing it since birth.'
T   ary Supplement

'T   story of a Julie Burchill heroine in a Julian Barnes
w   usk has earned all her eulogies.' *Literary Review*

'F   perceptive . . . a ruthlessly honest dissection of
m   asibilities.' *The Times*

Plea
Dych

RACHEL CUSK

The Temporary

faber and faber

First published in 1995
by Picador

This paperback edition first published in 2013 by
Faber and Faber
Bloomsbury House
74–77 Great Russell Street
London WC1B 3DA

Printed in England by CPI Group (UK) Ltd, Croydon, CR0 4YY

A CIP record for this book
is available from the British Library

ISBN 978–0–571–27211–2

2 4 6 8 10 9 7 5 3 1

For my brothers

*My thanks go to Sarah Lutyens
and Felicity Rubenstein for their diagnosis;
to Georgia Garrett of Picador for her consultations;
to my editor Katie Owen for her surgery;
and to Josh Hillman for his
excellent stitching*

One

In a call-box on Fortune Green Road, where Hampstead ends and Kilburn begins, a telephone was ringing. Francine Snaith heard it, and being possessed of the conviction that destiny had it continually in mind at any moment to summon her, felt it was intended that she should answer.

It had begun to ring just as she reached the top of the road, its call clear above the humming, dusky swarm of the pavement, and its imperative grew louder as she made her way alongside the throbbing traffic towards it. Several people walked quickly past the call-box, shaking their heads as if angered by its unsupervision, but one or two had stopped and were watching it with interest. The compelling pulse was loud in her ears as she reached the scene, and she felt herself drawn by it out of the crowd. In the glances this action drew she saw the natural acceptance of her distinction, and the busy pavement seemed to part before her. She opened the door, releasing its clamour into the street.

Once alone inside the shrilling enclosure, Francine was wrapped in warm air oily with urine and cigarettes, the manifestations of an anxiety she had often witnessed as she walked to and from the bus stop but to date had never shared; for the grooves of her daily routine, though rigid, at least ensured her safe passage past the brutalized individuals always to be glimpsed here, desperately shoving scrabbled coins into the hungry slit while from their downturned mouths Francine could occasionally hear snatches of a dark bureaucracy: 'Just one night', 'I'll pay you back', 'But you said you sent the cheque', and, most often, 'What am I supposed to do?' Her revulsion at these creatures was tempered by the safety of her distance from their misfortunes, and her confidence that the divide which separated them was fortified by sheer impossibility even permitted her to tend a small patch of pity for them. When she picked it up, the receiver was tepid and greasy with use.

'Hello?'

'Oh yes, hello,' said a man's voice, with an impatient sigh.

'Can I help you?'

'Well, yes, love,' said the man after a pause. 'As a matter of fact you can. Look to your left and you'll see a red door.'

Francine looked and was surprised to see it right there, as if it had just sauntered up and stood outside without her noticing. It was scarred with a peeling eczema of paint.

'I see it,' she said.

'Well, go over and ring the bell, if you would. Tell the bloke who lives there it's Mike for him.'

Francine placed the receiver on the metal shelf beside the phone and left the call-box. The door of the house gave directly on to the pavement and necessitated only a few steps to reach the bell. She rang it three times and when nobody answered returned to the call-box.

'There's no answer,' she said.

'Oh. Must be broken, I suppose. Try shouting up at the window on the top floor.'

'What should I shout?'

'Terry, love. Shout Terry.'

Francine left the call-box and returned to the front of the

house. A small group of people had gathered murmuring on the pavement. Having gained the impression that the situation concealed little personal profit Francine had been considering the possibility of escape from it, but the presence of an audience imbued her with exigence.

'Terry!' she shouted. 'Terry!'

Moments later she heard the pounding of footsteps and the window being opened above her. A fine snow of dry paint drifted down to her feet as the sash hit the top of the frame.

'Look, he *is* in,' said a woman nearby, pointing up.

A fat man with a dark beard put his head out.

'What?' he said.

'Mike's on the phone for you,' called up Francine.

'Oh, not again!' said the man, slapping his forehead. 'Tell him I'm busy, will you?'

He slammed the window shut and pounded off. A few seconds later the house began to shake with the sound of loud music.

'He says he's busy,' Francine dutifully relayed to Mike.

'I don't believe it!' said Mike. 'That bleeder owes me money! Three weeks I've been after him. Tell him I'll be round – go on, tell him, see how he likes that.'

'I can't,' said Francine. 'He's playing some very loud music.'

'Well, what's that got to do with anything? Chuck a brick through his window if he can't hear you. See how he likes that,' added Mike firmly.

'I don't think that's a very good idea. Why don't you write him a letter?'

'Who do you think I am? The bloody postman? I just want my money!'

'I've really got to go,' said Francine. 'Goodbye.'

She put the phone down and left the call-box. Moments later, as she walked down the darkening street, she heard it ringing again behind her. She turned into Mill Lane just as the street lamps were switched on.

She had been on her way home through the premature dark of an overcast winter afternoon from the local park, where she had spent a chilling, unsatisfactory interlude during which the rare and strenuous exercise of solitude had failed to warm her. She had gone there with the intention of substantiating the illusion of being out, lest the seeds of the previous night's party should, in her absence, bear fruit in the form of a telephone call; but also to get clear in her mind by a detailed reconstruction of events from whom she might, reasonably or not, expect one. She had been disappointed by the park, for having decided to grace the art of contemplation with her indulgence in it, it had not occurred to her that the proper accoutrements for its execution would fail to present themselves. The infrequency of her excursions into nature had given her vague, generic assumptions concerning its appearance, and in her search for the verdant scenery of thought she had not prepared herself for the discovery that such places might have problems of their own. The park was revealed to be a barren island circumnavigated by fuming rivers of Saturday afternoon traffic, unpopulated save by a small stream of pedestrians passing through it on the way to somewhere else. Lodged awkwardly on a bench at its perimeter Francine was comforted at least by the thought, which she met like an overnight train arriving from the previous evening's events, that the world was neither so complicated nor so exclusive a place as she had imagined.

Sitting there she remembered the dark, glittering room – an art gallery, she had been told – whose floor, to her secret and continuing concern, had been thickly strewn with dry autumn leaves. They had covered her feet with a light, rustling crust and she had had to kick them away with unfaltering vigilance in deference to the high-heeled shoes she had gone out and bought specially at lunch-time. There had been paintings on the walls, their violent, mangled surfaces quiet in the shadows like undisturbed car accidents, and she and Julie had looked at one or two of them, just as a laugh because no one had spoken to them yet, even though the room was alive, palpable with the proximity of flesh and the flash of faces. It had seemed like ages that they stood there on their own. Julie had been temping at the gallery for almost a month, and she kept pointing out people she knew.

'Why don't we go and talk to them?' Francine had said impatiently.

'Oh, we'd better not.'

'We look stupid just standing here.'

'Look, I'll find someone in a minute.'

While Julie had been craning her head around in search of an opportunity – so obviously, Francine thought, that it was almost embarrassing – a man with a bald head had suddenly come up and stood right in front of her. He was wearing an overcoat, even though they were indoors. To her surprise, he took her chin in his fingers and held it while he examined her face.

'Beautiful!' he said appreciatively, giving a chef's flourish with his hand.

Before Francine could say anything, he turned on his heel and swept off, his coat flapping behind him. She trailed him with her eyes in the hope that he would look at her again, but he didn't.

'Did you see that?' she said triumphantly.

To her annoyance, Julie laughed.

'Oh, that's just Fritz, one of the artists, don't mind him. He's always doing that to people. He'll probably say he wants to paint you next. He asked me to model for him once.'

'Did you do it?' She tried to hide her disappointment by looking nonchalantly around the room.

'Of course not – he'd have wanted me to take my clothes off, wouldn't he! Lara on reception says it's just his chat-up line.' She looked around too, her face haughty with experience. 'I'm not that stupid.'

Francine wondered if Julie was lying. She wasn't even that pretty. Fritz had probably gone off the idea, or maybe he hadn't even asked her at all. Also, she was so superior, acting as if her job was so wonderful and glamorous, when it was clear to Francine that everyone looked down on her. It *was* glamorous, though, being here: she had entered her own daydream and the fervent scene of her desire was all around her. The room was filled with the kind of faces she had looked at as if through shop windows, lovely, unaffordable things, the invisible throng of their luxurious, unimaginable lives springing up behind them. They glittered in their nocturnal majesty, a human zodiac cavorting across the heavens of fashion, far above the obstructed hives of office blocks, the blackened scuttling pavements, the swarming underground tunnels of the city they secretly commanded. It was everything she had hoped it would be – the proof that the things she wanted did exist! – and it only remained now for her to conquer the scene, to subdue its magic and train it with her own hand. Her envy of Julie distilled into a more palatable pity. She, after all, wore the public mark of her inferiority here, while Francine's mysteries remained intact.

'I love it here,' Julie said now, sighing. 'I could never go back to *corporate*. It's so uncreative.'

Francine wished that she could go off on her own, but then the girl called Lara that Julie had been talking about came up and started talking to them. She was quite pretty, Francine thought, but too fat. She had brushed her hair around her face to try and make it look thinner, but it was still obvious.

6

'I've just met these two hilarious blokes,' she said to Julie. She was shouting, even though the music wasn't very loud. A mask of perspiration coated her features with cellophane. 'They're a right pair of jokers.' She shook her head deliriously, as though their double antics had exhausted her. 'We had a right laugh. Do you want to come and meet them?'

'Why not?' said Julie, glancing sideways to give Francine a supercilious look.

Francine followed them across the room, dropping slightly back in case her evident separateness should tempt anyone to ensnare her. She felt a new sway in her body, as if the party's elegance were an element she had imbibed. Several people looked at her as she passed, and where their eloquent, penetrating eyes touched her she felt the tangible thrill of happiness. Lara and Julie plunged through a dense thicket of bodies and she stepped lightly along the path they beat until she sensed them stop ahead of her. For a moment she disengaged herself, luxuriating in the tropical heat of the room and the promiscuity of its possibilities, but then a hand thrust itself towards her in greeting.

'And who is this?' said a well-spoken male voice.

'Oh, that's Francine.'

Julie's voice appeared to come from a distance, her accent even more grating than usual in its pronouncement of the name. Francine felt her hand shaken in a disembodied, humid grip, but only after the bulk of Lara's back had shifted to one side did she see who held it.

'Stephen Sparks,' he said, reeling himself towards her along their joined arms and presenting himself. His face was flushed and handsome, and his hair stood damply away from his forehead. Their clasped hands made Francine feel suddenly as if they were linked in some intimate exertion and she permitted herself a pleasurable aloofness.

'Pleased to meet you,' she said coolly.

7

'And I you.' He bowed comically, as if he were making fun of her, but his eyes reassured her that he was merely trying to entertain and she laughed. '*Very* pleased.'

Another figure emerged from the crush and loomed at his side expectantly, as if to take part in the conversation. Stephen seemed unaware of him. Francine glanced at his face, but it appeared to be in shadow and she couldn't make it out. Stephen saw her eyes stray and he started round.

'Ah, Ralph!' he said, as if he were surprised. He ushered Ralph into the circle with his arm and smiled conspiratorially at Francine. 'I imagine you've come to pay court to Francine. We must all pay our homage to Queen Francine.'

'Hello,' said Ralph stiffly. He didn't put out his hand. Taking her cue from Stephen's dismissiveness, Francine didn't reply to his greeting. He lingered silently for a moment, watching her. 'It's an unusual name,' he said finally. His expression was pained, as if he had strained something.

Julie suddenly wriggled out from behind him and joined the group.

'Lara's been sick all down her front,' she announced. 'I had to take her to the toilet.'

'Is she all right?' said Ralph, ungluing his eyes from Francine.

'*Charmant*,' muttered Stephen, looking at her as if to re-establish their intimacy. She smiled her acknowledgement of it, a feeling of excitement tight in her chest. 'What do you *do*, Francine?' he said wonderingly, taking her in. 'Let me guess—'

'She's a secretary,' interjected Julie. 'Like me.'

'Really? Ralph's a secretary too,' said Stephen, winking at Francine to show that he was joking.

'Thanks,' mumbled Ralph.

'*Really?*' said Julie. 'I didn't know men were.'

'Are you an artist?' said Francine, keen to change the

subject. Ralph and Julie were now mired in conversation. It was really quite clever how Stephen had palmed them off. He laughed hilariously at her question, and she felt the mild disturbance of uncertainty while the taste of its sophistication was still on her tongue.

'Of piss, perhaps,' he said.

'Oh, right,' she said, not understanding him.

'Only joking. I'm a journalist.'

He said something else, but Francine was distracted by the enthralling mention of her own name beside her, in remarks the noise prevented her from construing. She could feel Ralph looking at her, and she modified the plan she had formulated for cooling off relations with Julie into a more direct resolve to telephone her the next day to find out what he had said. It was altogether a better idea, and should Fritz ever decide he wanted to paint her Julie would have no reason not to give him her number.

'How much do secretaries charge for their services these days?' Stephen was saying. He was laughing again, but his eyes held her through the disruption of his face and she was sure now that he liked her. The thought excited her. He seemed very aristocratic. 'I'd say you're at the top end of the market. Can I afford it?'

'Oh, it's only temporary,' she said, embarrassed that he had returned to the subject. 'Just until I find something more' – she searched for a word – 'creative.'

Stephen had laughed again and this time, not knowing what else to do, she had joined in. Their laughter had met and intertwined, rising confidently above the murmur of voices, the percussion of glasses, the sensuous thud of the music; and everything had seemed to crystallize for Francine then, as she felt herself truly enter the warm temple of privilege and partake of its sacraments.

A figure was moving along the path at a distance across the

park. An eccentricity of motion snagged Francine's gaze and with the sudden latent shock which signals the imminence of danger she fell from her reminiscences and plunged back into the present moment. She understood from his wild, loping walk that it was a deformed man, his hunched body flailing sideways like that of a crippled bird. As she watched, he struck off into the grass and began running in circles, light footed and graceful, as if he were dancing; then he stopped and gazed beatifically at the empty sky, flinging out first one arm and then the other in a seed-sowing gesture. He looked up, and before she could contrive to glance away he had caught her in his sights and begun lumbering over the grass towards her. Immediately Francine left her seat and started walking quickly towards the park gates. Her heart thudded and strained ahead, alert for the sound of footsteps behind her, but when she reached the road and looked back she saw the man standing beside the empty bench, talking and waving his arms wildly. She crossed quickly, grateful for the firm body of traffic which now lay between them. In the distance she could hear a telephone ringing.

Francine lived at the end of an isolated terraced row on Mill Lane, a long road which dangled like trailing spaghetti from the concrete jaws of Kilburn. The outer side wall of the building gave on to a tangled brace of railway tracks, which lay some way down in a wide incision stretching far away towards the cupped palm of the city like an arm of exposed veins, and which gave the house the precarious appearance of a cartoon character sauntering over a cliff. She had for almost a month been occupying the basement flat, which she had found in response to an advertisement in a newspaper. Janice, who had placed the advertisement, lived there with her. The flat was the fourth Francine had rented in the past year, and although lately she had begun to find certain aspects of Janice's behaviour far from ideal – in fact, altogether hypocritical – the loftier hopes for the arrangement which she had harboured when first she had moved in had so far prevented her from mentioning them. Janice was undoubtedly the sovereign figure in the history of her flatmates and although, once the first worship of unfamiliarity had faded, Francine had begun to see how she would scale and conquer this more sophisticated range, she required time to accustom herself to its greater challenge.

Before she came to live with Janice, Francine had shared a flat in High Barnet with two other secretaries. Her stay with them had been the briefest of all her tenancies, but she found herself occasionally looking back on it with a vague longing for the home which had included amongst its luxuries the ease of feeling contempt for those with whom she shared it. In return for the condescensions her sense of her own superiority had permitted her to make, Lisa and Michele had admired her unflinchingly, and when she announced her intention to move to a location more central to her expectations, had encouraged her to do so with the selfless wistfulness of plain sisters. Francine rather missed their easy company now, for at least they had all been going out to work, and she had enjoyed watching their eyes widen as she told them of her adventures in the City after their dull days at the local estate agent. Janice only did two mornings a week at a boutique in Hampstead, where she seemed to earn enough not to need anything else and was always getting free clothes, and when Francine came home in the evenings Janice would never ask her anything about her day. In fact, she often seemed to have forgotten that Francine went to work at all, and would say things like, 'So where have you been today?' Francine would tell her and she would say 'Again?' or 'Still?' and look vaguely sympathetic. Of course, on the days when Janice had to go in she would always make such a drama out of it, and would be in the bathroom for hours so that the mirror was steamed up by the time Francine managed to get in to do her make-up.

Nevertheless, she knew that she had been lucky to find Janice, and her first instinct that she would learn things from her which might result in personal advancement had quickly been borne out in the utter unfamiliarity of her habits. Often she had come back from work to find Janice curled on the sofa in a circle of lamp- or candlelight while night filled the rooms around her, irradiating an intimate warmth which, although it came in fact from the portable heater which panted continually at her side, seemed somehow to be the result of personal projection. Janice habitually remained indoors, where she would install herself before the television for the day, its volume subdued, on a bed of cushions, turning the pages of magazines and stirring only to glide to the kitchen in bare feet to make cups of instant coffee. Francine had emerged from her first startling plunges into this quite tangible aura of softness and languor with a hoard of rare and mysterious self-criticisms. Janice was thin and ethereal in appearance and whimsical in deed, and for the first time Francine found her own physique clumsy, her habits too regulated. Janice would wince at the bold voice Francine brought back with her from the office and shrink from the clamour of her return, watching with mildly astonished interest as she prepared her evening meal. It was unpleasant to feel so noisy, but Francine's dedication to matters of self-improvement could always overwhelm her pride and she accepted the proffered apprenticeship to Janice's atmosphere with subdued gratitude. Her affection for Janice once she had learned to resemble her more closely was certainly fond, but Francine's impulses for domination were beginning to rally from their exile. She wondered when their friendship would be established on its proper footing, with its missing element – the open acknowledgement of Francine's ordination to the exceptional – restored.

Francine had been surprised to discover that Janice didn't have a boyfriend, and the mood of instruction which still dogged their partnership had so far conferred its chastity also on Francine. Janice was more critical of men than other girls Francine knew. They were always ringing for her, though, and she would whisper into the phone, her lips at the receiver as if she were drinking from it, but she rarely went out. On those occasions when she did, two pale fingers of lipstick on her mouth, she would come back an hour or two later on her own. She never asked Francine to go with her, even though once Francine had invited her out with some people from work. It had annoyed her to see how all the men had behaved around Janice, and so many of them had asked about her the next day at work that she had felt quite insulted, especially when she considered that they had all been trying to get her own attention up until then. One or two had actually asked if Janice had a boyfriend and Francine had lied and told them that she did. Afterwards she had felt a bit guilty about it, but Janice had told her once that she was in love with a man who was getting married to someone else, so it wasn't absolutely untrue. Janice hadn't really mentioned the man again, except recently to tell Francine that it was the day of the wedding, whereupon she had drunk vodka straight from a bottle for several hours and then disappeared to her room. She had laughed about the men from Francine's office when they had got home and then done various quite funny imitations of them involving the type of snorting noises made by pigs. Francine had been forced to laugh, and after that she hadn't really been interested in them at all.

She crossed the bridge over the railway tracks and for a moment looked along its gorge towards the dark, distant crowd of buildings with its bright mass of nocturnal eyes. There was something in the vista which unsettled her and she hurried past it to her front door. As usual the flat was dark when she let herself in, but along the hall she saw a glow hint seductively from beneath the sitting-room door at Janice's presence and she went automatically towards it. Janice looked blankly up at her from the sofa when she entered the cave of the room's warmth, with the mild amnesia which Francine was always required to penetrate even after the smallest separation.

'It's ever so cold outside,' she said.

'Is it?' Janice received the message with wonder. 'God.'

'I went to that park, but it was pretty boring,' Francine confessed.

Janice picked up a packet of cigarettes which lay beside her and offered one to Francine. The gesture conveyed a certain intimacy and Francine took one gratefully. As she did so, Janice touched her arm lightly.

'Ralph called for you,' she said, keeping her hand there as if it were the conduit for her information.

'Ralph?'

Janice had pronounced the name with such familiarity that for a moment Francine was confused.

'Ralph.' She nodded darkly. 'He says can you call him back.'

Francine felt the pleasurable anxiety of an emergency. Janice held a lighter towards her and in its piquant illumination she ignited her cigarette and inhaled deeply. How had Ralph got her number? A dim memory of giving it to him promoted itself faintly but she pushed it back, enjoying instead the dramatic movement of Ralph from the shadows of her thoughts to their foreground. His assertion constituted a surprise, administering a forceful shock to her vanity. For a moment he glittered, but then his glory began to ebb as she admitted disappointment to her calculations. Why hadn't Stephen called? She summoned her memory of the evening's final exchanges from its confinement. It had been outside, on the pavement, while she was waiting for a cab with Julie, and Ralph had just been standing there on his own. Julie had written her number down on a piece of paper and given it to him, and he had acted as if he were surprised and then asked if he could have hers too. On the way home Julie had asked her what she thought of Ralph and she had shrugged.

'He's OK. I prefer his friend.'

'They both like you,' Julie had said miserably.

'He's got a heavy energy,' Janice said now through a thoughtful cloud of smoke. 'I could tell, even over the phone.'

Francine had looked for Stephen, glancing around secretly, but he had disappeared towards the end of the party and hadn't come back to say goodbye. She had given her number to Ralph, the moment dulled by disappointment, and then realized afterwards that Stephen could always get hold of her that way. It was probably for the best, she had thought on the way home, while Julie stared mournfully from the window of their cab. If she had given him her number herself, he would have thought she was desperate. This way he might even get a bit jealous. She had felt the satisfaction which customarily arose from the discovery of a personal advantage in the work of forces outside her control, and before long had gained the impression that the work had been her own.

Two

Ralph Loman woke to find he had become his best friend Stephen Sparks. The room – Stephen's room? Yes, he supposed it must be, although he had never been in Stephen's room before, an odd thing really – the room was cold, deathly cold, and blue with too-early light. It had been such a long night, a night busy with dreams. What a lot he had done! Just now he had been at a party – he had only just left, in fact – in a great glass place, a glass beehive filled with people. Everyone had been so kind. At one point a girl had given him an injection and for a while he had been terrified as something crept unstoppably along his veins, about to invade his heart; but then he had remembered that he was Stephen and felt an inquisitive rush of joy. It had gathered in him while the party murmured distantly, a beautiful, refracting thing, a lovely crystal suspended in his centre like a chandelier. He felt it there now, fading. His head hurt terribly. In fact, his whole body – Stephen's body, he supposed you'd say – his whole body hurt. He closed his eyes and sang silently. Birmingham, Lancaster, Crewe. Birmingham, Lancaster, Crewe. It sometimes helped to calm him on those occasions when he was not feeling himself.

Crewe, Crewe. He was awfully tired. Stephen's body tugged at him, weighted, escaping, a leaden anchor free-falling beneath the surface of things, then graceful as a dancer as sleep began to take the slack and he became light. He heard the rustle of bedclothes, felt one unfamiliar knee strangely bony against the other, and for a moment his mind raced and struggled. Stephen, yes. He opened his eyes again. Something loomed at the foot of the bed and a gorge of fear mounted in his throat. The chest of drawers. Birmingham, Lancaster, Crewe. He closed his eyes. The submarine light swam at his lids and he knew that when he opened them again Stephen would be gone and he would be alone, waking into the dead hours of an urban dawn as he always did. He kept them shut and waited, hoping that the ebbing tide of fatigue would drag him back down into unconsciousness with its diminishing fingertips; but the growing pressure of alertness in his head was forcing itself against his eyes in the effort to pry them open. As a child he had often lain like that in terror, knowing he was about to surface into the blue light, that awful, deathly light, his father lumpish and inert in the bed beside him, with hours to wait before sunlight broke like a raw egg over the room, ameliorating its unfamiliarity. There was never anywhere for him to go at that hour in the hotels they stayed in, nothing for him to do but lie still in that light which made it seem as if this time night would not progress to day, and which made monsters of the furniture while the patterned walls seemed alive with unspeakable creatures. He had seen spiders, crabs, even a lobster there. Once he had noticed a man lying on the floorboards during one of those dark dawns, a man in a bowler hat who was flat as if he were made of paper. He had smiled cheerfully at Ralph and tipped his hat, and Ralph had lain cataleptic with fear for a time which he could not quantify, his father sleeping beside him like a dead man, and had waited for this certain alchemy of night becoming day. There had been a picture on the wall opposite the bed and he had fixed his eyes on the black square of it until coloured lights danced before them. He remembered that picture still. As he watched it evolve from the darkness, he had known it primordially, off by heart. For a while it had been the only thing he knew. Birmingham, Lancaster, Crewe.

He woke again some time later. Cars were passing on the road outside and he heard a door slam, someone shouting. A beam of sunlight poked through a gap in the curtains. He had just been dreaming, something about a cripple and a horse, one of those wooden fairground horses with a shaft through the middle. It had been bobbing up and down, the way they do, except that there was no carousel. It had just sort of pogoed madly down the street. He turned on to his back and the warm ray settled across his face. A certain ripeness in the light made him suddenly suspect that it was late, and he jolted up in bed before remembering that it was Sunday and he didn't have to go to work. He looked at his watch anyway. The hands pointing at one o'clock seemed so impossible, so wild in their assertion that a great swath of time had gone by without his supervision, that he immediately got out of bed to look at the clock on the chest of drawers. Its remarkable confirmation filled Ralph with a curious elation at his feat of oblivion. The telephone began to ring in the sitting-room and he went obediently to answer it. He liked the feeling of running around after himself, the compact air that delay gave to a day. There had been times recently when he had felt imprisoned in the glass sphere of every passing hour, crawling from one orb to the next in an inescapable chain he sensed was taking him far from where he wanted to go.

'Sparks,' said Stephen when Ralph picked up the phone.

Ralph wondered where Stephen had acquired the irritating habit of answering the phone with his last name, before remembering that it was he, Ralph, who was answering and

Stephen calling. He felt a sleepy giggle rise in his throat as he saw through Stephen's trick, and was surprised to hear it emerge from his mouth.

'You're sounding girlish,' said Stephen.

'Sorry. I just got up.' He thought of telling Stephen that he'd dreamed of him but couldn't find the words.

'Aha.' His voice seemed further away, as if he were distracted. There was a rustling sound and then a heavy thud. '—last night?' he boomed into the receiver.

'What did you say?'

Ralph sat down and realized he was naked. His penis dangled grotesquely between the mottled trunks of his thighs like a hanging. The rough cloth of the seat cover beneath his bare buttocks reminded him of dreams he used to have in which he went unclothed and everything felt rather painful.

'I said – ah – what did you think of last night?'

'Nothing,' said Ralph, surprised.

A leaden disappointment hovered and then plummeted as he remembered the message he had left for Francine in the optimistic hours of yesterday afternoon. He had actually been relieved when the girl had said she wasn't there, his timid heart diving from his mouth down to the thrashing pit of his stomach, but her voice had been so warm and interested – had made him feel as if he was a prospect, a catch! – that for a while after he had put down the phone he had felt sure that things would go his way. The long vigil of evening had cooled his hopes, solidified them in ridiculous postures. He had become nervous, braced for the shriek of the telephone, jumping up every few minutes to rupture with activity the terrible membrane of silence which thickened around him. She hadn't called, of course, and he had watched television until his head ached and then plunged into the sleep from which he had only just awoken.

'Party,' mumbled Stephen. There was something in his

mouth. Ralph heard the click and hiss of a lighter, the suck of Stephen's breath.

'Alf's thing? The private view? That was Friday,' said Ralph sternly. 'Yesterday was Saturday.'

'Was it?' Stephen paused. After a while he gave a bark of laughter and began speaking in a silly, high-pitched voice. 'It's all become the most terrible blur.'

Ralph waited for Stephen to reproach himself but instead felt wearied by his own dullness, the tightening bondage of responsibility from which Stephen would never permit him to escape.

'Ah yes,' said Stephen. 'Alf's pictures. Bloody toss, if you ask me.'

'I didn't look at them much, I'm afraid. I don't think anyone ever does at these things. It's all so—'

'The temp!' interrupted Stephen, inspired. 'The tarty temp from Tunbridge Wells!'

Ralph was silent.

'Francine,' he said finally.

'Francine!' echoed Stephen. 'Yes! Lovely girl. Awful voice. Awful! Fran*cine*,' he mimicked.

'I've got to go,' said Ralph. 'I'm late for something.'

'I'd better run along. I was supposed to be at Mother's half an hour ago for lunch. She'll cook the cat if I'm not there to keep an eye on her.'

'Give her my regards,' said Ralph stiffly, although Stephen had already put down the phone.

He sat for a moment in his chair. The conversation had had a derailing effect and it was a while before he remembered that he was cold and hadn't had any breakfast yet. Stephen often did that, summoning and then abruptly dropping him so that he felt disorientated and lost afterwards. Disruption and confusion followed him like a weather system. These days, living outside Stephen's atmosphere, Ralph was more aware of what happened when he entered it, but at school, when they were younger, he had been under the siege of Stephen's presence most of the time. He rather missed it, despite feeling his humiliations more deeply now. The gradual severance of adulthood had left him not strong but ridiculous, marooned in his habits, so that when he saw Stephen he felt the more extraneous and lonely for the glimpses he had of their distant past. Besides, when they did meet Stephen was always spectacularly late, so that the very basis of Ralph's presence was untethered slavishness, a foolish injury with which he swelled with every passing minute. Once, Ralph had waited an hour and a half for him in a pub which was just around the corner from Stephen's flat. He had not been sitting alone at his table for more than fifteen minutes when an effeminate little man with wild eyes and an odd little beard – a goatee, like a courtier – had approached him and insisted on keeping him company. He hadn't spoken much, Ralph recalled, merely sat beside him occasionally sipping from a glass of beer and giving him a sweet, fleeing smile whenever Ralph caught his eye. At one point, he had suddenly leaned over and gripped Ralph's hand. His fingers were warm and surprisingly comforting. Had Ralph been less embarrassed, he might have wished they could have stayed like that, holding hands.

'Who's your girlfriend?' Stephen had said when he arrived, grinning unkindly. The man slipped quietly away with a curt nod of the head, and Ralph had felt inexplicably guilty. Nevertheless, he had stayed where he was, offering to buy Stephen a drink and even laughing with him about his strange companion. The man had caught his eye sadly from the other side of the pub and Ralph had felt dizzy with malice.

He went to the kitchen and opened the fridge, perusing it like a car engine. He had seen other men do that; not his father, of course, who would open the fridge door quickly and snatch something from it, as if worried that he would let the cold air out. One or two things lay inert on the metal shelves, like the contents of a morgue. A curling rubber leaf of ham languished in its collapsed packaging beside a small, waxy brick of cheese. He felt a wall of cold advance towards him and remembered that he was naked. There was a plastic bottle of orange juice lower down and he grabbed it, slamming the door of the fridge so that it recoiled jangling as if he had slapped it. He reached for a glass and then changed his mind, deciding instead to drink directly from the bottle. It was a cavalier gesture, and one which he felt led naturally on from his oversleeping, his nakedness, and perhaps towards a casual second phone call to Francine later in the day.

He threw back his head to make a funnel of his throat, and for a moment the acidity of the juice was appalling, poisonous. His scalp prickled as he felt it coursing cold across his chest and into his stomach. He tipped his head back further and drained the bottle, before tossing it across the room towards the bin. It landed instead on the draining-board beside the sink and skidded on its side into an arrangement of drying crockery. A mug shot over the edge and crashed to the floor, exploding into shards among which its handle lay intact, like an ear. Ralph stared for a moment at the miniature disaster. He considered leaving it as it was, but his sense of his own drama had collapsed and he propelled himself to the broom cupboard for a dustpan and brush. He penitently gathered up the fragments of china, wrapped them in a newspaper which lay on the kitchen table, and threw them along with the plastic bottle into the bin.

Some time later he slammed the front door and descended the steps, taking them jauntily two by two in an attempt to button up the mood of cheerful disdain which he had selected, as if from a drawer of tempers, to wear alongside his clothes. He felt better after his bath – could still feel its warm embrace on him – remodelled and fit for action. A determination to leave his mark on the day had driven him from the dragging influence of the flat, and he turned towards Chalk Farm Road filled with purposeful but undirected energy. In the distance he could see the brimming pavements flowing towards Camden Town and a plan to go to the market formulated itself, convincing Ralph that he had intended to do so all along.

The sun was bright but weak and gave the day a deceptive appearance, casting a patina of warmth which did not convert the essential coolness of the air. The naked trees lining the road strained towards the light, greedy for its faint catalyst to burst them prematurely into bloom. It was spring, Ralph supposed, that long and amorphous season into which winter would occasionally recover and summer remit like a lingering low-level illness, never quite gripping at the throat with certitude. He groped for a date and remembered then that it was still only February. The year stretched before him in all its unavoidable detail, the hundreds of days and thousands of hours which he would endure as if something more lay at their end than mere repetition. He wished that he could be tricked, as others seemed to be, by the close of each week, seeing in their false endings the imminence of some sort of conclusion, like a soap opera. He wondered why he had never fallen into step with this pattern of days, comprehended in the helpful clarity of a week's tiny eras – birth, growth, productivity, decline, dormancy, regeneration, played out beneath the celestial presence of longer phases of weather – a system which might ease the slow construction of his life. The year he had spent alone with his father, a chaotic tract across which no borders of time or habit were erected, had become in its elasticity the infinitely capacious repository of Ralph's failings and he placed this latest grudge firmly within it. How could he, who had spent the most formative year of his youth, the year in which he was most pliant, most liable to gel in whichever crazy mould was nearest to hand, had spent that year 'on the road', a hostage to his father's misfortune; how could he, then, be expected to see things as other people did?

He fed himself from the tributary of his street into the main concourse drifting towards the lock, and in the suddenly thick press of bodies felt his exposure ease as they gathered him in. He had had days like this before, days when his spirits would gutter or flare at each movement of life, when he wrestled hourly with his recollections, at once their victim and their hero. It was good that he was out, although even here in the open air his father's eyes were on him, shrivelled with whisky and immolated desire. He felt their reproach, as he always did when shrugging off portions of himself into the complaining vacuum of his absence. The problem was that it wasn't a vacuum at all. He was merely relocating things he disliked about himself, slapping up hasty walls around them, building twisted, ridiculous corridors, papering over their leaks. He had complicated himself with introspection. He felt a longing to demolish it all and start again. His father had been a master of evasion, blockading all routes to the past, bricking up vistas of the future, until all that was left of him was a tiny room in which a man sat in an armchair watching television. He had once been a boy scout, though; the only photograph Ralph possessed of his father depicted him at the acme of his scouting career, when he had risen from amongst the ranks to become their general. He wore a cap and cravat, and stared out beyond the lens with triumphant eyes as if towards vanquished hordes. Later, his mind would travel back to that glittering epoch and he would endeavour gently to tell Ralph of it, in a hotel room where rivers of Terylene cascaded from the mouths of his suitcases and the air was warm with the rank perfume of their take-away dinner.

'Dad, I'm reading,' Ralph would implore, raising his book

by the covers as if to shield him from the eye-watering woodsmoke of his father's recollections.

'Ah, yes,' his father would confirm, nodding. 'But a boy your age shouldn't have to turn to books for company. He should be outdoors with other boys engaging in some form of organized activity.' He would sigh and put his arms behind his head, like a man on holiday. 'What do you say we play a hand of whist?'

'Dad, I'm *reading*.'

Once Ralph witnessed his father getting into a fight – or failing to get out of it, in any case – in a pub in Worthington where they had gone one evening for pie and chips and where Ralph was permitted to drink his lemonade from a pint glass identical to that from which his father sipped beer with womanly daintiness. Ralph had deliberately left the translucent spume on his lip while his father wiped his own away, watching him closely as he ate and drank.

'Is it good?' he said after each mouthful. Ralph nodded. 'Never leave a moustache,' he counselled, handing Ralph a paper napkin. 'A gentleman never leaves a moustache.'

Already his father had begun to deliver his epithets in the defensive manner with which he touted Terylene, at once sheepish and proud.

'A gentleman,' he repeated, 'never has a sloppy lip.'

It was shortly afterwards that he saw his father, gone to the bar to refill their glasses, borne away from his view in a sudden clutch of strangers and swept out through the double doors of the pub beyond into the street, his bald pate bobbing as if suspended in water. Ralph had thought to follow him out, but the barmaid had come to the table with his second pint glass of lemonade and had instructed him kindly to drink it. He had done so while she watched, drinking it all down in one go as he had seen other men do until she had laughed and told him he'd burst if he carried on like that; and what with all the excitement he had quite forgotten about his father until he emerged back through the doors with his shirt hanging out and his cheeks flushed dark red in a grotesque approximation of youth and vitality.

'A word of advice, Ralphie,' he had said, sitting down heavily beside him. His belly heaved in and out frantically. 'Never show your wallet at the bar. Temptation, you see. The smart fellow always takes out a single note in advance.'

Ralph asked him if you could make yourself burst by drinking too much all in one go.

'Well, let's see,' said his father after a pause, furrowing his brow and screwing up his eyes intently. His upper lip glistened with sweat. He shook his head. 'I don't think it's likely. No, I don't think it's likely at all.'

Ralph would read in the evenings, devouring the pages of library books while his father dozed before the television with a hotel tooth-mug filled with whisky. Sometimes the empty glass would slip from his hand and he would wake with a start as it thumped to the floor.

'Must have dozed off,' he would apologize, rubbing his eyes and smiling crookedly. 'Good book, Ralphie?'

'Quite good.'

'Ah, I see. What's the plot?'

He crossed the lock and plunged into a sea of stalls, through crowds whose lumpy shopping bags thumped against his calves, past Indian men selling garish explosions of clothing and girls with dead eyes and chalky faces around which shreds of hair hung like seaweed. He headed down towards the fruit market, craving the perishability of its offerings. When he reached it the market was noisy, a field of combat where red-faced stallholders shouted like disgruntled babies while produce which seemed overly bright was fondled by people who evidently weren't.

'Can't you read?' roared one of them, as a woman in a

grubby knitted hat ran her fingers over a hill of oranges, touching them delicately like a blind person. She started at the sound of his voice, her eyes wide. 'What does that say?' persisted the stallholder. He pointed to a sign perched on the display, on which was depicted a large pair of melons with the warning 'Please Don't Squeeze' emblazoned beneath them. The woman removed her hands from the oranges and left them to hang inertly by her sides.

Ralph moved away quickly. Squashed fruit and bruised bits of vegetable lay trampled on the pavement, strangely ghoulish and unidentifiable, like the detritus of a serious operation. His foot slid on something pulpy and yielding, squelching beneath his shoe and oozing out around the sole. He limped along a few paces despairingly, trying to scrape it off against the kerb. It came away in smears, and by the time he managed to get rid of it he saw that he had spread it over rather a large patch of concrete. He looked around, embarrassed, and then walked awkwardly on as if nothing had happened. Moments later, recognizing the foolishness of his growing discomfort, he stopped at another stall and bought a bag of apples. The bag was made of brown paper and he had to hold it underneath to prevent it from giving way. He moved on, encumbered, through the nervous sunlight. As he approached the end of the small street he saw a well-dressed oriental girl bending over a large rubbish bin as if she had dropped something in it which she wanted to retrieve. She was exceptionally graceful, Ralph thought, fragile and luminous in that way Eastern girls were. People were looking at her as they passed. For a moment he thought ridiculously of offering to help her, but as he drew near he saw to his horror that the girl was clutching her belly with one hand and holding the other to her chest, while neatly depositing long ribbons of mucus and vomit into the bin. Her narrow shoulders shook slightly beneath her tailored jacket. He hesitated as a double wrench of pity and selfishness twisted in his chest. The girl would be grateful for kindness, he knew – she was alone, after all, sick and far from home! – but as he stood there the scope of the city seemed to unfold and chide him, bidding him to keep to himself, to go about his business in its common parts, its streets thick with souls, and then return directly to what was his, to what he knew. He permitted himself to walk past her. Later, walking back in the direction of the lock, he imagined himself stopping to help the girl, his arm strong around her convulsing shoulders, a handkerchief produced to smooth over her glistening lips. She leaned weakly against him, her eyes filled with tears and gratitude. He strained guiltily to return to her, but his legs carried him stubbornly on.

Once, a few years before, he had stopped to help an old woman who had fallen over in the street. It was late and he had come upon her lying on the dark pavement with her skirts around her waist, her mottled legs veined and appalling in the street light. She had smelt unspeakable as he bent down, the awful stink of cheap beer and neglect, and when he tried to pull her skirt down over her legs, fumbling with it ineptly in a parody of male adolescence, she had opened her bleary yellow eyes and watched him helplessly, as if he were an assailant.

'It's all right,' he had said awkwardly. 'You're going to be all right.'

She had not been wearing underwear, and her flesh had looked both wizened and bloated, androgynous somehow, identifiable as female only by the bloodless lips of her genitals. A trail of ooze glistened over the tops of her thighs; and Ralph had felt a sudden surge of aversion, not physical revulsion exactly, but more of an intellectual certainty that there was nothing here for him, that to stay would constitute a defection from hope, from aspiration, from the business, the responsibility, even, of being himself. The street had been deserted, he remembered, and there was no one to see him as he left her there, scarcely believing what it was he was doing, and walked slowly on his way while her mute eyes burned at his retreating back.

He stopped at a stall and began fingering cloth, not knowing what he was touching. Some girls were laughing near by and there was something in the sound which caught him and made him look up. Francine Snaith was standing no more than ten feet away from him, with a girl he did not know but whose voice he recognized from the telephone as that of her flatmate. A bolt of surprise stunned him and he drew back slightly, instinctively shrinking from an encounter. Francine was holding by its edge a piece of red silk – a shirt, he could see – while the animated stallholder waved his hands operatically, never taking his eyes from her. Ralph watched her face in profile, drawn by it into something approaching a trance. Her unconscious features welcomed his eyes, proclaimed themselves the property of appreciation, and as he travelled over the pearly surface of her skin, the symmetry of its ridges, the dark pool of her hair, he felt oddly as if he were touching her. She carried an aura of astonishing clarity about her which made everything else appear blurred, as if she were at the focal eye of a camera constantly trained upon her. The stallholder took the shirt by its other edge and they held it between them with an intimacy which struck Ralph as almost painful. Finally he nodded his agreement, and the tranquil surface of Francine's face broke and made a smile. She dropped the shirt, opening a leather bag which hung from her shoulder and extracting a single note. Her activity buffeted him with waves of troubled longing. The stallholder folded the shirt carefully – caressed it! – and Francine took it, saying something to the girl beside her. She closed her bag and looked up. He had been so intent on observation that he had forgotten she could see him. Suddenly her gaze was upon him and their eyes collided before either could contrive to look away. Far from giving him the advantage of preparation, Ralph found that his minutes of secret gazing had rendered him awkward and detached. For a moment he could do nothing but look. Francine's face was blank, and the thought that it was consciously so, that she was deciding whether or not to recognize him, flashed upon him during dreadful seconds. Finally, before it was too late, he found himself again and waved his hand. At the signal she hesitated momentarily, as if trying to place him, and then smiled her open acknowledgement.

'What a surprise!' he called out as she approached him, pronouncing the words rather too loudly in his determination to be the first to speak. He cursed himself for yesterday's peremptory telephone message. If only he had known, how much better it would have been to have left things to chance! He felt heavy with the guilty scent of his desire, a desire no response had aired, in which he had been left to steep, and which now emanated a rank odour of rejection which shamed him as keenly and publicly as if he were unwashed.

'Yes,' said Francine, reaching him. Her eyes were downcast, and it was a moment before she revealed herself to him. He examined her shyly again in disbelief, as if looking for some mistake in her face which might release him from his giddiness. She looked very calm, not with the suggestion of relaxation or dullness, but rather as if animation did not occur to her. There were no traces of it on her skin, and it struck him as he watched how carefully she held herself that she was surprised by her own beauty, that her custody of it, her refusal to wear it out with base uses, was a constant responsibility. The surprise of her eyes when finally she looked at him almost took away his breath.

'How are you?' he said.

'I'm fine.'

She was wearing a jacket too thin for the cold, and he noticed fondly how her hands had crept within its sleeves for warmth.

'Good.' There was a pause, and Ralph felt a terrible blankness envelop his thoughts. For a moment he could seize on nothing which would deliver them from the oncoming silence. 'I always make the mistake of coming down here on a Sunday,' he said suddenly, to his own relief. 'I forget what it's like. Each time I swear I won't do it again, and every week I find myself back here elbowing through the crowds.' He gestured vaguely, like a man doing magic tricks.

'I like it.'

There was another pause which almost took Ralph to the brink of his endurance as he waited for some sequel to qualify this bleak statement of their differences. Over Francine's shoulder he could see the other girl waiting, shifting irritably from one leg to the other. She caught his eye and gave him a sudden, encouraging smile. Francine was gazing downwards again. Her eyelashes were so thick and dark against her pale cheek that he wondered clumsily if they were false.

'Well—' he said finally, looking around him in a manner suggestive of departure. His heart writhed with such acute embarrassment that he could feel no disappointment through it, just a humble acceptance of his own foolishness which rendered him desperate to put a stop to the encounter as quickly as he could. 'Well, I suppose I'd better be off.' To his astonishment he saw something happen in her face as he spoke, a small acknowledgement of exigence which inflamed him with hope. 'Did you – would you like to meet up some time?' he said hurriedly as she watched him. Panic gripped at him as things slipped outside his control, like a silent prisoner escaping over a moonlit roof. 'Just say – please do say if you'd rather not. I'll quite understand.'

'All right.' She smiled faintly. 'Why not?'

'It's just that when you didn't call back,' he rushed on, 'I thought perhaps you weren't – for whatever reason—'

'Call back?' She furrowed her untrammelled skin with a child's perplexity. 'I didn't get any message.'

'Yesterday!' cried Ralph, a suffocating relief welling up in his throat. 'I spoke to your flatmate – she said she'd tell you.'

'Oh, she probably meant to,' said Francine wistfully. Her eyes implored him and she glanced behind her. 'But things have been – a bit difficult with Janice lately.'

Ralph's righted injury combined with this whispered confidence to fill him with new allegiance. He felt himself swell before Francine's fragility. In the distance, Janice's serpentine eyes glowed with cunning.

'Really?' he said. His eyes pricked ridiculously with the forewarning of tears.

'Yes. It's, well – never mind. I'd better go.'

'Listen, if you need anything, I mean if there's anything I can do—' She was retreating from him into the crowd. 'I'll call!' he said.

Three

Francine Snaith was lodged in the gloomy oesophagus of the Metropolitan Line, where her enjoyment of the single customary pleasure of underground travel – that of observing her reflection in the dark windows opposite her seat – had been obstructed since Baker Street by the disorderly herd of standing passengers which had been driven by overcrowding down the narrow corridor in front of her. The enforced contemplation of a mis-shapen male belly which rose from a sea of pinstripe and thrust itself towards her had been bad enough at speed, but since the train had suddenly and inexplicably shuddered to a halt Francine's ears were filled with the acoustics of its physical proximity. She heard breath complaining from obstructed nostrils above her, and from much closer the whining sounds of blockage. The mountain heaved alarmingly before her eyes. There was a gurgle of clearance and then the rush of fluids draining. Above the forest of flesh, a canopy of inquisitive faces turned at the sound. Francine closed her eyes, lest the thought of this hot, human filling in a dark pastry of steel and black earth should inspire feelings of panic. From the deluge of silence, a rank and humid mist of sweat rose thickly. The sea of bodies shifted impatiently, swelled and settled. Just as the stoppage seemed most permanent, the train suddenly lunged forward with a jolt as if it had been punched. People gathered themselves to a rising dissonance of coughs and clearing throats. Francine stirred also in anticipation of her imminent release as the train sped darkly through the tunnel. Finally the rolling scenery of the station slid tiled past the windows, its appearance an order to begin work on the already botched canvas of the day.

Minutes later, Francine was walking briskly to the front desk across the hushed marble reception hall of Lancing & Louche. She announced herself to the man sitting behind it, who picked up his telephone to dial Personnel.

'Frances?' he said, screwing his face up uncomprehendingly.

'Fran*cine*.'

'Yes, we've got a Francine for you in reception,' he said into the receiver. He paused for a moment, listening, and then laughed. 'That's right. Yes.' He guffawed and put down the phone. 'Take a seat over there, love. Someone'll be down to fetch you.'

Francine did not feel like sitting down, but the porter's eyes were on her and she knew that such mild anarchies were disturbing to those in whose jurisdiction they occurred. She crossed obediently to the other side of the reception area where a bank of brown leather sofas waited. A muted rabble of voices was growing along a corridor near by, like a dog barking behind a closed front door, and their amplification as they entered the vast hall caused her to start. A group of men in dark, expensive suits burst through the glass doors and passed her as she sat down. Several of them glanced at her as they walked by. Their voices lowered once they were past her and then erupted into loud laughter. One or two of them looked back. A middle-aged woman came through the glass doors behind them, her aspect telegraphing the search for a misplaced object, and Francine stood up.

'Francine?' The woman smiled and held out her hand. Her

teeth were large and yellow, and saliva glittered over them as if with the threat of mastication. 'I'm Jane. Thanks for coming. Do you want to follow me?'

Francine followed Jane back through the glass doors. From behind her blonde hair appeared not to move as she walked, whisked into stiff peaks like beaten egg whites. They stopped at a wall of lifts and Jane pressed a button. Francine straightened herself as they waited and breathed deeply. The impending mountain of the day rose reluctantly before her, with its steep slopes of novelty and idle plateaux. Had she been able to walk in the fresh air after her journey perhaps she would have felt better, but the ascent directly from the station to the office block gave her the impression that she was still trapped in the now-carpeted intestines of a dream.

'Did you have far to come?' enquired Jane as they stepped into the lift.

'West Hampstead,' said Francine. 'It's not far.'

She could feel Jane's eyes examining her, intimately but impartially like a pair of doctor's hands.

'I'm pretty, aren't I?' she almost blurted out. She had opened her mouth to speak. 'Where do you live?' she said.

'Welwyn,' said Jane.

'Gosh,' said Francine. 'That must be a long journey.'

'Actually, it's very convenient.'

The lift rose like a lump in the building's throat. Jane's perfume, warmed by the confinement of her skin, dispersed and settled around them in a musky cloud. Francine felt a strong desire to escape.

'You'll be working for Mr Lancing himself,' said Jane as they approached the top floor. She smiled. Her vast, moist teeth were alive, and seemed to perceive more than the tiny, carbonized eyes above them. Francine felt it was appropriate to look at them while she spoke. 'Don't worry, his bark is worse than his bite.'

The doors opened with a sigh and they emerged into a windowless corridor identical to that which they had left below, except for a gold-plated 5 stuck to the opposite wall in place of the large G downstairs. The brown carpet beneath Francine's feet absorbed the noise of her shoes, amplifying instead the swishing sounds of clothing and the quick exchanges of their breaths. Jane turned to the right and began walking briskly, and Francine hurried to keep abreast of her. She felt disturbed by Jane's air of permanent unfamiliarity, until she remembered that Personnel were always like that. She never usually saw them again after the first day. Francine was often left with disembodied impressions of people from these first intense exposures, a moustache here or large bosom there, a smell or a set of teeth, which together formed an area of clutter in her mind like spare parts littering a garage floor. Occasionally one of these strange, useless memories would rise unbidden in her thoughts and she would find herself unable to remember how she had acquired it or where it belonged. She would suddenly recall jobs she had done from which she could not retrieve a single face, while those faces which had become separated from their owners would drift about among her recollections like detached and meaningless ghosts.

'This way,' said Jane, listing suddenly and sharply to the left. She opened a door and the brown, mummified silence of the corridor was all at once broken by the familiar chatter and hum of the office and a bank of dull natural light emanating from the large windows to the far side. Francine followed Jane into the room. She felt dazed, as if she had just emerged from beneath deep water. The office was instantly recognizable, a flat, immaculate vista of steely geometry and manicured synthetic fibres, its variations in tone all conducted in the key of grey. Through the windows the low cloudy sky and iron hives of companion office blocks were visible. From the fifth floor one could see other fifth floors, the heads of buildings like a crowd of adults.

Several people looked up at the intrusion and Francine suddenly remembered herself. It was one of the advantages of her position that her novelty, the most fragile of all her arts, rarely had the opportunity to wear off. There was a perceptible lull and swell as things shifted to accommodate her. One or two people allowed their glances to linger like tenacious guests into stares. Seconds elapsed and eventually everyone bent their heads, or turned to gaze blankly into computer screens while their fingers tapped at keyboards in an imitation of tedium. Francine's eyes swept the surface of the secretarial pool and then rose to confront what instinct informed her was a masculine inspection. The man wore a dark pinstriped suit and was examining her in an authoritative manner. His desk was on a raised podium, like a car in a showroom. Francine looked away and then back once or twice until the persistence of his stare caught her eyes and held them. At that moment he assumed a bored expression and dropped his attention back down to the slim pile of pages in front of him. He made a mark or two on the top sheet with a heavy gold fountain pen and crossed his legs away from her.

'This is Francine,' said Jane loudly. She threw her voice in the direction of another man on the far side of the room and then followed keenly after it like a dog chasing a stick. The man wore a pinstriped suit identical to that of his colleague, but sat behind a desk whose podium raised it just perceptibly higher. At the sight of Jane advancing briskly towards him he stood up and put out his hand, as if anticipating the transfer of a baton. His gesture had been automatic, but as he comprehended the nature of the interruption Francine saw him waver in his maintenance of it, his arm flopping feebly as if the mechanism designed to retract it had suddenly failed.

'Francine, this is Mr Lancing. Francine will be looking

after you,' said Jane, raising her voice for Mr Lancing in the manner of a matron in an old people's home.

'Hi,' said Mr Lancing in an American accent. The blood appeared to flow back into his dysfunctional arm and it twitched perkily, inviting Francine to shake it. He had a boyish, grinning face over which a map of age had been laid as if artificially. His clear eyes peering through the tanned and withered skin gave him the appearance of a child wearing a rubber mask. 'Great!' he said enthusiastically.

'Hello,' said Francine, shaking his hand.

Mr Lancing continued to grin at her and she noticed a slightly dead expression behind his eyes.

'Well, that's the introductions over with,' said Jane. 'I'll just show Francine to her desk, Mr Lancing.'

'Give 'em hell!' said Mr Lancing. He clenched his fist and punched it into the air.

Jane laughed shrilly. 'We will, Mr Lancing,' she said.

Francine's desk was a right-angle of grey counter-top positioned near the foot of Mr Lancing's podium. The desk was fenced in by a capacious window to the side and a wall on which shelves were hung to the rear. Along the shelves were arranged a large number of box files, their vertical labelled spines inscribed like tombstones. In front of the desk stood what appeared to be a coffee station, a small table on which a kettle fumed in a dry and dissolving landscape of shiny brown pools and white hillocks of sugar, interspersed with tiny dark granular boulders, stained spoons, and damp fists of used teabags. Francine's objections to this arrangement were strong and immediate, not least because it formed a second channel of interference – the first being the rows of files – which permitted the unrestricted access of office traffic to her territory. She moved behind her desk and saw that it put her in view of the whole room. From beyond the plastic plain of the desktop, a chirping forest of computers appeared to monitor her movements with their single unblinking eyes. She wrestled for a moment with her faint-heartedness, knowing that if she cowered from this corporate ecology she would disable herself for survival within it, becoming victim to a new range of cruelties whose invisibility did not lessen her faith in their existence. Mr Lancing and his colleague sat atop their rival podia, dumb and vigilant as marble dogs at a gate.

'I'll just run you through one or two things,' said Jane. She manoeuvred her broad hips round to the other side of the desk, as powerful and clumsy as a car. 'Do you mind if I just sit on your chair for a minute?'

'Not at all,' replied Francine. In such a place territories were as quickly and fiercely marked out as they were returned to their anonymity. She moved to stand behind Jane so as to observe her instructions. On the chair, the cheeks of her buttocks were forced sideways like a tomato crushed underfoot.

'You'll be in sole charge of Mr Lancing's diary,' said Jane, lifting a large ledger from the far end of the desk. It had scraps of paper stuck to its cover and protruding from amongst its pages, scribbled relics of other hands. She opened it and began to leaf through the blueprints of days long since passed, with their emergencies of meetings and lunches. The diary was thick with arrangement and rearrangement, its pages gnarled into relief by the hieroglyphics of rounded handwriting. 'Here's today's schedule,' said Jane, turning to reveal a fresher page. '11.30 Haircut' read Francine.

The phone on her desk began suddenly to shriek. Francine started and stepped automatically aside so that Jane could pick it up.

'Let's see if you can answer it,' said Jane, revealing her large teeth.

'All right,' Francine replied, bright with loathing. She picked up the vibrating receiver, and in the imperative of its sudden silence felt necessity overpower apprehension. 'Mr Lancing's office,' she said smoothly.

'Gary there?' barked a voice in reply. Its American accent took her by surprise, disabling her comprehension as if it were a foreign language.

'Excuse me?' she said, after a pause.

Jane lifted her head like a guard-dog detecting an intruder.

'I said gimme Gary.'

Francine paused.

'I'm afraid I don't know who Gary is.'

'Who is this?' said the man impatiently.

'Francine,' said Francine stupidly. She felt herself beginning to drift away and pulled herself back sharply. Jane writhed beside her in her seat. 'I'm new here,' she added. Her blunder had brought heat to her face.

'Well, Francine, all I can say is you *must* be pretty new,' said the man. 'Gary's your boss, honey.' There was a pause. 'Ha! Ha!' he suddenly shouted. 'Ha!'

Francine giggled politely.

'We're not on first-name terms yet,' she said.

'First-name terms!' said the man after a pause. 'Ha! Gary! Gimme Lancing, honey. That all right for you?'

'Who shall I say is calling?' said Francine, keeping the warm edge of humour in her volce.

'Jim – no, Mr Vernon. Ha! Tell him *Mr Vernon's* on the line for him.'

'Just a moment, Mr Vernon,' said Francine.

'Nice to know you, Francine,' said Jim as she put him on hold.

'Mr Lancing!' she called firmly, humming with success. Jane's examination burned beside her and she turned away slightly, blocking her out. Mr Lancing looked up, his mouth agape.

'Somebody call me?' he said.

'Mr Vernon for you,' said Francine. He appeared confused and she waved the receiver helpfully.

'Put him on.'

Mr Lancing gripped his phone expectantly and Francine ran her eye down a list of numbers attached to her extension. She located his number and put the call through.

'Hello?' said Mr Lancing loudly, as if uncertain whether his voice would travel down the wire without reinforcement.

'Well,' sniffed Jane as Francine turned triumphantly to face her. 'You seem fairly confident. You shouldn't have any trouble coping.'

'Oh, I'm used to this sort of thing.'

'I think you'll find this position rather more demanding than what you're used to, actually. Mr Lancing is a very important man.'

'I think I'm going to like him.'

'Well, I think the point is rather more whether he likes you, isn't it?' Jane's teeth made a menacing reappearance. She stood up and smoothed her furrowed skirt tightly over her hips. 'Let me know if you have any problems.'

She eased herself out from behind the desk and walked towards the door.

'Bye, everyone!' she called out when she reached it. One or two people looked up but there was no audible reply. Jane smiled widely and disappeared.

As soon as she had gone, Francine saw Mr Lancing's colleague move smoothly from behind his desk and approach her across the office, his eyes fixed with studied absorption on a piece of paper in his hand. She sat down, busying herself with Mr Lancing's diary. He loomed before her and she bent her head in concentration.

'I haven't had the pleasure,' he said finally.

She looked up and he smiled urbanely. He was younger than Mr Lancing and quite good looking, Francine thought, but his handsomeness was fatigued through over-use and his skin had a slightly thickened, curdled quality suggestive of decline. His belly strained at the waist of his trousers. As if sensing her looking at it, he pulled it in sharply without removing his eyes from her face.

'I'm Francine.'

'Roger Louche, co-Director,' he said, putting out his hand. She shook it, and was surprised to feel coarse hair on his skin beneath her fingers. The intimacy of her discovery seemed inappropriate in the atmosphere of the office and she felt herself begin to blush. 'Glad to have you with us, Francine.' He sat down on the edge of her desk, his manner abruptly changed. 'So how long do you think you'll stay?'

'As long as I'm needed,' said Francine, shrinking from the proximity of his bulk. From its fringes she could see one or two of the other secretaries watching them. 'I'm only temporary.'

'Oh, don't say "only"! We need girls like you around here, otherwise we'd die of boredom. It'll be nice to have something good to look at for a change. No, don't be embarrassed!' He lowered his voice and leaned towards her. Close up, his face was large and porous. 'You're a very attractive girl. It's nothing to be ashamed of.'

Francine giggled with mingled pleasure and anxiety. At the sound he stood up again suddenly and dropped the piece of paper on the desk in front of her.

'Type that up for me by lunch-time, will you?' he said, turning and walking back to his desk.

Francine watched his retreating back with astonishment. The piece of paper had slid from her desk to the floor and she bent to retrieve it. When she re-emerged she saw Mr Louche watching her from his podium. She caught his eye and he looked away. Francine sat with a beating heart. She wished Jane would come back. An older woman sat at a desk identical to Francine's at the foot of Mr Louche's podium. She was plump with short permed hair and wore a cardigan over her shoulders instead of the tailored jacket worn by most of the other secretaries. Francine hadn't noticed her until that minute, but now she realized that the woman must be Mr Louche's own secretary. She sat for a moment, paralysed by the necessity for asserting herself.

'Hey you!' said Mr Lancing suddenly. 'You!'

Francine looked up and saw that he was speaking to her.

'Yes, Mr Lancing?'

'Get me Bill,' he said, picking up his telephone and dialling a number.

Francine waited for further instructions but Mr Lancing had begun speaking into the receiver. She searched her desk for a list of numbers which might help her and soon found a plastic wheel bristling with hundreds of cards at the far end. She began to flick hopelessly through them. Beside her, Mr Louche's letter lay unresolved.

'It's a vanilla reit, dumbo,' said Mr Lancing into the phone.

Her own telephone rang and she froze at the sound. It shrilled again and she picked it up, but as she opened her mouth to speak she suddenly lost all memory of where she was.

'Hello? Hello?' said a man's voice impatiently.

'Yes, hello!' said Francine. 'Can I help you?'

'Don't they teach you how to answer the phone over there?'

'I'm sorry, I was—'

'I need Lancing,' said the man.

'He's on the phone,' said Francine shortly, desperate to be rid of this latest interference.

'Well, do you take a message too, or do they just programme you to pick it up?'

'Who may I tell him called?'

'Tell him it's Bill.'

'Oh, Bill!' gushed Francine gratefully. 'I know he's been trying to get hold of you!'

'I was here,' said Bill, audibly shrugging.

'I mean, I know he *wanted* to speak to you, I don't know if he's actually *tried*—'

'What is this?'

'I'll just see if I can get him off the phone for you,' said Francine, jamming her finger over the hold button. Mr Lancing was still talking, his back turned towards her. 'Mr Lancing!' she said. 'Mr Lancing!' When there was no response she snapped her fingers in desperation and the other secretaries raised their heads in horrified unison. Eventually Mr Lancing looked round.

'What?' he said, holding the receiver against his neck.

'Bill's on the line for you.'

'Oh, put him on!' he said, waving his arm. 'Dial the other phone. Larry, can you hold a second? I gotta talk to Bill,' he added, although the telephone was still pressed to his neck.

'Just putting you through,' said Francine, releasing the hold button. To her despair, the handset was emiting a dull tone. 'Hello?' she said, pressing buttons indiscriminately. 'Hello?'

'Where's Bill?' said Mr Lancing.

'I think I lost him,' admitted Francine.

'Well, get him back!'

'But I don't have his number—'

'Larry? You still there? Sorry, we got a new girl here. Look, like I was saying—'

Francine replaced the phone and fixed her eyes on the desktop. They stung with tears and she held herself rigid until they receded. Finally she stood up, Mr Louche's letter in her hand, and walked determinedly to his desk.

'Excuse me?' she said, standing before him. He was reading something and didn't look up. Beside him his secretary sat neatly tapping at her keyboard, her eyes fixed on the screen. Apart from her fingers, her soft body was motionless. 'Mr Louche?'

'Sorry, yes?' he said, looking up in surprise. His face was blank.

Francine felt herself grow cold with anxiety. She held the letter before him.

'Mr Louche, I don't think I'm supposed to do this.'

He was silent for a moment.

'Why not?' he said finally, as if he were interested.

'I've been employed to do Mr Lancing's work.'

'You've been employed,' said Mr Louche slowly after a pause, 'to do whatever you're told.'

A sudden faintness stole over her.

'But surely,' she persisted, smiling in an attempt to infuse her words with charm, 'surely your own secretary should type your correspondence?'

'Barbara has enough work to do,' said Mr Louche.

At the sound of her name, Barbara turned her head and stared at Francine with mute eyes. Her face was very plain. The three of them were locked for a moment in silence. Francine turned and went back to her desk, the letter still in her hand.

At 11.25 Francine reminded Mr Lancing of his haircut. He hadn't spoken to her since her earlier mistake with the telephones, and although she feared that his silence was the signal of his displeasure, she was relieved at least that he seemed to have forgotten about Bill.

'See you later,' she said foolishly, as he put on his suit jacket. The collar was turned up and she wondered if she should tell him.

'I'll be back!' he said with a crooked grin.

Their eyes met as if by mistake, and she saw his dim with the lack of recognition. After he had left the office, she imagined him seeing his upturned collar in the barber shop mirror and wished that she'd told him. He would know that she had seen it. She turned to her computer screen and began to type Mr Louche's letter. His writing was neat, and she was glad that she didn't have to go to his desk and ask him to explain anything. Before long she had finished, and seeing how easily the task had been accomplished she felt oddly warm with gratitude for her humiliation. She fussed with it, adding touches on the screen to improve its appearance. In a moment of inspired alertness, she took down one of the files of past correspondence from the shelves behind her and looked at one or two of the letters to make sure that she had typed Mr Louche's according to the correct format. Finally she printed it out and, crossing the office, placed it before him on his desk. He read it while she stood there, without looking up. After a long time, he raised his head.

'Good girl,' he said, smiling brilliantly.

Four

Ralph unlocked the door to his flat and as he entered the dark, motionless hall experienced that momentary qualm of ownership which, even after three years of it, still lightly besieged him sometimes when he returned alone at the end of the day. When he had first bought the flat, he used to come home in an eager, questioning mood – often as early as he could – as if it were a lover or a new child, wondering what it had been doing during the hours he had been away. In those days it had represented a form of welcome to him, a region in which his focus was undisputed and reliable. He supposed that he should have worried about intruders or burst drains in that moment of reunion, and prepared himself for the sight of the spilled guts of drawers, the sounds of dripping and desecration to greet him with their anarchic protest at his absence; but his flat had always been as good as gold, sitting waiting for him with an expression either of independence or of neglect, depending on whether he'd left it tidy or not, and in the end he had begun to regard it merely as another cloistered annexe of himself, a space into which the stuffy chambers of his heart and head had gradually overspilled their contents and rendered indistinguishable. He had grown impatient with its inability to be transformed, beyond the small, angular puddle of letters which sometimes gathered by the door and the staring red eye of the answering machine which could occasionally be found resuscitated and blinking with life when he returned, and although of course he was grateful that the glassy eyes of its windows hadn't been smashed nor its contents ravished with violence, still, he wondered what it would look like afterwards.

Two calling-cards from taxi companies lay on the hall carpet at his feet and he stepped over them as if demonstrating his indifference before an invisible audience. Halfway down the hall he turned back and went to pick them up, deciding instead to find them useful and perhaps pin them on the kitchen noticeboard. With this in mind he continued back down the hall, bypassing the sitting-room where the tawdry drama of the answering machine might or might not have been playing.

The kitchen made a spectral tableau in the falling gloom of early evening, the rigid great-aunts of the chairs around the table, the fridge a tall, stern butler hovering in a corner, the face of the clock obscured to a halt by shadows. He switched on the light and felt immediately comforted by its generic familiarity, its resemblance to other kitchens he had seen. Putting the cards on the table, he opened the fridge and was rather pleased to see a bottle of beer in it, for a moment having no memory of actually buying one. Its further contents – margarine, milk, a yellow square of cheese sealed in plastic, something leafy on one of the lower shelves – reminded him of his trip late the night before to a mini-market two streets away, a dingy place in whose overcrowded aisles nothing ever seemed real or distinct enough to purchase, but where nevertheless he had gone in a sudden burst of life and bought the beer with the intention of its meeting him the next evening in precisely the manner it was now doing. The bottle had been lukewarm and dusty when he took it from the market shelf, but in the cold sunlight of the fridge had been transformed into a green and frosted icon, which in turn elevated the items around it to a more appealing plane. He took the beer and, seeing the cards still lying on the table, picked them up and threw them into the bin.

From the dreary distance of his shabby third-floor office on the Holloway Road, Ralph often looked forward to his three or four solitary evenings at home each week. The fact that, once he had fled the fabricated world of the office and felt the memory of himself begin patchily to return on his bus journey home, he no longer needed to be on his own, seemed continually to elude him in his social calculations. Sitting exposed at his desk he would crave isolation, unlimited draughts of time alone amongst his possessions, but the relief of escape drained him and he would vainly wait for the spring of selfhood which the rock of his daily round had seemed all day to be blocking to begin to flow. Instead, there was merely a resounding emptiness, which made him suspect during his long hours of loneliness that the alien exercise of doing work which did not suit him had forced him to change, moving him further and further from the mouth of his resources until he had become stranded and unable to find his way back. He would often read or listen to music as the night deepened outside, familiar habits which now, however, he would find himself asking for whom or what he did them. His points of reference had grown dim, his signposts muddied: sensations and ideas would arrive and then get lost, circulating around the junctions of his mind, unable to find a connection.

There had been a time, he supposed, when he had not felt this powerlessness, when, had he but perceived his own fluidity, he might have escaped the machinery which was now making him; but he had been so eager to fix himself that all the more discreet aspects of his volition had been swept along by this one great desire for *something*, and he had followed the first course which presented itself as if it had been ordained that he should do so. He had tried, of course, after he left university, to formulate some plan for his own betterment, but it hadn't really surprised him to find, when he searched himself for ambition, merely the desire unobtrusively to survive. He had applied for the types of jobs which had become familiar to him through the talk of his peers, had latched himself wearily on to their futures and jogged behind as they rushed towards them, but his inability to imagine that he might be put to some use which would manufacture as its by-product his own happiness meant that the waves of rejection which his activity generated had washed back over him warm with his acceptance of them. He had attended his only interview gratefully, and in the fever of examination did not think to test the position – an inexplicit editorial role on a free local newspaper – for its own merits. Relieved at having pulled off twenty minutes of pleasant conversation with Neil, his boss, he had not considered the future of lengthy encounters by which he was now daily assaulted. Neil had offered him the job there and then, telling him he was the only graduate who had applied; a revelation which at the time Ralph had obscurely taken as a compliment.

'I'm something of an intellectual myself,' Neil had said, straightening a tie across which autonomous golf clubs roamed.

The paper was a dreadful thing. Neil wrote most of it, copying stories assiduously from a heap of other newspapers on his desk while Ralph transcribed television listings and local events. Roz, the secretary, typed them up uncertainly. The majority of its flimsy pages were occupied by local advertisers and a long classified section, with which Ralph had at first been fascinated – the things people tried to sell! On his first day he had found one which read 'Pair of brown men's shoes, one missing, £5', and had made his friends laugh telling them about it – but at which now he could scarcely bear to look. The office was terribly cramped, although Neil told him that once the paper had occupied the entire third floor of the building. Since then it had been shouldered into its small corner by a more successful copywriting firm, whose suite of rooms encased behind giant plate-glass windows displayed immaculate grey prairies of executive carpet and desktop. The *Holloway Journal* emerged weekly from the compressed adjacent clutter, and seeing as it had little organized means of distribution – Neil had tried hiring door-to-door delivery boys, but found out that they were just dumping their consignments in the nearest bin – it was mostly touted on the pavements outside the building where Neil could keep an eye on things. Much as Ralph tried to avert his gaze from the paper during the week, he could not avoid witnessing its fortunes when he left the office on Friday evening. It pained him to see the feeble trajectory of his labours, and the fact that the scrawny boy buckling beneath the weight of his bag couldn't even manage to give the things away – Ralph watched passersby shy from his thrusting arm, digging their hands in their pockets as he approached them – meant that he usually felt compelled to accept a copy himself and display it as proudly as he was able until he found somewhere to throw it away unseen.

Nevertheless, the pay he received, like the work he did for it, was automatic, and Ralph would feel the soothing rhythms of his stability even through its worst oppression of him. He would occasionally rise with thoughts of liberation, but feeling himself teeter dangerously on the brink of change would withdraw quickly back into the ever-knitting security of his routine. His only alternative – that of transforming the fixed nature of his work – had been removed before he had even seen out the first month of his employment. He had attempted to infuse his listings with something of his own personality, but to his humiliation Neil had routed out every flourish and confronted him with its lifeless form.

'What's this "seminal" lark, then?' he had demanded once, brandishing a sheet of Ralph's copy before him. Ralph had lovingly ascribed the term to one of his favourite French films, which was showing on television that week. 'Is that dirty or what?'

It had been possible to accept his intransigent portion with mild amusement, and now he rarely strained beneath its strictures. His job paid him enough, and was capable, as long as he observed some restraint in his description of it, of standing up to the glancing attention he generally received. He did not require, for the time being at least, more than that.

The answering machine was undisturbed, and with the possibility of human intervention more or less ruled out for the evening, Ralph sat down with his beer and drew up the blind with which the distractions of his journey and return had concealed his thoughts. All week he had felt his mind leaning towards the prospect of his oncoming evening with Francine, a process which seemed so to have corralled every part of him in agreement with it that the customary position from which he saw things appeared to have altered. The ballasts of his life, he knew, were too flimsy to protect him from such slippage, and though he had tried, really there was nothing else he wanted to think about. He had negotiated with himself what he saw as a compromise, caging his wild and fluttering thoughts in the stronghold of their one agreed liaison, and he was relieved at least that he had managed to prevent his desires from running ahead to a region of fantasy where they would almost certainly perish.

He had telephoned Francine the day after their miraculous meeting – he saw it as that now, a wonderful and significant chance that had been given to him, like a golden key – and the boldness which his good fortune had inspired had seemed to round up the miscreant possibilities and force them into an orderly march in his favour. Francine had been at home, and had even answered the phone instead of Janice – whom he now treated, in his own mind at any rate, with the greatest mistrust – and he had secured their evening with such an assertion of will, such *force*, really, that when he had put down the phone after what he had already decided should be the briefest possible conversation, the communication which would least allow for any mistakes on his part and consequently any second thoughts on hers, he had felt quite unlike himself.

She was to come on Thursday, the day after tomorrow, to his flat. He had felt rather churlish about that, but they hadn't been able to decide on a place to meet on the phone – he had foolishly left it up to her, thinking that was the gentlemanly thing to do, and the poor girl had been quite at a loss – and detecting the approach of a conversational abyss in which he would be bound to undo himself, he had told her to come here. They could have a drink, he said, and then decide together where to have dinner. She had agreed, although not, if he was honest, in a way which particularly betrayed whether she thought it was a good idea or not, and that was when he had commandingly ended the conversation.

He would have to decide on a restaurant in advance, of course, and then casually suggest it to her as if it was a regular haunt, but so far nothing had seemed quite right. He had no car – public transport was out of the question – and besides, after making her come to his house it would seem silly then to go to another part of London. He wrestled once more with the handful of local places he knew, coming inevitably again upon their shortcomings. He never really went to restaurants, in fact. He and his father had always eaten in pubs, and at university he had never had enough money, and now he just didn't like them much. It was an area in which he felt even less able than usual to take control: he disliked being besieged by choice and felt embarrassed by the waiters, not only because of the strange contract which decreed that they serve him, but because their youthful, insolent faces, their snobbery, their very apparent *desire* to be mastered, rendered him hesitant and effete. They would invariably find him out, too, becoming deaf when he made his order, leaning forward and saying 'Excuse me?' and forcing him to repeat it, always seeming to find something in the loneliness of what he had chosen for himself to eat which merited a smirk and the implication of mockery.

He supposed he could cook dinner himself. He had done that before. The room had grown darker around the circle of lamplight in which he sat. He got up and switched on the overhead light. He would need to cheer things up if they were to spend the whole evening here. He could buy some flowers, and he'd have to clean the bathroom and get some nice soap. He remembered a conversation years ago with Stephen – what was it he'd said? – about what to do when a girl was coming round. Stephen had recited this list, as if he'd read it in a book, for God's sake; things like leaving letters around with exotic stamps, and what else? Oh yes, some kind of intriguing book lying open on the coffee table – actually, Stephen had said by the bed, but that was out of the question. He had gone too far, of course, talking about half-finished poems on the kitchen table and God knew what else. Ralph laughed aloud.

Ralph's flat was to the north of Camden, in a small labyrinth of identical streets where most of the houses were only two storeys high, like a cloned village. The area was bounded and bypassed on either side by two large roads along which streams of traffic ran, prevented from forging time-saving tributaries through the tiny residential island between them by a number of no-entry signs, dead ends, and tortuous one-way systems. This lack of circulation gave the area a curiously bloodless air, Ralph thought, an atmosphere of blockage which, though he valued the parochial quiet it guaranteed, sometimes made him forget the city which lay around it.

He had chosen Camden without hesitation when he had decided to buy somewhere to live, using the small but still inexplicable amount of money his father had left him. He knew things were probably cheaper elsewhere, but when he was younger he and Stephen had always used to come to Camden, during the half-terms and holidays it had mysteriously been decided he should spend with Stephen and his mother. Stephen's mother lived in west London, in a white mansion house surrounded by embassies. Ralph could remember seeing the large black cars installed with dark, motionless silhouettes roll silently past the kitchen windows, their bright flags writhing in the breeze. Stephen's mother was forgetful about money and Stephen would sometimes elicit his 'allowance', as it was called, from her twice in one day. Stephen's allowance, Ralph knew, in fact arrived regularly at his bank from his father, who lived abroad, but if she was party to it Lady Sparks never referred to their arrangement. In her vague way she always seemed rather frightened of Stephen and would rifle nervously in her purse at his request, producing a fistful of notes and offering them to him as if he were holding her at gun-point.

To his initial embarrassment and later concern, she gave Ralph money too, and although his stomach would knot with anxiety at the thought that she might pay him in front of Stephen, she never did. She would leave the money in his room or catch him on his own, her manner cool and confusing with discretion, and afterwards she would sometimes stroke his hair. He was grateful for it, of course, for he had little money of his own – just what his father had left him in a policy for his weekly upkeep, the rest to be collected when he came of age – and Stephen always liked to do expensive things when they were in London. Lady Sparks seemed to know just when his supplies were dwindling, and having learnt the secret of her acuity Ralph cultivated a slightly fearful respect for her. She was a small and elegant woman, so unlike the memory he had of his own mother, with a distracted, aristocratic voice and the redundant manners, the despairing aloofness, of a displaced, abandoned queen. She could unnerve Ralph if he was left alone with her for too long without the emboldening presence of Stephen's bravado, by looking at him so blankly that he thought she was mad. He knew Stephen had had a brother when he was very young who had fallen out of their car on a motorway and died, and although he sometimes thought that Lady Sparks perhaps liked him because of the brother, and might even want to adopt him as a replacement, the sight of her pale, empty eyes told him that she didn't feel that way at all. Stephen would do imitations of her when they were on their own, rolling his eyes back into his head and speaking in a feeble, effeminate voice until Ralph cried with guilty laughter. He said that his father had divorced her so that he could marry his French girlfriend Isobelle, with whom he now lived in a big house in the French countryside. Stephen went to stay with them sometimes during the summer and Ralph would have to go to London alone, where he crept nervously through the great, cool rooms to avoid the drifting ghost of Lady Sparks and more often than not kept to his bedroom and read during the hot days. Usually it was only for a week or two, though, and while Stephen would often say that he was going for Easter or Christmas, or for the two whole months of the summer, when the time came more often than not something 'came up' and he didn't go. Ralph had never met Stephen's father, or Isobelle, whom Stephen used to describe to the boys at school, claiming that he had once hidden in a wardrobe in their bedroom and watched them having sex through a crack in the door. They had two small children with French names which Ralph couldn't remember.

They would usually go to Camden in a black cab hailed in the street by Stephen. Ralph would sit in it, filled with the inebriation of awe and with a sense of how randomly this grace had fallen upon him, how little it had to do with anything that had happened to him before. He wondered now if his own occasional but nevertheless illogical habit of taking cabs existed in deference to those cloistered journeys, which he looked back on amazed that his younger self had felt no embarrassment when emerging from them into the cheerful anarchy of Camden High Street. The area had a significance for him, though, which he did not wish to escape: they had sat in pubs, had looked at people unlike themselves, had bought records and even 'scored', as they had called it, from skinny fetid men in the street – not like now, Ralph thought, when Stephen seemed to have a minion for every drug he used, a book full of telephone numbers to be dialled at all times, the late-night ringing of the bell. Stephen had used to 'skin up', another phrase which now seemed foreign to him but which once he had had tamed on his tongue, in broad daylight, and Ralph would take panicked nips at it, not really feeling anything. It couldn't have been very good, he thought now. He had taken things since which had made him feel so far inside himself that his voice was like a megaphone in the pit of his stomach trying to project things out of his mouth.

He smiled as he trudged over Camden Lock with the two bags of shopping he had bought at great but unheeded expense at a delicatessen opposite the Tube station. Even then, he remembered, Stephen had used to change his voice, adopting a colourful proletarian twang, like something out of an Ealing comedy, through which his precise vowels would protrude like limbs from an ill-fitting set of clothes. These days the contrast was less amusing, for the two had almost merged into a single all-purpose voice. When he telephoned Ralph, Stephen would often say things like 'all right?' instead of 'hello', or 'see you later' when Ralph wasn't going to see him later at all.

He reached his street, changing the bags to opposite hands. He had told Neil he was going to the doctor and had managed to get away early, something he had used to do frequently in the first, desperate months of his job. Eventually, though, things had changed, not at work but in his own acceptance of it: he had come to believe that there was nothing else, that this was the life that had been laid out for him, like a meal at a stranger's house, and that if he didn't like it he must change until he did, for there was nothing else.

It was not quite dark yet, the sky watery and blue with the aftermath of the afternoon's cold sun, but the air had grown thin and icy and Ralph was surprised to see children in T-shirts wheeling and chattering round the street on their bikes. They were a familiar motif of summer to him, but he hadn't seen them over the past few months and they had changed, had strange, brutal haircuts and new versions of their faces.

'Hello,' he said none the less as he passed them.

They looked round at him but didn't reply, their compressed mouths bursting with suspicious humour. As he reached his flat and took out his keys he heard a volley of cries behind him.

''*Allo*! '*Allo*!' they shouted in voices effete with vaudeville mimicry.

He shut the door, hoping they wouldn't be there by the time Francine arrived. He tried to imagine her in his road, a strange and beautiful fruit suddenly appearing on the bare branches of the sentinel winter trees which lined it. For a moment he felt faint at the prospect of the evening ahead, his responsibility for it, and almost decided there and then just to take her to a restaurant and be done with it. He put the bags of food on the kitchen table and sat down with his head in his hands. A thread of self-consciousness stole through him as he did so. He was the picture of despair, like somebody in a film. He laughed aloud at his own comedy. He would do exactly what he had set out to do: he had bought food and wine, had rendered the flat unrecognizable with order the night before, had even had his hair cut on the Holloway Road at lunchtime.

'Get the doctor to do something about your hair, mate,' Neil had said, folding over with his own hilarity, when Ralph had left for his fictitious appointment at four o'clock.

He stood and went to look at himself in the hall mirror. The cut made his face appear rather beefy, giving it the exposed, foolish look of a passport photograph. He ruffled it a bit and saw a spray of dark filaments fall gently to his shoulders. He turned away from the mirror, his face itchy and hot. He had planned to do the cooking first and then get himself ready at the last minute. He had ruled out the temptation to make something elaborate: it wasn't much of a temptation in any case, as his preliminary skim through his only cookery book – a strange fifteenth-birthday present from Lady Sparks, with garish photographs of prone crustaceans spewing lumpy substances from their backs – had informed him that he possessed neither the utensils nor the skills even the simplest dish demanded for its creation. He would make a risotto, something he had learned to do as a student; never properly, of course, merely approaching it by intuition and experiment, until finally he'd made it for a group of friends who'd called it risotto and said how much they'd liked it. This time, he had bought expensive things to put in it, which probably could have formed something more impressive if he assembled them in a different way, but the expansive, forgiving framework of the risotto offered an indispensable form of insurance against disaster.

He went to the sitting-room and looked at the answering machine. There was a message on it, and he regarded it for a moment with foreboding as he realized it might be Francine, saying that she couldn't make it after all. He pressed the button and heard Stephen's voice saying something clipped, which sounded like 'let's see' – probably 'it's me', Ralph thought – then a kind of long sigh and the clamour of the phone being put down. Everything was fine, then.

Some time later, Ralph lay in the bath. Next door, the risotto lay in the oven, warming. He had been too frightened to taste it, but he knew there was something wrong. At first it had been too liquid, and he had added more rice, in his enthusiasm rendering the whole thing rather glutinous, its parts indistinguishable. More worrying, however, was the peculiar smell it emanated, which Ralph had attempted to track down to some infestation of the fridge or kitchen cupboards but which finally he had had to admit was the perfume of his offering to Francine. He had attempted to identify it – it was a bitter, floury smell – from the parade of ingredients from which he had assembled the dish, but it had resembled none of them. In the end he had tried to disguise it with the addition of stronger presences which he had hoped would somehow crowd it out. The spices he had added had succeeded only in transforming its colour, against which he had had no complaint in the first place, and he had been forced to resign himself and place the muddy, odorous mass in a large dish in the oven.

The incident had burdened him with a sense of indifference

which was prolonging his lazy, lukewarm immersion dangerously close to the half-hour zone he had cordoned off for last-
minute preparations. His bath had thus far been a nihilistic
event, an exercise in detachment involving the objective
scrutiny and contemptuous dismissal of each immobile, ghoulish part of his body. In the day-dreams with which he had
readied himself for Francine's arrival, the bath had been a
hearty, foamy affair, a steamy and fragrant series of whale-
like dives and merry purgings, from which he would emerge
tousled and shining to spray and slap himself with pungent
substances. Only enforced contemplation of the inescapable
and fast-approaching evening succeeded finally in urging him
into a cursory scrubbing, and he rose from it dripping and
slightly more cheerful, thinking of how he and Francine could
laugh together at his risotto and how all he had to do was
relax. His hair didn't look so bad in the bathroom mirror
either, and after one or two different attempts his clothes
seemed all right too. He went back to confront the hall mirror,
and found that he had improved himself.

In a moment of largesse, filled with the growing sense of
his own urbanity, he decided to open a bottle of wine and
drink some of it, just to show Francine that he knew how to
be sociable with himself. She wasn't due to arrive for half an
hour yet, taking into account the fifteen minutes by which he
assumed she would be late, whether by accident or design. He
opened the oven door and peered in through the crack. His
oven had a light in it which gave the risotto the appearance of
a museum exhibit, a dish of planetary matter brought back by
astronauts, or a porridgy alien captured and held hostage. He
slammed the door shut and opened one of the bottles of red
wine he had bought at the delicatessen. Sitting at the kitchen
table with it, he realized that he hadn't spent an evening –
well, this kind of evening, anyway – with a woman for a long
time. He had *thought* that he had, of course, but the quite

suffocating excitement and fear with which he currently trembled explained to him why he had felt so awkward on those occasions, almost as if he didn't care what happened during them. He had cared in the hours before a liaison, going through the imaginary evening like a diligent tourist would a guidebook, marking every highlight; and then registering his disappointment on arrival at each reality with equal thoroughness. This time, he had tried not to think about anything beyond the moment of Francine's arrival. His unfamiliarity with her rendered his conjectures flimsy and unenjoyable, and it was a testament to her superiority, he thought, that the idea of imagining her in unplayed scenes appeared all at once rather lewd and inappropriate. He had always thought that love, or even infatuation, took him a long time to make, an old-fashioned business which would eventually produce a high-quality emotion. If he was honest about it, though, Belinda was the only person he had really loved, and when he first met her he had instantly felt much the same as he was feeling now. The disbelief at the beginning that she had agreed to go out with him, gradually eroded by the fact of her continuing presence; really, it had been the most amazing thing. He had felt disbelief at the end, too, but events had made it true, a sickening succession of votes cast against him until he had had to concede that he had lost.

His glass was empty and he poured more wine into it. He never saw Belinda now, hadn't seen her for two years actually. She had tried to be his friend, he supposed, but he had messed it up, unable to stand the sight or sound of her, really, everything she did without him hurting him. She had said that had upset her more than anything else. It made him laugh. He laughed now, the sound ghostly in the empty flat. At least she didn't see Stephen either, pretty much the only good thing to have come out of that time. Not that Stephen cared, of course, but it would have made Ralph's main achievement of the last two years – never thinking about Belinda – that much more difficult. He was thinking about her now, though, he could feel himself doing it. He drained his glass and held the bottle once more at its rim. His hand shook, and the two glass lips chattered against each other loudly. At the sound, a quite unstoppable feeling of fear began to steal over him. He had worked so hard to compress all of that, to hammer it down and keep it somewhere out of sight, but here it was springing up in all its large, noisy mockery, and for a moment he couldn't remember how he had ever managed to crush and contain it. He tried to think of something else – Francine, that was right – but everything around him suddenly seemed so foreign and far away that he could not place himself within it. A great shiver shook him as spools of memory began to unreel messily across his thoughts, scenes hurtling by in the gallop towards the blackest part of himself, the only thing he ever thought of as true and yet it was so fantastic, so easy to deny – as they had both denied it! – that he thought he had cut it off for ever, that he would never go there again. He clenched his fists on the table and felt something burn at his eyes, so hot and dry that it seemed wrung from the tight and boiling ball of his heart. His misery struggled and was born; and when it did so everything seemed to stop, to accept the impossibility of going on, as if he had some place in the world where he reigned, a small place where he could say the sun wouldn't rise tomorrow if he didn't want it to.

The doorbell rang, and Ralph jumped in reflex as the loud voltage pealed through him. Its alarm dispersed slowly into silence, and it was a while before it reconstituted itself in his thoughts. Francine was at the door. Everything seemed foggy and submerged, and he stood up heavily, realizing that he felt quite drunk. He set off down the hall, his footsteps loud as earthquakes in his ears.

Five

Francine stood outside Ralph's front door and used the delay between her ringing the bell and his answering it to make some last-minute adjustments to her appearance. She unbuttoned the jacket she had been forced by cold to fasten during the walk from the Tube station – she had compared the two styles several times during the day, before the large mirror in the ladies', and had concluded that the open front was more flattering – and inspected the blouse beneath to make sure it had not been deranged by its period of enclosure. It was slightly flattened and she plucked at it expertly until it hung in a more becoming fashion, casting as she did so a keen eye over the glimmering vista of her stockinged legs. They appeared undamaged by their journey, but she craned her head and twisted first one leg and then the other to afford her a view from behind, just in case. She had debated bringing a set of different clothes in a bag to work so as to change into them at the end of the day and thus appear more casual, but when she considered that the tailored suits and high-heeled shoes she wore to the office revealed her to her best advantage, the necessity of travelling directly from the City to Ralph's flat appeared to provide the perfect excuse for remaining in them.

The street was quiet and motionless, and in the absence of

its activity Francine felt the thin, freezing night air penetrate her clothing and touch her skin. Ralph was taking a long time to answer the door. The thought of his panic pleased her, but in view of the fact that she had lingered shivering at dark shop windows on the way to ensure the expiry of a full half hour beyond the time on which they had decided, she had expected him to be straining with anxious readiness for her arrival. She turned on her heel in irritation so that her back was to the door – he would certainly get the message when he finally decided to open it! – and wearily assumed an aspect of contemplation towards the street. It was really very cold now, and she knew that the pale skin on her nose and chin tended to become inflamed in such conditions. The thought kindled a flame of indignation at her predicament, and she had just turned to ring petulantly a second time when she heard a sudden thunder of footsteps and the rattling of locks as the door opened.

The hall behind him was dark, and Ralph seemed different standing there from the person Francine remembered. In the grey illumination of the street lamps his face looked severe, almost unfriendly, and there was something complex in his unfamiliarity which sent a tremor of aversion through her. For a moment he didn't say anything at all, and without his direction Francine found herself unable to act. Experience had created the expectation that her reception would be a warm and windless affair, a meteorological certainty brought about by the constant current of her attractions, and she naturally shrank from the coolness of Ralph's greeting.

'Hello,' he said finally, still standing in the doorway as if he had no intention of permitting her to progress beyond it. A strong instinct informed Francine that things were not proceeding in the correct way.

'I thought you weren't in,' she said. Her voice twanged unkindly in her ears, forgetting its recent lessons in intonation, but the sight of Ralph made her feel horribly as if she didn't care what he thought. In fact, the situation was growing every minute less acceptable – why was he making her stand there in the cold, looking at her with that rude expression? – and had the rejection it implied not compelled her to endure it for the purposes of investigation, she felt sure she would have turned around that minute and gone home. All at once, as if sensing their arrival at the threshold of an impossibility, Ralph, although apparently at the expense of some effort, underwent the necessary transformation.

'I'm sorry,' he said, the pale plate of his face breaking into a smile. He turned and switched on the hall light. 'I was on the phone when you rang the bell and I couldn't seem to get away – sorry, do come in.' He stood back to allow her in, his cheeks suffused with colour as he ran a hand over his hair. 'Sorry, you must be frozen – sorry, come in. How are you?'

In the light of the hall, Francine felt the situation returning once more to dimensions she recognized. She looked at Ralph and was alarmed to notice a curious dark stain on his lips, like blood. He smiled again reassuringly, ushering her with his arm towards an open door on the right.

'It's just through there,' he said. 'Go ahead.'

Her inability to comprehend it, as well as Ralph's belated restitution of the appropriate behaviour, encouraged her to forget what had just happened. She followed his directions and found herself in a large, warm room glowing with lamplight. Its welcoming atmosphere exerted an immediate improvement upon her spirits, and she even managed to summon some enthusiasm for the thought of how flattering the gentle light must be to her complexion.

'I'll just get you a glass of wine,' said Ralph from the doorway. 'Make yourself at home.'

He disappeared and moments later she heard the proper sounds of the kitchen, the thump of cupboard doors and the clink of glasses. The room was really quite elegant, and although Francine thought the presence of heavy curtains and shelves full of books and what looked like second-hand furniture a bit old-fashioned, still it had a kind of authority which she judged to be pleasing. The floor was wooden – a feature she knew from magazines to be fashionable, and for which she awarded Ralph credit, notwithstanding the fact that she secretly thought the effect somewhat miserly – and there was a fireplace at the other end with a mirror over it. She immediately crossed the room and stood in front of it to see if the ordeals of the interlude between her last reflection in the office toilets and her arrival here had wrought any unwanted changes. Surprisingly, she actually looked improved by the exercise, and she peered more closely, suspecting the dim light of concealment. Magnified, the image was still pleasing and Francine regarded it with satisfaction. She had never known her appearance not to be well behaved, but she was wiser than to let this consideration relax her discipline of it.

Ralph's footsteps sounded down the hall behind her and she lowered her gaze to the mantelpiece, where she was confronted by a photograph of Stephen Sparks in a silver frame. His presence surprised her, and she greeted it with mingled bitterness and excitement. It was a close-up of his face, although she could see his hair, which was much longer than it was now. It looked unfashionable and rather silly, she thought disappointedly.

'Here we go,' said Ralph, putting two glasses on the table.

The stain had disappeared from his lips, and the sight of his short hair made Francine warm to him. He came and stood beside her at the fireplace.

'Stephen in his hippie era,' he said, nodding at the photograph.

'I like your flat,' said Francine. The presence of the

photograph suggested something complicated which might interfere with the now-smooth transmission of Ralph's interest in her. Unconsciously, she hoped that Stephen would be admonished from the mantelpiece by the sight of them together. 'How much do you pay?'

'What? Oh, I don't – I mean, I do, but I own it.'

'Really?'

Francine's sense of her own foolishness was ameliorated by her pleasure at his ownership. She felt the reassuring thirst for conquest rise in the wake of this newly ingested information.

'Well, it's only small,' Ralph said. 'Here, have some wine.'

He handed her a glass. The wine was red, and she felt a slight cooling of her admiration as she wondered why he hadn't given her a choice, or at least offered her something like a gin and tonic instead. When he had suggested drinks she had vaguely imagined them having cocktails, with a lustrous cherry speared by a parasol. Red wine tasted bitter to her, and in any case she thought people only drank it at dinner-time, not before. The memory of their unpleasant doorstep encounter began to rally from its consignment, and with it came the recollection of their telephone conversation, in which Ralph had been abrupt and not at all polite. At the time she had been quite impressed by his assurance, though, and this factor, along with Ralph's flat, his now improved manners, and his really not unpleasing appearance, rose in battle against Francine's disaffection. She waited to see what his next move would contribute to the conflict.

'Do you know, I didn't even ask you if you *wanted* red wine,' he exclaimed suddenly. He made a gesture with his hands which suggested impatience with himself. 'It's just that it's all anybody seems to drink these days – sorry, would you have preferred something else?'

'No, I love it,' said Francine, immediately taking a mouthful as if to mark it territorially. It tasted acrid and rather dirty.

Ralph glanced at her and then looked down. He wasn't looking at her as much as she had expected: when she had met him by chance that time in Camden Market his eyes had kept bounding towards her, two shining, hungry dogs straining on a leash, and she wondered why the more comfortable element of his ardour had been exchanged for this new atmosphere of restraint. It proved difficult to locate a solution to this mystery which pleased her, and she abandoned it with the thought that the very darkness of Ralph's motives at least guaranteed an intensity of which she was confident of being the object. He drank from his glass, tipping back his head slightly so that most of the wine drained down his throat. He wiped his mouth with the back of his hand and then looked at it.

'Do you mind if I smoke?' said Francine.

'No, please do – please, go ahead.'

She put down her glass and crossed the room to find her bag with a sense of liberation in the movement and the noise of her heels knocking against the wooden floor. The commotion seemed also to arouse Ralph.

'Have you come straight from work?' he said, raising his voice behind her.

She rummaged gracefully in her bag and came back across the room towards him before she answered. His eyes, awaiting her reply, were fixed on her as she approached.

'Oh, yes. I often have to stay late. Would you like one?'

'Oh – OK, why not?'

His tone was warmer now, and the exchange of the cigarette manufactured a successful intimacy. He met her eyes, and Francine felt confident that she had magnetized his thoughts and was drawing them out of their dark recess towards her. She was unused to having to do so much to secure her victories: the normal pattern of such engagements invariably permitted her a defensive position, from which she would admit or repel foreign advances. Ralph's seclusion, however, demanded some form of attack, and the discovery of a small but none the less unexpected body of resistance barring the path to his surrender was beginning to inspire in Francine the idea that what lay beyond it must be of greater worth than she had thought.

'What exactly is it that you're doing?' said Ralph. He seemed to comprehend the stiffness of his own question, and added: 'I don't believe I've ever even asked you.'

'I work for the director of a company in the City,' said Francine. She waved her cigarette distractingly. 'I don't have a light.'

'Oh – let's see, there'll be some matches in the kitchen. Come on, I'll give you a guided tour.' He led the way across the sitting-room. 'So is your director a bit of an ogre?' he said over his shoulder. 'It sounds like he works you very hard.'

'He does.' Francine followed him. 'But a lot of it's my own work too.'

'How's that?' said Ralph.

'Well—' Francine was glad that he couldn't see her face. 'I'm trying to learn a bit about the business.'

'So is this a long-term thing?' They entered the kitchen and Ralph began searching the counter-tops. 'For some reason I thought you did temporary work.'

He opened and shut drawers loudly. The end of a metal bottle-opener flew up and jammed at a right-angle from one of them, and Ralph tried unsuccessfully to slam it shut two or three times without noticing the impediment. His face was red, and in the strong light Francine could see it was covered with a boisterous mask of sweat.

'I can't seem to find them – oh, hang on, I can just light it from the cooker, can't I?'

He put the cigarette in his mouth and bent down over the hob, turning a knob with his hand. A ring of blue flame leapt up towards his face and he shied slightly, straightening up seconds later with the smouldering cigarette still hanging from his lips. An oddly sweet smell of burning drifted towards Francine in a cloud of cigarette smoke, and she saw that Ralph's face was screwed up as if a bright light were shining in it.

'There we are,' he said, handing her the cigarette. His voice wavered with physical strain. 'Can you light yours from that?' He rubbed his hand across his face as she lit her cigarette and then touched his eyebrows tentatively with his fingers. 'Oh dear,' he said.

'It's a nice kitchen,' said Francine, looking around to avoid giving the situation her attention. Suddenly she remembered a time, a few years ago, when she had gone to meet a man in a bar which was in a basement and had a long, steep flight of steps down to the entrance. She had stumbled and fallen all the way down, and although the pain had been severe, she had picked herself up, examined her clothing to make sure that no trace of her accident remained, and had walked into the bar as if nothing had happened. Fortunately, there had been no one else on the stairs at the time to witness her mishap. When she got home that evening, she had found large, black bruises across her back and legs which had taken weeks to disappear.

'Thanks,' said Ralph, composing himself. He leaned against the cupboards and drew deeply on his cigarette. 'Which business is it that you're learning?'

For a moment Francine couldn't think of what he was talking about.

'Oh, I'm sure you don't want to talk about this,' she said, smiling. 'It's pretty boring.'

'No, I'm interested,' said Ralph. 'I don't know anything about the City. I just twiddle my thumbs on the Holloway Road all day writing things that no one's ever going to read.' He laughed, as if to himself. 'Tell me what your company – what's it called?'

'Lancing & Louche.'

'There you go! You'd never find Lancing & Louche on the Holloway Road. Tell me what they do.'

'They're financial,' said Francine. Her thoughts writhed against the bent of the conversation.

'What, an investment bank?'

'That sort of thing.' She looked around her as if she had lost something. 'I think I've left my glass in the other room.'

'Oh, sorry – let's go and sit down, shall we?'

Francine headed gratefully for the hall. For a minute Ralph didn't follow her, and when she looked back she saw him rubbing his face. He blinked his eyes fiercely several times, his eyebrows moving up and down as if in astonishment, and then turned to the oven and opened it. Sensing Francine standing there, he straightened up guiltily.

'Look, I've got a confession to make,' he said. 'I know I said we'd go to a restaurant, but then I thought it might be nicer to have something here instead. What do you think?'

The news of a confession had set Francine's heart thudding and it was a minute before she could understand the meaning of what he had said. When it came, the revelation was something of a disappointment. She was immediately gripped by the suspicion that he had lost interest in her, and didn't want to be put to the expense or effort of taking her out. The sundry collection of clues which, when amassed, testified to Ralph's odd and irrational character reinforced this conclusion; but vanity told a different story, and Francine shortly found herself more attracted to the idea that he wanted her all to himself, in a shuttered seclusion where developments could be allowed freely to unfold.

'Oh, I'm not that hungry anyway,' she said, weighing up the sacrifice of a restaurant's glamour, with its opportunities for public appreciation and its tokens of private expense, against this new and uncertain plan. 'Don't go to any trouble on my account.'

'But I want to!' Ralph replied. 'I mean, I already have, it's in the oven – I don't know if you'll like it very much, that's all. It's only a risotto.'

His presupposal of her agreement to having dinner in his flat was held in the balance, Francine felt, by his already having prepared it. She had heard of girls beings asked to dinner and expected to help, or worse still to do the whole thing themselves. It was not what she had hoped for, but nevertheless Francine could see how Ralph's behaviour could be construed as heroic when she described it to Janice and perhaps one or two of the secretaries at work. That it was 'only' a risotto was more unsettling, but her ignorance of risotto, combined with its admittedly exotic sound, left her no choice but to attribute his qualification to modesty.

'I love risotto,' she said, finding, as the word fell easily from her lips, that in fact she really did.

Six

The blind was up over the kitchen window and Ralph could see himself clearly reflected in it, a strange photograph of a private, incoherent moment into which he could gaze and fall. The tide of self-absorption began mounting again in his veins, as it had all evening, and when it drummed insistently behind his eyes he turned away from the window and began busying himself at the kitchen counters to drive it back down into the pool of his stomach.

It required a surprising effort of belief to remember that Francine was in the next room, waiting for the dinner he had said he would bring if she could just leave him alone with his mess for a few moments, and although he knew that the wine had no doubt dampened the ignition of thought and made him an obscure, heavy creature of uncertain impulses, his malfunctioning sense of contingency was lodged in a deeper place more resistant to immediate repair. It was strange to think of how he had travelled so steadily towards this evening with Francine, his destination the object of joyful anticipation, his means of conveyance sure beneath the friction of nerves; the certainty that time would bring it to pass, and that for once he had the heart for the journey, making him lower his guard against the inevitable intervention of other forces to disrupt his passage to happiness. And yet really there had been no other forces; it had all happened as he had hoped it would, except for the one thing that of course he hadn't expected, the derailment of his own desires!

He had felt a kind of dark exhilaration at moments during the evening, an almost gleeful disbelief at the scandalous abscondment of his proper feelings, and yet his inability to experience the correct sensations in Francine's presence revealed him to himself in the sinister light of dreams, where the sight of a familiar face is accompanied by the sudden recognition of an unglimpsed evil behind it. He had thought that he knew every channel of himself, the capacity of each vat of his heart and mind and the vacillating measure of spirits within them; but here was a vast, unpatrolled space, a great cellar to which he had rarely opened the door but where he now knew the debris of his disappointments was still stored. Such things he had thought incinerated, long since consigned to dust, but now he had caught the diluted stench of it all over him he knew the residue of his miseries still lived in him, leaking its deleterious perfume daily into his thoughts. Nevertheless, he had always regarded his wounds as things inflicted on him by other people, and it was odd to be spoiling something for himself. He supposed it had happened because Francine had expected him to lead her, had been unable to draw him away from his descent, until he had found himself wishing she would just go home and leave him to plunge back into his darkness.

She had been something of a disappointment to him, in fact; he could admit that now that his hopes for the evening had subsided. When he had opened the door and first seen her, he had had the impression of someone who shouldn't have been there at all, someone so unrelated to his own life that for a moment it had seemed impossible that the drinks and dinner would still go ahead. It was her clothes, probably, a strange executive uniform which was as resistant to his sensibilities as armour and which made her presence at his door seem unnatural. He knew she must have just come from work, and yet he hadn't been able to find enough in the personality of her job to fill its outward appearance, and he was left with a sense of her as a strange mannequin who had come to pose in his sitting-room. She was beautiful, of course, but her beauty could find no conduit through which to flow to him: it remained forcefully packed in her face, a disruptive presence.

Of course, he had made a complete fool of himself, spinning idiocies for conversation, capering with the mimicry of charm in the absence of all his better qualities. It had astonished him to discover that even so she was willing to shine for him. He had expected her to be filled with the skills necessary to find him out, blade-sharp with social acumen, but she merely went along with it all with an air of slightly dumbfounded accept-ance, for all the world as if his madness was something of which he had mastery! Then again, perhaps the poor girl was only being kind in trying to normalize him; or perhaps, Heaven help her, she too felt herself to be on trial. In his mind he rose and regarded their situation from above. From a larger perspective, things hadn't been so bad. They had drunk and conversed in a civilized manner, and now Ralph was going to serve dinner. He saw them eating it, their bodies cold and private beneath their clothes, his thoughts swarming at the glass of his eyes.

He removed the risotto from the oven, and was amused by how appropriate its unfathomable horror now seemed. It looked uglier than ever, aged by its long, dry stint in the heat, and Ralph considered sacrificing it to save the evening in its death throes, dropping it on the floor and taking Francine out to a place where the noise of life would perhaps provide them with a clue as to their part in it, and where by imitating the people around them they could improvise their own little drama. Fatigued suddenly with drink, he decided against it. It would be unwise to animate the strange creature they made together and watch what he knew would be its ghastly, fleeting dance. He just wanted to get through it, tunnel through the hardest, shortest route which would deliver him to solitude.

He loaded everything on to a large tray and bore it down the hall and into the sitting-room. Francine was on the sofa and Ralph felt a sudden impulse of pity for her, for he had given her nothing to do while she sat and waited, and his relentless tidying had deprived the surfaces of the room of interest. She had the neat, apprehensive appearance of someone awaiting an appointment, and his pity was overcome by a fresh surge of bewilderment at her presence there.

'Here we are,' he said brightly, desperate to rouse her. 'Do you want to come and sit down?'

She got up from the sofa and walked carefully towards him, and he suddenly saw that her mystery was an effect of her silence, a knowing vacancy in which people were invited to construe their own versions of her. He wondered why he had not perceived this before, and supposed it was because he too had construed, had projected a manic, bumbling effusion of self before an inscrutable object.

'Where did you learn to cook?' said Francine as he put the dish in the centre of the table.

'What? Oh, nowhere. As you can probably tell,' he added, gesturing deprecatingly at the risotto. 'How hungry are you?'

She looked about her.

'Have you got any candles?' she said.

'Um – yes, yes, I should think so.' He found the request disconcerting, a demand for romance which made him appear churlish; yet it wasn't really a demand, it wasn't, *Haven't* you got any candles?; it was more of a plea. 'I'll just find some.'

There were two candlesticks on the mantelpiece with the matches he had sought earlier beside them. He thought of his ridiculous performance at the hob, where he had singed his eyelashes and eyebrows, and, had he not had it cut, would probably have set his hair alight too. He hadn't wanted to draw attention to himself by rushing to a mirror, although Francine hadn't seemed to have noticed what had happened. He glanced at his reflection now in the mirror over the mantelpiece. There was an unfamiliar expression on his face, a sort of garrulous stupidity, and he barely recognized himself. His eyebrows seemed unharmed, though, and he picked up the candlesticks and went back to the table.

Once the candles had been lit and the lights turned off, Ralph had to admit that things looked better. The risotto had receded into a vague landscape of earth-brown hillocks, the glasses shone palely like translucent moons, and he found it easier to focus in the softer illumination on Francine's face. The candlelight was a levelling element, a warm and buoyant pool in which their separateness seemed less brutal. Francine, too, seemed to respond to its gentleness, and as he watched her, only half listening to her reply to a question he had asked, he felt the gradual melting of his reserve send trickles of feeling through him. The lurching disorientation of his drunkenness settled into a more benign and fertile detach-ment, and he noticed that Francine was more attractive when she was animated and that her dark eyes were wonderfully eloquent in the dim light.

'Are we ever going to eat this?' he said almost gaily.

'Why not?'

She laughed and looked at the risotto with mock-suspicion. He picked up the serving spoon and brandished it comically, warmed by the flicker of friendliness.

'Many reasons,' he said sternly. 'But we haven't time to go into them.'

'Right.'

She laughed again as he plunged the spoon into the centre of the resistant crust and tried to pry some of it loose.

'Need to get some muscle behind it,' said Ralph, standing up and leaning forcefully on the handle of the spoon. A large clod sprang from the dish and was catapulted into the air. 'Oh God – where's it gone?'

Francine collapsed into giggles as Ralph searched the area around the table. His mind was humming with humour and he played the fool, crouching down and looking under a rug to fresh shrieks of laughter. He felt drunk again, a light and ebullient sensation which lifted him above his inhibitions and made a success of the smallest things.

'It's escaped,' he said, standing up. 'We'll have to send out a search party.'

'Never mind,' said Francine.

'Shall I try again?'

She nodded, her face alive with responses to him. She leaned forward encouragingly and Ralph was all at once dizzied by her acquiescence. She was *offering* herself to him – she *wanted* him to accept her; it was all he had to do! – and he suddenly saw where it might end. He met her gaze for a moment and felt a clear current pass between them. If he understood it correctly, he was being given an opportunity; there would be no further tests, nothing for him to do but accept it. Excitement leapt up in his throat, unchained. The tangible presence of a fantasy unalloyed by a complex object was so altogether new that it struck him with the force of a revelation. He wondered shamefully what Francine's requirements were, and searched his memory of the silly evening for the mysterious point at which he must have met them; but then he realized, in another bright shaft of comprehension, that she was merely different from other girls he had known. There was no baffling maze through which he was expected to fumble his way, trying to make a good case for himself according to the tortuous laws of confluence. She perceived herself – and this thought caused the spoon to tremble in his hand as he fearfully met her eyes once more and clearly saw its confirmation there – as an object of pleasure. Her profit, her share, was simply that he should do so too.

'You'd better duck,' he said, digging his spoon in a second time.

She put her hands amusingly over her face and bent over the table. He forked the risotto out of the dish and howled with laughter as it splintered into grainy fragments around them. Francine's face was wide with comic astonishment and her eyes brightened with approval of his performance.

'I did say I wasn't that hungry,' she said.

'Did any of it get on you?'

'I don't think so.'

She sat back slightly in her chair and smoothed her hands slowly over her blouse and skirt. Ralph felt a fresh lurch of disbelief as he watched her. She met his eyes and giggled.

'That's good,' he said.

A pause shimmered, filling the room, and Ralph knew his moment had come. For a second he drew back, hovering on the edge of action. His body seemed to swell and bloom around him, its machinery unfolding, and he suddenly felt the heaviness of his own flesh, the million pumping intricacies beneath it. He walked stiffly round to the other side of the table and felt the air thicken around him as he forced his way through it. Francine was watching his approach and as he drew near he saw something in her eyes which he couldn't identify. It occurred to him dimly that his touch would be her triumph, and when he did it, clasping her cool hand in his, he experienced a sudden flash of loss at the unfamiliar feel of her skin. He put his other hand on her shoulder, anchoring himself, and his hands felt all at once so implicated there, so guilty with greed, that it seemed as if a strange glue had trapped his fingers and was preventing him from removing them. Francine raised her head and looked at him, a faint smile on her lips. He knew then the impossibility of escape, felt doors slam around him, and his struggle stiffened and died.

'Shall we sit on the sofa?' he said.

The words were loud in his ears.

Seven

The day had been very tiresome, and when Francine shut the front door of her flat against the windy, dark grey late afternoon, she had a satisfying sensation of slamming it also on the administrative harness of the office and the dumb moon faces yoked within it. It had been dark all day, the great wads of cloud pressing down and sending people scuttling through the streets as if beneath the sole of a large, descending boot. The atmosphere of force had found its way into the building: there was a sudden assertion of regimes, a resistance to leisure, and when the rain began to hurl itself against the windows people bent their heads and worked faster.

She had anticipated an idle day, one in which she would sit and steep pleasurably in thought, perhaps sharing a little of it with anyone who happened by her manner to scent the presence of a drama; but instead she had been driven reluctantly into productivity, with not even a stint by the photocopier or a run to the Italian café near by for the office cappuccinos to provide any opportunity for reflection. Her night away from home had left her with an enlarged sense of the personal, and combined with the detachment wrought by little sleep and the red wine, the cuffs and chains of duty were tight and painful. By the end of the afternoon a helmet was clamped around her aching head and her tongue was thick and bitter with instant coffee. At five thirty she left the office for the weekend, not even lingering to be ensnared in the customary Friday evening drift of the City to the local pubs.

She had phoned Lynne at the agency that morning to ask if she had any work for the next week, and Lynne had said that Personnel at Lancing & Louche were pleased with her and wanted her to stay on. There might be a chance of a permanent, Lynne said, seeing as the lady away on leave was still phoning in sick and didn't know when she'd be back. She was called Sally, and Francine disliked her for the fact that, even though Sally was middle aged, overweight, and had greying, frizzy hair – facts revealed in a framed photograph of Sally dancing in a disco opposite a bald man with flailing arms and red eyes which Francine had found on her desk – Mr Lancing kept calling her Sally as well. Sally was a 'career' secretary and had been there a long time: she had put luminous pink stickers with her name on on all her files and a large one on her telephone extension too, as if to remind herself of who she was in case anyone called for her. She had a pair of slippers in flowered material which she changed into when she got to work. One of the secretaries had told Francine that when she found them beneath her desk, positioned neatly side by side in front of the chair as if Sally had been snatched from them by illness where she sat. Francine had put them in a drawer, along with the photograph, the roll of stickers, and a manicure set which also belonged to Sally, feeling confident that her superiority would bring its own rewards.

She was glad she would be staying at Lancing & Louche for a while: it was a big company and she liked the youthful commerce of the corridors, the legions of smart secretaries, the young men with sleek hair who rushed in and out of the broking rooms, the hushed acres of carpet and confidential mahogany doors of the executive floor at the top of the building where meetings were held. She was usually asked to

83

take coffee into Mr Lancing's meetings, prepared on a tray by one of the aproned women in catering and handed to her outside the door, and although she disliked its suggestion of servitude, the sudden silence and raised circle of heads as she entered the room made the duty more gratifying. Their eyes followed her to the door, and sometimes, after she'd shut it, she could hear different tones in their voices and the occasional burst of meaningful male laughter.

Her last job had been a two-week assignment to a dingy little office behind Waterloo station – normally she only worked in the City, and she was sure Lynne had sent her on this job to get her back for the one before, where she hadn't left on very good terms and they'd complained to the agency – working for a fat man called Mr Harris, who wore brown shirts with stains dotted like islands over the expanse of his belly. She didn't know what Mr Harris did, even at the end of her two weeks. The business of the companies she worked for rarely had any bearing on the work she was expected to do. Mr Harris received few telephone calls and his correspondence was featureless. She spent most of her time typing long lists of figures and addresses into a database.

She was alone in the office with Mr Harris, and the slack pace of trade meant that he was obsessed with everything she did, rushing over to her desk when she opened a file or typed a letter to make sure she was doing it properly.

'You'll get the hang of it,' he would say encouragingly, while Francine prickled with irritation beside him. He would stand too close to her, his open mouth emitting clouds of rancid breath, and often a tiny rain of saliva would spatter across her desktop. He watched her continually, making comments about her mood and habits or the expression on her face.

'You like your coffee,' he would nod if she got up to make a cup. He would offer her biscuits, custard creams which he kept in a drawer, and she would refuse them. 'That's how you keep your nice slim figure, isn't it, Francine?'

Normally Francine found it easy to understand her life at the office. Her rank and station were clear, her duties and regalia always the same, her employer a distant, regimental figure whose peculiarities were generally substantial enough to be discussed at lunch-time. The band of her cohorts was genial, and usually manufactured a set of easily grasped distinguishing features on the surface of a deep homogeneity. Every office was at pains to possess its own character: 'What do you think of this place, then?' people would ask Francine at the end of her first day, and although she never really thought anything, they would proudly tell her that she would get used to it in the end.

With Mr Harris, though, Francine had begun to feel as if she didn't know who she was. Without the armour of a corporate identity, she had felt him clawing at her person, simulating a hideous intimacy which for the first time revealed to her the precarious contract on which her position was founded. Her transience normally safeguarded her liberty, but locked in with Mr Harris's fascination the days had seemed long. His presence had become hourly more predatory, and although Francine knew that the termination of his lease on her was not far off, the fingering, probing quality of his ownership subdued her into the belief that it would never end. She became listless in the evenings, avoiding her reflection in the windows of the Underground train as she made her lonely journey to Waterloo the next morning. At the end of two weeks he asked her to stay on and she said that she had another job to go to the next week. She didn't tell Lynne what she had done.

'I'm sorry about that, Francine,' Mr Harris had said, drawing close to her as she stood straining at the door with her coat. His skin was stodgy and pale, and his eyes quivered like tinned fruits in the jelly of his face. 'It's meant so much to me having you here.'

Afterwards Francine had hurried down to the station, the grim scenes of her unhappy lunch hours clinging to her as she passed. It had taken a long time for the elation at her freedom to come, and she had only really felt it when Lynne phoned to tell her about the job at Lancing & Louche and sounded quite friendly, as if nothing had happened. She had even said that they only sent their top people to Mr Lancing, although in her sensitive condition Francine had detected a note of warning in the compliment.

She turned on the kitchen lights and put her bag on the table. Janice had left dishes in the sink, minutely and elegantly smeared, and a carton of milk stood open on the sideboard. A note on the table said that she had gone out for the evening. Irritation provoked a tightening in Francine's head, and she felt the slight tumult in her stomach which was the residue of being unable to distinguish her thoughts by discussing them with someone else. She never really assumed control over events until she had related them in some form: untold, their reality was too pressing, still sullied with the awkwardness of the moment. Once she had presented them to an audience, they came back to her purged and confirmed, interpreted, ordered scenes which could then be filed in memory. Given the unsociable nature of her day, she had hoped Janice would be on hand when she arrived home. She remembered that it was Friday night, and the thought of spending it alone worried her for a moment, until she conjured up the dispensation of her activities the night before. She was recovering, and would prove it with a long, scented bath, an arsenal of beauty treatments, and a relaxed posture later on the sofa with a magazine.

Thus intent, Francine visited the sitting-room *en route* to her indulgences and listened to the messages on the answering machine. Two were for Janice, one of them the imperious manager of the Hampstead boutique, the other a man with a rough voice saying something that Francine couldn't hear very well. Her mother's clearer, complaining tones followed, asking why she had to have that silly machine on the whole time and would madam like to phone her when she got in, although not if it was past ten o'clock. Then it was Ralph, saying that he'd enjoyed last night and he hoped she hadn't felt too awful at work because he certainly had. His voice sounded incongruous and polite beside the others.

Francine immediately began the business of not returning Ralph's call, going into the bathroom and turning on the taps. She looked in the mirror above the sink and was surprised to see that her face was haggard beneath an unfamiliar mat of lank hair. The idea that Ralph had wrought this change with the pummelling effect of his attention – wanting to talk to her before she'd even walked through the door! – was interesting, but the seeds of melodrama were blighted by the realization that his message had contained no suggestion that he wanted to see her again. In the more productive state of mild uncertainty, she removed her tired, twice-worn clothing and set about the lavish business of restoring herself while fingers of steam began to creep warmly over her skin.

In the bath, she reflected on the fact that her mother had lately seemed to be enjoying a new lease of life, which, while it didn't succeed in blunting the voracity of her interest in Francine's affairs, suggested the renewal of activity in her own. Francine didn't think about her parents very often, having some time ago realized that the profitability of her association with them would never again reach the modest peaks of her childhood years – unless they died, of course, which was a horrible thought – but she did occasionally solicit her mother's attention, and maintained a relationship with her over the telephone which was useful in times of shortfall, when other confidantes could not be located or were found wanting. Maxine Snaith's appetite for information was considerable, and allowed Francine the rare luxury of being asked more questions about herself than she really wanted to answer.

Her parents had never visited her in London, and although they frequently mentioned the fact that there was always a bed for her in Kent, both parties seemed to consider the terms of Francine's emigration so extreme as to lend her absence a certain finality. Since Frank, Francine's father, had taken his retirement, a journey to London had been mentioned more frequently, but Francine had soon discovered that the foreign flavour of the idea made it easy to forestall. If the disincentives of bombs and bad weather failed, she could always say that she was very busy at that particular time, and Maxine would grow meek with awe and with the possibility of encountering things that she didn't understand, making a trip later in the year sound much more acceptable.

Francine was Frank and Maxine's only child, and they had united their names as well as their bodies to form her. The experiment had certainly been a success; almost too great a success, in fact, for their hazy understanding of their own union made its exotic and turbulent fruit the object of a slightly fearful contemplation. Frank and Maxine hadn't really known one another for very long when they'd got married – Frank had proposed to Maxine over the telephone from Maidstone, and had been away on business in Leicester right up to the wedding – and Francine had arrived so rapidly that they had straight away been sent into inescapable orbit around her and never really got the chance to catch up with each other. The fact that Francine resembled neither of them gave their grouping a somewhat alien atmosphere, and although any two of them could conjure a certain intimacy on the common ground of the third's absence, seated around the dinner table in the evenings things were often awkward.

Francine's sex and her fast-developing loveliness eventually swung the tide of affiliation in her mother's favour, and Frank became an increasingly extraneous presence in the house. The forces of femininity were, he soon realized, inward-looking and indifferent to his conquest, and he was not even required to do the slavish work of offsetting them. Francine's vanity had been tended at the roots by her mother's determination to witness and enshrine every new development, and Frank was relegated to the position of a patron observing with a slight, helpless horror the spectacle his generosity has permitted to be enacted.

Maxine's devotion to Francine's physical triumphs and the social victories which the future would undoubtedly bring permitted her time only to give herself attention of a somewhat indifferent and secondary nature. She was not an attractive woman, made from small bones which easily accrued quantities of bluish, intractable fat in their own defence. She found it hard to see herself clearly in the glare of Francine's superiority, and she grew detached and confused in matters of her own upkeep. At the hairdresser's she never really knew what she wanted, and would allow the woman to run free with her uncertain creative powers, manufacturing whimsical, ill-realized styles which didn't seem to belong to her. She would occasionally look at herself in the mirror and would feel a mild perturbation, dutifully applying blocks of make-up to all the recognized places. The apparently meaningless reservoirs of flesh around her body she regarded rather more fearfully, and took to palliating them with the consumption of brightly coloured milkshakes instead of food. As this cruel practice became more frequent, it eventually replaced all the memories of varied and seductive forms of nourishment she had accrued during her life with the simpler image of a tall glass filled with brown, pink, or cream liquid – colours which she came to associate with the meals they represented, preferring the brown one, for example, for the evening meal – and as she shrank Maxine wondered if there would come a day when she wouldn't be there at all.

Frank, although slightly fearful of the vacancy in his wife's eyes, approved of her diminution. They had long since set up twin beds in their room, but even so he liked the idea that his wife would be seen as a woman who could control herself. It suggested that she cared what he, and other people, thought. He did find her means somewhat repellent, and although she still made his usual breakfast and cooked the evening meal, the fact that she insisted on drinking those revolting things while he was eating was, for Frank, too public an expression of her problem. He would have liked to be able to tell his friends that his wife ate like a bird, but the shaming nature of her diet led him to keep it to himself.

Since she had left home, however, Francine had several times entertained the suspicion that her parents had united in her absence, flowing together over the space she had once occupied until their surface was so smooth that she might never have been there at all. Her mother's interest, of course, could always be recruited with a telephone call, but there was something masculine in her interrogations now, a desire for more substantial evidence of progress than had previously been required, behind which Francine detected the conspiring hand of Frank. It irritated Francine to hear how Maxine had blossomed in the wake of her desertion, dyeing her hair blonde, wearing gold jewellery, her face fashioned by a make-over.

'You should see your mother,' Frank would boom, picking up the extension in the sitting-room while Maxine regaled Francine with her improvements from the kitchen. 'She's a corker.'

She had even given up her milkshakes, she said, in favour of a local exercise club which she had joined, where she had made new friends. The emergence of features in Maxine's life meant that she expected to be able to talk, and even answer questions, about them.

'You haven't asked me how Body Conditioning went,' she would complain to Francine at the end of a call.

The consequence of this trend was that Francine called less often, and felt a vague and disturbing insecurity at her exclusion which, although it coincided with her desire to pare down her connection with her parents, removed from her hands all the pleasure of doing so. She had disappointed them, she knew, in her last year or so at home: they had safeguarded her through school and secretarial college, beneath the assumption that a lucrative deal would subsequently take her off their hands; but she had frittered herself, in their view, on flashy types with few intentions, getting herself a flighty reputation and probably scaring off any chance of a decent prospect into the bargain.

Francine's long life before the mirror, however, had given her different ideas about her own destiny. When it came, she felt sure that she would recognize it as clearly as she did her own face and that it would be a similarly pleasurable vision. She was so careless of her parents' qualms that it was an effort to remember them at all in her schemes, and she would always feel mildly surprised when their judgements rose up in the dust of her activities. None of it was serious, in any case. She was merely awaiting the opportunity, sure that it would come to her, to move on to greater, if unspecified, things.

It was in this mood of scornful assurance that she had allowed herself to be flattered by the attentions of the manager of a local software company, where she had been stationed for three weeks' secretarial work. He was young and rather attractive, and when his wife came into the office one lunch-time Francine was surprised and somewhat dismayed to notice that she was quite beautiful and that David behaved like a silly, devoted dog around her. If she was honest, Francine had to admit that up until then David had done a good job of concealing his interest in her. She hadn't really intended to do any harm, but she was always interested in testing her powers, and she perceived in this situation perhaps the greatest challenge they had yet received. After his wife had gone, she had lingered around his desk with the pretence of activity, wondering what effect her mere physical proximity would have. When nothing happened, she launched a more deliberate offensive, subjecting David to amplified versions of several devices tested and found to be successful in other trials. One night she stayed late, offering to help him with his work, until it grew dark outside and they were alone in the office. They had talked, and Francine had cleverly steered the conversation towards the personal. David had revealed that his wife ran a local advertising agency and often didn't get home until late herself. In answer to Francine's questions, he admitted that he did often have to make his own dinner and occasionally even iron his shirts, and she gave him her utmost sympathy. The next day, she had made sure to meet his eye frequently and they had shared several intimate glances. Eventually, after more than a week, he became flustered and tried angrily to grab her behind a filing cabinet when no one else was looking. She waited for a few days before she gave in, and one lunch-time he took her to a hotel. He must have told his wife what he'd done the same evening, because she appeared at the office the next day with a red, ruined face and started shouting that she wanted to know which one it was. Francine had fortunately retreated to the toilets as soon as she caught sight of her, but one of the other girls had told her that David had had to ask his wife to leave the office. He barely spoke to Francine during her last couple of days at the company, and remembering his rudeness at the hotel and the fact that he hadn't even bought her lunch, she felt that he had behaved quite badly.

News of David's indiscretion spread quickly through the town, and over the next few weeks Francine experienced a distinct and unpleasant cooling of manners towards her as she went about her business. In this change of climate, her dormant hatred of the place where she had grown up suddenly sprang and flowered. She didn't exactly feel guilty about what had happened, but when she looked up at the dinner table and caught her parents' troubled eyes on her, it occurred to her how enjoyable it would be to go somewhere else. One evening she told them of her intention to move to London, and to her surprise they hadn't seemed particularly upset and had said it was probably for the best. Francine had really only made her announcement with the purpose of getting used to the idea, but when her father said that he would give her a thousand pounds to get her on her way, she sensed that things were moving rather more quickly than she had anticipated. Still, she was glad of the money, which gave her the satisfaction of thinking that, all in all, things had worked out for the best.

She rose from the bath and lost herself for a while in the generous administration of resources to all her surfaces. Finally she donned her bathrobe and drifted to the sitting-room to telephone her mother.

'Yes, love,' said Maxine wearily when Francine announced herself.

'Don't sound too pleased,' snapped Francine, who disliked her mother's latest habit of inferring that her life was one of constant, complex demands, when Francine felt sure that she was only watching television with Frank.

'Don't start, Francine. What is it?'

'What's *what*?' She would have put the phone down there

and then, had she not wanted to discuss her evening with Ralph. 'You asked me to call you.'

'Well, we hadn't heard from you for so long,' sniffed Maxine. 'I just wanted to know you were still breathing.'

'How's your class?' said Francine, knowing the enquiry would put her mother in a more communicative mood. Not wishing to hear the answer, however, and confident that it would be lengthy, she put the receiver down on the table and went to the kitchen to get a glass of orange juice. When she returned, she could hear her mother's voice squeaking with alarm from the abandoned telephone.

'Francine! Francine!'

'I'm here.'

'Where did you go?'

'I was listening to you talking about your class.'

'I told you, I didn't go this week. I've hurt my back – as if you were interested!' She gave an unbecoming snort of laughter. 'Francine, it's very rude to just go off when a person's talking to you. I don't know what gets into you sometimes. Your father and I sometimes sit for hours trying to remember what terrible thing it was that we did to you. I know you think my aerobics is boring, but it's very important to me and—'

'Sorry,' said Francine.

' – and you haven't even asked how your father is yet.'

'How is he?'

'He's been unwell, as a matter of fact. We thought he had cancer.'

Such excursions into tragedy were a frequent feature of Maxine's conversation.

'Really?' said Francine. She lay back on the sofa and examined her freshly shaven legs.

'But the doctor said it's just a bit of constipation. He's got to cut down on his fats. Not that I ever give him fatty foods,

94

mind you. I learnt that lesson long ago with my own problems. Still, we'll get by.'

There was a clamour on the line as the extension was picked up.

'I'm fine,' bellowed Frank. 'Just a bit bunged up is all.'

'Good,' said Francine.

'And what's madam been up to? Out all night, I don't doubt, causing trouble.'

'Catting about!' interjected Frank helpfully.

'Oh, I've been busy,' sighed Francine, relaxing into a cushion. 'I've got a new job.'

'The last one didn't last long,' said Maxine suspiciously. 'Why can't you seem to hang on to anything?'

'It was only temporary, Mum. This one's much better. The agency thinks it'll be permanent.'

'What's it involve?' interrupted Frank.

'It's with an investment bank in the City, working with the director.'

Francine enjoyed their bewildered silence.

'Make sure you hang on to it,' said Frank finally, hanging up.

'How's that Janice? Frank and I think she's a very nice girl.'

'She's fine.'

Maxine had a habit of drawing unshakable conclusions about people from the way in which they comported themselves on the telephone.

'You're still getting on, are you?'

'Of course we are.'

'There's no "of course" about it, Francine. You've quite ruined my new address book, what with all the crossings out. You can be very difficult to live with sometimes. Believe me, I'm the expert.'

'Thanks.'

'You say you've been busy,' said Maxine after a pause, her manner warmer now after the exercise of her resentments.

'I've been out a lot.'

'I'll say you have. I've got to know that machine of yours so well it invited me round for tea.' Her laughter shrilled down the phone.

'I went to a party in an art gallery.'

'Very grand,' said Maxine, catching her breath. 'Anybody nice there?'

'Oh, I met a lot of people. Journalists, mostly. Everyone was really nice.'

'So nobody special.'

'I just said, lots of people!'

'I suppose they don't have names.'

'Well, there was a journalist I liked called Stephen, and a friend of his called Ralph.'

'What sort of friend?' said Maxine darkly.

'Just a friend,' said Francine, exasperated. 'He invited me to dinner at his house.'

'And what does the friend do for a living? He's the arty type, I suppose.'

'He works in television.'

'I see. You're going to tell me next he's going to put you on it.'

'Don't be stupid.'

'Watch your mouth, young lady. I suppose he can cook, too.'

'He made risotto,' said Francine. 'He owns a flat in Camden.'

'Well, that's what he says,' said Maxine. 'But you never know, do you? He might have it mortgaged up to the hilt. Why didn't he take you out? Is he tight?'

'You don't know anything,' sighed Francine. 'Everyone has dinner parties these days.'

'Pardon me for living,' said her mother.

Afterwards, Francine felt dissatisfied by the conversation. She wished Janice would come home. Eventually she got up and walked restlessly around the sitting-room for a while. She wondered if Ralph would call again, and realized that he might have been trying all that time she was on the phone to her mother. Finally, she sat down on the sofa and picked up a magazine.

Eight

Camden Road was a flooded river of cars and from the top of the bus Ralph had watched the traffic jam take on the irremediable, erupted look of a disaster. For a while the packed chain of dirty, disparate metals had been forcing itself thickly through the gates of the traffic lights in a unified triumph of will, but suddenly it was as if the crowd of cars had lost faith in the principles of their community and people had begun breaking from lanes in an attempt to escape, skewing themselves across the white lines and nudging into other hostile queues to a rising clamour of horns. Ralph knew that he should get off the bus and walk the last half-mile to the office, but he was hindered by a strange paralysis, an inability to free himself from this vision of chaos in which he seemed so to belong. Unchained and let loose in the streets, who knew where he might wander? On a Monday morning such as this, when his membership of the city was an imprisonment and the emergent self the weekend had allowed to roam must be forced back into its cell, it was better that he should be delivered defeatedly to his door.

His patchy performance in the closing stages of the previous week made the proper execution of the day imperative. He had been distracted on Thursday, his mind crowded with what proved to be unplayed scenes, his body bent on leaving early, and on Friday he had been morose and unwell. He had run into debt and must use today to replenish his reserves of good conduct. Once their taste was acquired, such disruptions of routine could, he knew, lead to larger rebellions. Ralph feared the prospect of his own disobedience, and although he had never really detected in himself any sign that he might one day decide, for perhaps no reason other than perversity, not to follow the path that necessity had laid down for him, still he remained vigilant against the possibility of his insurrection. He couldn't afford to entertain ideas of his own freedom: once admitted, he could not be sure of ever persuading them to leave. It was not that he judged himself particularly prone to being led astray, but he had always ascribed the right to build fantastical, foolish plans as belonging to those whose foundations were secure. He didn't regard the people he knew as dependent, exactly, but he felt sure that they would never be permitted to slide into poverty or destitution: there would always be someone, some relative who could be dug up and appealed to, someone who would feel pity or guilt at their demise. Ralph was alone, and although sometimes he could go for weeks without really thinking of his solitude, some deeper instinct always remembered it. It was a mercy not to think of it too often, in fact, because when he did he would often grow angry or morose at the relentless contingency of everything in his life; and what was the point of self-pity if there was nobody to pity you for it? He had learned to accept certain things: the inescapability of work, regardless of whether he enjoyed it or not; and the possibility that no one might care if he lost everything. Stephen would *mind*, probably, but he couldn't be counted on really to care in any useful way.

Ralph supposed that his situation carried within it the danger of relying too much on love to swaddle him in illusions of security. That had been the problem with Belinda, really, because he had somehow got the impression that his orphaning, his terrible aloneness, was one of the things for which she loved him. She used to ask him about it all the time, wanting to know exactly when each beam had rotted and given way and how he had felt as the sky and ground came terrifyingly into view; and he would enjoy watching her face soften with sympathy as he told her, knowing that his subscription to things he hadn't really felt, but knew none the less to be tragic, would make her care for him. In the end, though, the feelings gave him no pleasure, for they were impersonal, humanitarian things, and Belinda had grown tired of it as her love curdled to pity and then, he feared, contempt. He suspected that the lack of visible evidence of how he had come to exist made people uncomfortable with him. For a while, certainly, he was unusual, but eventually he was only odd and difficult to fit into the scheme of things. He had come to regard his solitude as a principle by which people felt it correct to act, a feature which generated its own response: he had been deserted, therefore it was possible, necessary even, to desert him.

Stephen was different, Ralph supposed, in that it never seemed to occur to him not to be Ralph's friend. Their alliance was what Ralph imagined to be brotherly, an unquestioned linkage which demanded no particular profit or return and which didn't seem to have arisen out of personal choice. It irritated Ralph that he sometimes wondered why Stephen stuck with him; partly because he knew it never occurred to Stephen to wonder the same thing about Ralph, but largely because his criticisms of Stephen were deep and should not have manufactured a sense of good fortune at Stephen's friendship as their irrational by-product. He supposed it was an unreformed conviction of their schooldays, when Stephen had been a princely character whose patronage was an asset.

If Ralph was honest it had been his only asset, the thing that had got him through it all.

Stephen had never asked about Ralph's parents, although when his father died at the end of Ralph's first year at the school and he had had to go to Stephen's house for the summer holidays, Stephen had been kind to him in a clumsy way and patted him on the back once or twice. When they went back for the new term, they had gone on a school trip. As the bus wound its way through the outskirts of the town, Ralph had suddenly recognized the road in which he had lived with his mother and father when he was younger. He had gazed out of the window and as they approached his old house he had turned to Stephen to point it out.

'*Plebsville*,' Stephen had said before he could speak, following Ralph's eyes through the window. He made the hilarious vomiting noise which they had lately been using to signal disgust or contempt. For a moment Ralph had a strange feeling in his stomach, but then he had made the noise too and had sat back in his seat, glad that he hadn't said anything.

It made him sad to think about that now, although he scarcely remembered his mother any more and the confused, itinerant portion of his life with his father had long since supplanted the old house with a set of diffuse, unrelated memories. He remembered running into their bedroom, though, early in the morning, and climbing up on the bed beside his mother in her nightdress. Her bare arms used to seem colossal to him, riven with a delta of frightening veins, but he had loved the way she smelled in the mornings. Later in the day she would be perfumed and distant, but in the morning she had a human smell, a smell of herself, which made him burrow against her like an animal. She was called Angela, although remembering her name made her recede even further in Ralph's mind. His father had always called her 'Mother', which now struck Ralph as strange, but at the time had seemed a natural extension of his partnership with his father against her hygienic and dissatisfied leadership.

'Better shape up,' he would whisper to Ralph, as his mother swept in some nameless fury through the small rooms of their house. 'Else Mother'll have us.'

The bus had heaved itself past the traffic lights and was now thundering down the Holloway Road towards Ralph's stop. Returning from his recollections he felt all at once rather lost and he reminded himself of the suddenly distant necessity for getting off the bus and going to work. He stood up, clinging to the metal poles as he staggered along the swaying platform. His body felt large and heavy, as if he had just woken from a dream and found it newly so. The bus stopped and he disembarked. Hurrying along the pavement towards his office building, he saw himself calling for his mother through the quiet house when he came home from school one day, worrying that she wasn't there. He had used to call her 'Mummy', and he remembered now that she hadn't liked it.

'You sound like a little pansy,' she had said, emerging wearily from the bedroom as he stood calling her in the hall. Her face was full of secrets. 'What's wrong with "Mum"?'

He opened the door and walked quickly across the foyer to the stairs. He hadn't thought of that in years.

'Good weekend?' said Roz, who sat opposite him.

Their desks were pushed together at the front to form a square, a contact Ralph found obscurely intimate. Roz was in charge of the office computer and had discovered how to play games on the screen. She would sit for hours at solitaire, or a faster game involving spinning meteors which made explosive noises, and Ralph would grow infuriated at the incessant clicking and the blank rapture of Roz's face, sighing and clearing his throat to no avail.

'It was all right,' he said.

'What did you do, then?' said Roz after a pause, her hand still clicking on the desk as she spoke.

'Not much,' said Ralph. He bent over his work and began writing something.

He occasionally felt guilty about his unkindness to Roz, for she was always interested in him in her slow, impervious way. She would ask him questions with apparently no memory of repetition or rebuff, retaining nevertheless the few blunt details he was obliged to divulge about his activities outside the office and stringing together a little narrative from them of which it pained Ralph to be the subject. He was ashamed of his feelings of physical repulsion for Roz's pale, doughy form, her big moon of a face with its round eyes and slack, wet mouth. He would find himself watching her occasionally in wonder at her almost impossible plainness and sometimes she would catch him doing it and would reveal her teeth in a mirthless, fleshy smile.

He didn't know much about her, for her fascination with Ralph's life seemed to carry within it an almost dutiful apology for the monotony of her own. She lived with her mother in Hendon and she didn't have a boyfriend. He had asked her about boyfriends when he first started the job, trying to be friendly, but something had lit up in her eyes which told him it had been a stupid thing to ask. The result of his enquiry was the flailing rapport which now plagued him daily, and it was with dumb misery that he realized Roz liked him – and, worse, that she was now irreversibly possessed of the conviction that he liked her – and that no amount of curtness would ever erase his early blunder. He had encountered girls like this before, big, silent girls who required only the acknowledgements his politeness obliged him to offer for their sad, obedient devotion to be forever nourished. At university there were several of them, and they would stop and greet him in the street, standing before him with the mute expectation that he would talk to them, until he had to excuse himself quite rudely and would go on his way with his heart thudding angrily in his chest. He perceived in their attentions some notion of affiliation, a disquieting recognition of his hopelessness which hurt him more than the disdain of loud, confident girls who had made the same discovery.

Roz never asked Neil any questions, although they talked all the time in a way Ralph knew he could not imitate; chatting about things they'd seen on television, or reading a tabloid together while they ate their sandwiches. Neil would ask her how her mum was, what she was seeing at the cinema that night, would even joke about who she was going with, and yet Ralph had never once seen her fix Neil with that dogged, injured look which suggested an outstanding debt awaiting payment. The worst thing was how, on a Monday morning, Roz would unfailingly ask him, with a dull glimmer of painful anticipation in her pale eyes, if he'd met anyone new over the weekend. The question was so audacious to Ralph, and yet bespoke a joyless void of opportunity so horribly familiar to him, that he always answered it awkwardly. His embarrassment made it sound as if he cared that he hadn't met anyone, and would often inspire Neil to shrieks of effeminate laughter from the other side of the office and a high-pitched rendition of some song about searching which Ralph vaguely recognized.

'Did you meet anyone new over the weekend, then?' Roz asked now, her fingers momentarily stayed from their clicking but still poised over the handset as if ready to annihilate Ralph with an electronic pulse.

'Yes,' he said suddenly. He heard it fly from his lips and

saw Roz jerk slightly, as if the murder of her hopes had been too swift even to feel. Her eyes welled with water and for a moment Ralph wondered in terror if she was going to cry. 'Yes, I did, actually,' he continued hurriedly. 'I've got a new girlfriend.' The words were large and clumsy in his mouth, as if they didn't fit.

'What's this?' shouted Neil from his desk. 'Ralph's got a new bird? You got a bird, mate?' he said, getting up and coming over.

'What's she like, then?' said Roz.

'Oh, I don't know,' said Ralph. The conversation was unbearable to him. He could scarcely believe he had started it. 'She's very pretty.'

'What's her name?' persisted Roz, as if in the hope of finding some ground on which she could conduct a contest.

'Francine. She's called Francine.'

'Fran*cine*,' howled Neil. 'Fran*cine*. Not a frog, is she?'

'I don't think so,' said Ralph irritably.

'Where does she work? What's her job?' said Roz.

Ralph looked at her with horror.

'She's a secretary,' he said.

Roz didn't speak to him for the rest of the day, but the Morse of her clicking informed him that an injustice had been perpetrated against her.

Ralph's indiscretion haunted him that evening at his flat, and although he tried to subdue his memory of it by the devotion of his energies to domestic tasks, the resistance of his surroundings to further regulation so soon after the previous week's reforms permitted his thoughts to churn and race as he drifted desultorily through a series of minor activities. His slip rose up before him everywhere he looked, monstrous in the familiar, cautious landscape of his communications, and although he knew his customary reticence made a more terrible spectacle of his transgression than perhaps it really was, it seemed ridiculous to try and change the way he saw things merely to diminish it. His preposterous and meaningless untruth appalled him, not because of any fear of it being found out – although the thought of Francine overhearing his conversation with Roz made him grow hot with shame – but more for the burden the very idea had placed upon him, which seemed in his quiet hours to have handcuffed and marched him considerably closer to its fulfilment.

He had telephoned Francine the day after their extraordinary evening, calling secretively from the office in the afternoon when he knew she would still be at work. For him the message had been a polite escape, a gesture to his own sense of how these things should be brought off, nevertheless making it clear, he thought, that their evening had been a pleasant but unique occasion. He supposed everyone had their own set of rules to be applied in such cases, measures long since drawn up by experience to curb the impulses of feeling. He had arrived at his own judgement swiftly, barely able to touch the raw memories which burned in his thoughts as he sat at his desk, but the unavoidable glimpses he had had of their blurred, complex images urged him to parcel up the whole affair and consign it to history. His hangover had been mingled with something darker and more sticky, a strange, guilty sense of himself whose taste he remembered from childhood. He had behaved oddly, had borrowed feelings he had no wish to own, and his desire to forget the episode could not be fulfilled merely through the partial erasure of its worst moments. It had surprised and somewhat irritated him that Francine had called him back late that same night. She had obviously interpreted his message as a statement of infatuation – an impression gained no doubt from its precipitance, the very thing he had thought would inform her of his retreat –

and being caught off his guard, his confounded politeness had prompted him to compensate for their silence with the acceptance of another meeting with her during the week. He thought it odd that she could take him for such a fool, and yet still wish to prick him into a semblance of pursuit.

He didn't exactly regret their evening together, merely the silliness that had gone before it. He had wrought such things in himself, such breathless spirals of hope and despair, for all the world as if he had had nothing better to think about. The ghostly apparitions of wisdom astonished him with their many illusions and tricks, making one quite sure of the existence of something which in the next moment vanished. In the end, though, the discovery that really he was just like every other man filled him with a horrifying form of relief. It was a burden to consider oneself different, and what had he done but for once in his life take something cheaply? And afterwards, what more than feel every man's mild ache of redundancy, and the desire to move on from what was empty to what was full? For a while, certainly, it had fascinated him to see how little he could care about Francine while sharing with her what he regarded as the most precious and precarious intimacy, but it was no more than a callous experiment with himself which would prove nothing. He had emerged from it belittled, sullied with the memory of what felt afterwards like his own violation.

Their night remained oddly bereft of recollections, for all that. Searching for its reality, he found only his phantoms of thought, a heap of discarded disguises garish by daylight. She had insisted on darkness, and in it he had felt lost and detached, his body given a command for which he had feared drunkenness and muddled desires would render it unfit. He wondered what amnesia it was that time and time again generated a pleasure in the anticipation of an act which was almost always destroyed by its fulfilment. In the end he had not been as awkward as he would have thought likely, but he had been so intent on giving a correct performance that it only occurred to him afterwards, straining to remember what had happened in the darkness, that Francine had done nothing at all. The acquiescence which had so struck him modulated at the first touch into submission, and in the very granting of her permission he had felt her sudden absence, as if she had what it was that she wanted and was leaving him to the business of his own pleasure. What struck him now was how confident she had seemed that this was enough, but for him the privilege had been a lonely one. He had finished it all quite quickly and had surprised himself by going straight to sleep. When he woke up in the morning she wasn't in the room, and he had found her in the kitchen, sitting fully dressed at the table with a piece of toast on a plate in front of her. It was then that he had felt most unnerved by her. He had tried to make a joke of it, saying how much more organized she was than he, but she had looked at him as if she didn't understand what he was talking about. When she left he had gone back to bed and lain inertly for half an hour, his head aching and blank.

He abandoned the evening's regime and made a sandwich, carrying it into the sitting-room with the intention of eating it in front of the television. As he sat down on the sofa, the thought of his claims for Francine came round again on the trundling wheel of his consciousness. It all seemed rather comic to him now, and he smiled at his own foolishness. He supposed he hadn't behaved very well, but he would be kinder to her when next they met. He turned on the news, and felt all at once overwhelmed with contentment at the warmth of his flat, the correctness of its comforts, his freedom to be alone there, while beyond the drawn curtains the city night began again the long drama of its uncertainties.

Nine

When Mr Lancing was in the office the atmosphere was one of siege, and his community laboured towards the goal of his next disappearance with dedication. When he had gone, to a meeting or to lunch, his large desk remained his monument in the centre of the office, bedecked with the insignia of leadership. If the meeting was in the building, his suit jacket often stayed behind, hung on the shoulders of his high-backed chair as vigilant as a sentry, with his briefcase to heel on the floor beside it. During these periods his presence seemed more imminent and the office was guarded, its revolutions whispered beneath tapping fingers and shrilling telephones, while neat, resentful stacks of finished work automatically accrued on his desktop. If the meeting was elsewhere his exit was triumphant, with a car to be called and his briefcase prepared, and in the wake of it there rose the euphoria of actors after the performance of a play. His people would sit back in their chairs behind his retreating figure, flushed and smiling, and a celebratory coffee would be made.

Francine searched Mr Lancing's diary, of which she was the caretaker, and found to her concern that he had no meetings at all that day. He had arrived at his desk earlier than usual, rolling up his sleeves, and his jacket decorated the back of his chair with an aspect of entrenchment. He was reading a report Francine had typed for him the day before, his forehead wrinkled with concentration.

'What the hell is this?' he shouted, apparently to no one in particular.

The telephone rang and Francine answered it.

'Good morning, Mr Lancing's office.'

'That Gary?'

'No, this is his secretary. May I ask who's calling?'

'Tell him it's Buck.'

Francine pressed the button which put the line on hold.

'Mr Lancing!' she called loudly. Mr Lancing frequently failed to respond to his name, and Francine had concluded that he must be slightly deaf. He looked around, as if wondering where the noise had come from. 'Mr Lancing, Buck's on the line for you.'

'Buck?' he said. 'Who's Buck?'

Francine considered her options. She had already offended several of Mr Lancing's close associates by returning to their line when he failed to recognize them and questioning them further before allowing them through. She had got to know most of them by now, but she couldn't remember Buck having called before.

'He's American,' she said hopefully.

Mr Lancing gave the matter some thought. Suddenly he grinned and bounced slightly in his chair with excitement.

'It's Buck!' he said. 'Why didn't you just put him on?'

Francine did so, and moments later the telephone rang again.

'Is that Sally?' said another American voice, this time belonging to a woman.

'I'm afraid Sally doesn't work here at the moment,' said Francine.

'This is Sylvia,' said the woman.

'Oh, hello, Mrs Lancing,' said Francine. She had spoken to Mr Lancing's wife several times before and still occasionally had to explain Sally's disappearance. 'This is Francine.'

'What a pretty name,' said Sylvia vaguely. 'Listen, is Gary there?'

'He's taking a call at the moment,' said Francine. 'Is there anything I can help you with?'

'It's our son's birthday tomorrow, Francine,' said Sylvia. 'I was calling for some gift ideas. Is there anything you could suggest?'

'Well – how old is he?'

'I believe he'll be eleven years old tomorrow, Francine,' Sylvia sighed. 'My little baby, all grown up.'

'What about – what about a bicycle? No, I suppose he's already got one.'

'A bicycle?' said Sylvia. 'Gee, that'd be fun. I don't know. You say he's already got one?'

'I thought he might, that's all.'

'I was actually thinking we could get him some stocks.'

'Socks?' said Francine.

'No, stocks, you know, like stocks and shares. Maybe you could talk with Gary about that.'

'All right,' said Francine.

'Thank you so much, Francine. Do you know when Sally's coming back?'

'I don't know.' Francine was beginning to tire of the conversation. 'She's ill.'

'I bet you're hoping she'll get *worse!*' said Sylvia. She shrieked with laughter.

When Mr Lancing had finished his conversation, Francine approached him about the matter of the present.

'I thought a bicycle would be nice,' she said, growing more attached to her own idea.

Mr Lancing looked pensive. His hair was unkempt, as though he had forgotten to brush it. He looked as if he were wearing a wig.

'Which one is it?' he said.

'Which what? Oh, I see, the one who's going to be eleven.'

'And you want to buy him a bike?'

'It was only an idea. Your wife thought he might like some stocks.'

'Stocks?' Mr Lancing's face lit up. 'That's a great idea! He'll love it, he can hang the certificates on his wall!' He motioned with his hands, demonstrating their placement.

Francine went to the ladies' and stood behind the locked door in one of the cubicles. After a while she came out and looked at herself in the large mirror for a long time. When one of the other secretaries came in, she washed her hands and went back to the office. Mr Louche was cutting something from a magazine at his desk with a pair of scissors. He carried the severed page over to Mr Lancing and placed it in front of him.

'What do you think?' he said, beaming.

Francine was standing near by and she leaned over slightly so that she could see what it was. It was a full-page advertisement for underwear. A girl with dark hair lounged on a sofa clasped in small pieces of lace.

'How about that?' persisted Mr Louche. 'Isn't she something?'

'She has a very kind face,' agreed Mr Lancing, nodding. 'She looks as though she'd be very nice.'

Mr Louche returned with the picture to his desk. Moments later Francine saw him sticking it to the wall behind him with a drawing pin. At one o'clock, Mr Lancing and Mr Louche put on their jackets and left the office for lunch.

'Bye, girls,' said Mr Louche from the doorway.

Francine left soon after them, trying to look as little as

possible as if she were going on an expedition to the shops lest the others ask her to buy sandwiches for them. That had happened on her first day, when she had been eager to be pleasant and had asked if anyone wanted anything because she was going out. She had spent the entire lunch hour queuing in a sandwich shop with a list saying who wanted butter and mayonnaise and which of them liked salt and pepper. As she left the building and launched herself into the swarming pavement, she was met by the familiar volley of glances of which she had eventually tired in Kent; but the homage of London's streets never failed to uplift her with the suggestion that here, at the centre of it all, she was still everything she had believed herself to be. At first she had sometimes felt fearful that the unexceptional landscape of her old town had been too flattering a foil, but now it seemed to her that people had never really *looked* at her there, that she had been out of scale and incomprehensible to them. For the first time, she was really being appreciated. The fact that this appreciation as yet took such an insubstantial form – a deep and searching look, sometimes an expression of brazen pleasure, occasionally even a comment – worried her only mildly, for she felt sure that time would see its maturation into something more useful. It was just a question of staying in the light long enough to be seen, of keeping herself above the surface; and although Francine had faith in her own buoyancy, lately she had seen glimpses of a subtle, unexplained terror, that if ever she disappeared from view, she would sink and sink with no one to save her.

Francine ate her sandwich at her desk. By the time she had finished, it was not yet half-past one, and she felt the day drag at her with its unsparing hours. A murmuring quietude had settled on the office after the excited swell of Mr Lancing's departure. The other girls sat turning the pages of magazines. Lorraine was on the telephone at the desk next to Francine's.

'Really? *Really?*' she said.

Francine had nothing to read. She wished she had bought a magazine when she was out. She thought of calling Janice, but when she considered it more closely could think of nothing to say. She found her eyes running automatically along the typed lines of a letter in front of her, which she had printed out for Mr Lancing before lunch and which now awaited his signature. Her mind emptied with the exercise and when next she looked at her watch she saw that five minutes had passed. Boredom did not usually trouble her, for her contemplations were large and continuous, and often seemed more real and colourful than her physical activities. The facility with which she found her thoughts could slip away, hurrying back to the subject of herself after the interruptions of circumstance, meant that generally she relished these vacant interludes, filling them with the enactment of things passed or to come, and even occasionally with vivid scenes featuring people she had invented and was unlikely ever to meet. Sometimes her absorption would develop into a state of trance, the crowds of her consciousness dispersed to permit higher meditations which, although they could be achieved more easily in front of a mirror, were still accessible merely through the memory of one.

On this occasion, however, as she tried to think of the meeting with Ralph scheduled for the evening ahead, she found that her mind would not pleasure her. There was something in their connection which made the contemplation of it hostile to her enjoyment, and when she touched on it, even wrapped in the deepest clouds of illusion, her thoughts came back to her punished as if an electric shock had repelled them. Dimly she knew that her telephone call, made at the end of that long Friday evening during which she had battled and lost against resolution, had been a mistake. Despite the warm contrivances of her imagination the horrible truth it had fleetingly revealed sent its chill through every passage along which Francine tried to approach their arrangement. She was unused to analysing the motivations of her admirers and the memory of Ralph's resistance, the ultimate defeat of which had permitted her to inter it in the deepest tomb of the forgotten, began to struggle again with life. He *had* behaved oddly that evening at his flat, but the subsequent improvement in his affections had led her then, as it did again now, to suppose it the product of nerves, a facet of his shyness or perhaps even his intelligence – a mystery in which she had little interest except in thoughts of the more interesting consequences of its enslavement. In the end everything had happened as it always did, but in this case the greater difficulty of achieving what was recognizable left Francine with a certain reluctance to abandon the scene of her hard work. After all, she could have just turned around and gone home right at the beginning, there on the doorstep! The fact that finally he had done what was expected of him was her only place of refuge, but even there the suspicion that something was wrong tracked her down.

His coolness on the telephone could, after all, have been nothing but a habitual return to restraint, a sort of tic out of which it might take some time to train him. She examined their conversation warily in the light of this new theory. He had been polite, but there had been something weary in his voice when she had announced herself, a tone disconcertingly similar to that deployed by her mother only a few hours earlier. Afterwards she had alternately comforted and upbraided herself with the memory of his reserve, one minute assured that his manner was merely the proof of his being a different 'type', the next horrifyingly tempted to believe that, even so, one or two of the same rules must apply, and that if he'd wanted to see her he would have asked. Truth laboured over this point, fatigued but resilient. Try as she might to camouflage the fact that she herself had suggested they meet, the material of fabrication was simply not there. Not thinking about that particular aspect of things at all had proved her only escape, but she felt its haunting presence.

She switched on her computer and stared at the awakening screen. Her thoughts had made this long journey several times over the past few days, and as often as not arrived at defiance. As she began to type another letter for Mr Lancing, she resorted to the secondary pleasure of thinking how cool she would be with Ralph, how obvious it would be that she didn't care about him, and, in a triumph of regained authority, how she might not even turn up at all.

'That's a bit keen,' said Lorraine, putting down the telephone.

'I've got to leave early,' said Francine.

'Up to something special tonight, then?'

'I'm meeting my boyfriend,' said Francine, an enjoyable feeling of satisfaction warming her limbs as she said the words. 'He's taking me out.'

'*Really?*' said Lorraine.

It had been milder that day, and even though darkness had fallen Francine found that she could walk with her coat unbuttoned. If she walked briskly enough, it flew behind her in a manner she interpreted as romantic, and the intermittent revelation of her legs by its flapping drew the inquisitive glances of Camden High Street.

The anxiety which had moored in her stomach all day suddenly began to churn her juices as it propelled itself in circles of apprehension. She felt uneasy with the desires that had brought her here, a shady, duplicitous tribe of impulses with whom she did not normally do business. The street was crowded, and clashing waves of frenetic music burst from the noisy, brightly lit façades of open shops as she walked by. Several people had stopped at the window of an electrical shop and were gazing dumbly at the silent, animated screens of televisions. She pushed past them, depleted by the imperviousness with which they blocked her way. The thought of Ralph waiting for her, far from strengthening her against the vicissitudes of her journey, left her only with the unpleasant suspicion that her arrival was not urgently required. She drooped slightly and summoned again the possibility of going home, leaving him to sit there alone, punished by thoughts of her. The idea fortified her with enthusiasm and she quickened her pace. A man was approaching her along the street and she could tell from the intent angle of his face that he was trying to fix her eyes with his own. She met his glance and was surprised to find it irritating, filled with suggestion, with promises of whose emptiness she was suddenly assured. It occurred to her that these men who looked at her, these hungry strangers, were taking things from her without giving anything in return. She wondered why they should be permitted to visit her face so freely and then move on, as if it were but the distraction of a moment.

She reached a turning and stopped as a glowing lava of cars erupted from the traffic lights and flowed hotly across her path. Crossing it seconds later she recognized ahead the bar in which they had arranged to meet and she found herself hurrying towards it. She was late, a genuine ten minutes appropriated by a long wait for the Tube. She felt momentarily comforted by the sudden reality of time, the forceful packing of it after a day of empty, ghost-like hours which had haunted her one by one, each with its own ghastly tincture. Ralph had protested at meeting her in Camden, saying that he ought to come to West Hampstead, but to Francine the idea had sounded too much like a favour, a kind visit after which he could walk away free. She wanted him embroiled in scenes of himself from which he could not escape.

She saw him as soon as she arrived, sitting at a table in the corner with a newspaper. The bar was not crowded and her entrance was unimpeded, but as she swept past tables, glad again of her dramatic coat, and felt faces turn gratifyingly towards her, she was disappointed to notice that Ralph himself did not look up to observe her finely judged approach. The interlude somewhat restored her possession of herself, however, and as she sat down opposite him the sudden calming of her fractious uncertainties allowed her to manufacture a radiant smile.

'Francine,' said Ralph, looking up from his paper.

Francine was satisfied to see a look of surprise flit across his face, and knew that he had forgotten how beautiful she was. She was glad they had arranged to meet in a bar. The almost tangible force of public opinion around her – people were still looking round, she could see them from the corner of her eye! – seemed to offer some security against the disaffections solitude might have admitted.

'Sorry I'm late,' she said softly, forbidding the triumph which surged in her thoughts from exiting importunately through her mouth. She considered advancing the reason for her delay and then decided against it.

'Don't worry, I was enjoying catching up with the papers. What would you like to drink?'

Francine felt a mild chill of disappointment that he should have found her absence so productive. She noticed that he was wearing the same clothes as he had done the last time she had seen him, and could not decide what it meant.

'Oh, I'll have red wine,' she said. As Ralph looked around for a waiter, she glanced at his glass and saw that he was drinking beer. 'So what have you been doing lately?' she said.

'What?' He craned his neck and flapped his hand ineffectually. 'Oh, ignore me then, you idiot.'

Francine turned her head and immediately caught the waiter's eye, drawing him with a smile to their table. She was relieved by the distraction. Her attempt at conversation had given her an odd sensation of nakedness.

'You're good at that,' said Ralph once the waiter had disappeared. A slight grimness about his mouth kept the remark short of a compliment. 'I can never get them to see me.'

Francine's thoughts were alarmingly empty. She wished that she had rehearsed a topic, or, now that she knew Ralph read them, at least looked at a newspaper over lunch.

'So what have you been doing lately?' she said again.

'Me? Oh, not much.' He looked better than he had before, and when he met her eyes she felt a tug of attraction. 'I haven't done any reading for ages, so I mostly just caught up on things I'd been meaning to finish. Oh yes, and I went to see that exhibition at the Hayward.'

'Really?' said Francine, who had been unaware of 'that' exhibition but resolved to visit it as soon as possible. 'Did you enjoy it?'

'Well, it was all right, but a bit thin, didn't you think?'

'Oh, I haven't had time to go yet. I'm going over the weekend.'

She glanced at Ralph and caught the shadow of a strange smile on his lips. It gave her the idea that he might be thinking things about her which conspired against the impression she was attempting to make, and she grew diffident from the injury, looking down at her hands in silence until the waiter came with her drink.

'What about you?' said Ralph in a more kindly tone. 'How was your weekend?'

'Oh, exhausting. I went out every night.' She remembered

her telephone call to Ralph on Friday evening. 'Except Friday, of course. I never go out on Fridays.'

'Why not?'

'Well, I like to have an evening to myself, just to relax, you know. I read a lot,' she added.

'But why Friday? Why not Sunday or Monday?'

'I don't know.' Francine was growing uncomfortable with his line of questioning. She remembered the night they had first met, a Friday night. 'Anyway, I do go out on Friday if there's a party or something.'

Ralph looked perplexed.

'So what sort of things do you read?'

'Magazines mostly,' said Francine. 'They're not just about fashion – they have really interesting articles as well.'

Ralph's eyes brightened and she felt satisfied that she was beginning to understand him.

'And what about books?' he said. 'Do you read books?'

'Oh, yes.' Francine named one or two of her favoured authors, those in whose thickly gathered pages she had found the best confirmation of her own ideas about how the world worked. Ralph didn't appear to have heard of them. 'Perhaps I've got the names wrong,' she said, giggling for his benefit. 'I'm not very good at remembering names. Normally they get passed around the office so you don't get to keep them for very long.'

'I see,' said Ralph. 'Would you like another drink?'

'Thanks,' said Francine. The red wine had flushed her cheeks and she felt her spirits begin to rise. Ralph had been drinking slowly, but now he drained his glass with conviction and set it firmly on the table.

'I think I'll join you,' he said. 'We might as well get a bottle.'

Watching him, she caught an expression on his face for which she was unable to find an explanation. It was as if he had forgotten she was there, and looking at him she had a sense of glancing through a window at something she shouldn't see, something private. Seconds later he caught her eye and the expression disappeared hastily, as though he were embarrassed. She had sat many times at tables such as this, the face opposite her but a mirror in which her successes, her charms, every flicker of her loveliness were clearly reflected. Ralph's face was unkind to her image, and Francine was unnerved by her suspicion that behind his barred eyes whole worlds turned, lives of thought were born and flourished, and that at the centre of its operations was a presence before whom she was powerless. She shrank slightly from this unpleasant notion of his complexity, and then returned with redoubled boldness, determined to conquer it.

'Have you had many girlfriends?'

The force of her own words surprised her and she saw that their penetration had been considerable. His eyes widened at the question and he drank fiercely from his glass. She wondered why she hadn't enquired of history before for clues which might make him clearer to her. Generally she wasn't interested in what people had done before they met her, but Ralph didn't talk about himself as much as other men.

She watched him drain his glass and swallow. She was only sipping at her own wine now, remembering the lethargy and the strange feeling of desperation which had been the residue of their last evening together, and with her restraint had come a sense of advantage as Ralph mechanically sank the bottle's level.

'Not many,' he said. His eyes met hers. They were unfathomable now, two dark little wells into which suddenly she was afraid to look. He poured more wine into his glass and it gushed dangerously towards the rim. 'There was a girl called Belinda who I knew at university. We were together for a year or so. I suppose she was my only real girlfriend.'

The mention of Belinda – what a ridiculous name! – and university drove Francine back into silence. She disliked the inference made by this twin assault that she was not the star of his experiences. Normally on such occasions, the present moment was firmly declared the climax of all that had gone before, but Ralph appeared to have said his piece and it seemed unlikely that any comforting codas would be added. This talk of 'real' girlfriends was unsettling. Belinda's isolation, the very thing Francine would have imagined left her a clear field, made her seem all at once mountainous.

'I suppose you've had a lot of men,' said Ralph.

'Oh, not really,' Francine hurriedly replied. She found his comment peculiarly insinuating, and attempted to defuse it with protestations of innocence. 'All the men I meet are so – so shallow. I mean, they only really want one thing, and once they've got it – well—' She looked down at her hands. 'It's harder for girls, you know.'

'I suppose so,' said Ralph, who appeared not to be listening.

Outside it had grown colder and a whip of wind stung Francine's legs as they turned into the High Street. She wished that Ralph would put his arm around her as a signal of protection against the night and the lonely waste-cluttered pavement, beside which demon-eyed cars roared too close, illuminating phantoms of litter leaping in the wind. People waited at a forest of bus stops, their faces ghoulish and grey. Someone was shouting on the other side of the street, a man walking slowly alone, his bearded face turned to the brown sky.

'I'll walk you to the Tube station,' said Ralph. 'It's on my way,' he added, although she had not objected to his inconveniencing.

He had drunk most of the wine in the end, and Francine had waited while his eyes grew liquid and bright and his face dismissed its guard for some unruly outbreak of interest, but now he seemed withdrawn and composed. His unrelenting manner as he marched her to the station fuelled her dread of the imminent solitude of the Tube, the precarious walk home, the emptiness of return as she unlocked the door. She wished fiercely that things were going differently, but the sound of her desires had never been more faint. They were apparently to have no effect on what was actually going to happen. The situation was, she had to admit, out of her control. She wondered, walking silently beside him, how he had escaped her. What was wrong with him? If only he would do something, make some acknowledgement of those qualities others had always found exceptional, it would have been easier for her defiantly to take her leave of him intact. His indifference was compelling, bound her in inaction, and she feared most of all the thoughts that would visit her once she was released from it.

Just then a smartly dressed man passed them on the pavement. He pinioned her with a searching look and then moved his glance to Ralph, smiling his approval quite openly before he walked on, leaving an ether of expense and the sound of tapping footsteps behind him. As if automatically, Ralph's arm moved up and placed itself across Francine's shoulders. The warm flood of her satisfaction filled recesses parched with anxiety. They drew level with the Tube station and stopped.

'Would you like to come back?' said Ralph, as if the idea had only just occurred to him.

'If you like.'

Francine looked at his face and saw nothing there. His features were absolutely still, and in the draining, neon-lit darkness he looked unnervingly like a photograph. To her surprise he suddenly leaned forward and hugged her, his body stiff and awkward against hers. His mouth was pressed against her ear.

'What do you want from me?' he whispered.

She pretended she hadn't heard, and soon they were walking in silence towards the Lock.

Ten

These days, when wandering through his memories, Ralph would occasionally stop at the door behind which his dead love lay and would decide to go in and visit her. Lying in her vault she seemed beautiful to him, luminous and intact, the pall of sickness faded, the lines of agony smoothed, the scars of his autopsy invisible, all erased by the artful undertaking of time; and while her ghost still sometimes haunted him, a mischievous poltergeist caught in the echo of his own essential unchangingness, or hers, he felt in her recollection a sense of peace, a certain sculptured completeness which was altogether new.

Yes, he certainly felt differently about Belinda now – not that Francine had changed him, of course, merely moved him further away from the person he had been by provoking actions which did not seem to belong to him – for in learning again to speak the conjugal tongue, he had discovered new expressions of bitterness, a whole vocabulary of dissatisfaction, which in hindsight made him understand things about Belinda whose meaning had at the time escaped him. What he had heard as harmony, he now saw, had in the end sounded to her ears as an intolerable dissonance. In acting her part – if only he had been able to do it sooner, how much he might have saved himself! – he had brought his own sympathies to the role, and there was something compelling in the act of forgiveness, the gentle, invigorating climb towards empathy, which made him want to savour it and draw it out. He was treading a narrow path, though, and when he strayed from it, tempted towards the rocky reaches of the irresolvable, he would come back shaken by the knowledge of how many parts of himself were still dangerous. It was then that he most wanted to know in what state he had been preserved by she whom he considered so respectfully; and then passed quickly on from the thought, frightened by what it might tell him, as if past a rainy day funeral to which no one goes, a grave on which fresh flowers have never been lovingly placed.

Despite his busy hours spent marshalling the riotous crowd of things that had gone for ever into a more disciplined formation, these weeks with Francine – how many weeks? Perhaps only four? – had been accompanied by an encroaching consciousness of his own isolation. From it he looked back to the time before they met as if towards a distant mainland, discovering longings within himself, not for the extinguished joys it harboured, for he could still admit that they were few, but for its familiarity, the memory he had of being recognized there. He supposed he had felt a similar dissociation from himself when he had first met Belinda, but it had been a holiday feeling, an ecstatic celebration of escape. He had used to tell her about the place from which he had come, inflating its horrors, not realizing that she would eventually return him to it. He would enjoy presenting her with the shameful fragments of his past in the knowledge that she would fit them together to make something different.

Once, when he was very young and his parents still lived together in their house – a memory more disappointing than precious, a good beginning made ridiculous by what came later – he had been sitting on the edge of his parents' bed while his mother 'lay in'. She often did that at the weekend, her pillows banked behind her, the frill of her nightdress making a doll of her recumbent form, and he had used to think that she suffered from a brief but regular illness which afflicted her only on those particular days, days when he wanted to play and the house to be full of life. Later, when she really did fall ill, the resemblance of her confinement to those mornings made it seem natural to him, a state to which she had always been going to revert. On this particular morning, he had found something on her bedside table, a mysterious plastic contraption like a large straw, with a funnel at one end and a smaller inner cylinder which slid in and out of the larger one.

'What's this for?' he had said, holding it up and trying to make a toy of it by sliding the cylinder in and out.

'Never you mind,' his mother had snapped, reclaiming the object from his curious fingers and putting it in a drawer beside her.

'But what's it *for*?' he had insisted. Her censorship had shown him a glimpse of something dark and confidential, and he attempted to work it out himself so that he could present her with the answer.

'You'll find out when you're older,' his mother had replied; and he had known then that it must be something to do with *sex*, that unwanted inheritance which promised one day to explain things which now seemed comic and unbelievable. The odd thing was that he hadn't found out later, when sex was as familiar to him as he feared it was ever going to be. It had haunted him, a missing clue, a cipher for his inadequacies. His failure to encounter it devolved accusatorily back upon him, made worse by the fact that even in his enlightened state he still couldn't begin to conjure up a use for the silly thing. Then, one evening, he had found one in Belinda's bathroom, lying nonchalantly on a cluttered shelf among shampoo bottles and jars of face cream. For a moment he had been paralysed by the sight, but the sudden and tangible appearance of the symbol filled him with a heedless determination to decipher it. He took it back with him to the other room and held it before her.

'What's this?' he demanded.

A mild astonishment lifted her features, and even through his agitation he felt a fist of love clench in his chest for the way expressions settled on her face like butterflies.

'It's for thrush,' she said calmly. 'You put this pill on the end of it, a huge sort of horse pill, and then just shove it up.' His face must have been entertaining, for she began to laugh as she watched him. 'Don't look so horrified,' she said. 'You did ask.'

He told her about his mother and saw her amusement become kinder and more genuine. She liked to hear of him as a little boy, and he sometimes feared that her feelings for him found a more natural object in that younger incarnation.

'What on earth did you think it was?' she said.

'An erotic sex toy,' he admitted gamely, playing the fool. Belinda's revelation had made him feel quite light headed.

'But how—?' She began to shake with laughter, wiping tears from her eyes. '*Really?*'

He sensed a thread of mockery in her voice, and for a moment he didn't understand how he had changed from an object of sympathy into one of ridicule. A flash of anger tore through him, not at her, but at his mother, for seeing in his young, pliant face a future in which this scene would come to pass. Her failure to save him from it, to make the world easier for him, seemed to constitute evidence of a horrifying neglect, but thinking about it later, he saw in it something far worse, a submission to indignity, the certainty of a terrible homogeneity which made the future as inescapable as the past.

The sense of imprisonment within his own faculties which had haunted Ralph then still plagued him, and lately he had found that the wide and insuperable border which lay between himself and Francine, rather than lending him a prouder definition, had made him feel more than ever sealed up inside himself. In the beginning he had fancifully imagined that their differences might eventually be fertile – she had said so herself, in fact, reading to him from a magazine in that impervious way she had, about the attraction of opposites – but once or twice he had glimpsed himself lost in the bleak open spaces of their conversation and had since abandoned the hopeful examination of their prospects. Had he been going to put a stop to it all and return to the imperfect but comfortable life which only a few weeks ago had been in his grip, that moment when he had diagnosed a fatal sterility in their situation was the time to have done it. Now, however, his senses were no longer vigilant against novelty, and although he had developed no real liking for the element in which he currently lived, custom made it harder to remember Francine's insinuations and thus extricate himself from them. His early posture, redolent of imminent departure, had disintegrated into an attitude of collapse from which thoughts of change or movement were hazy and reluctant. He was waiting, he supposed, for an outside impulse to direct him towards action, knowing that his own mechanisms had failed and their authority been superseded by that of circumstance. His resolutions visited him like ineffectual salesmen, and although he had often persuaded himself with the memory of his most recent meeting with Francine to draw their history to a halt, the subsequent encounter would invariably demonstrate the intractability of the status quo in the face of his attempts to suborn it.

'I think I need to spend some time on my own,' he had even said to her one evening, his heart growing wild in its cage of timidity.

They were sitting in his flat watching television, a habitat in which at first he had been benumbed with sorrowful incredulity, but which was becoming every day more familiar to him. Francine had certain programmes she liked to watch, and their recurring nature formed a schedule from which, he soon found, she could not be derailed. The appearance of such habits had been swift, and the hostility of their tastes meant that their diversions rarely blended to form an impression of mutuality. The depth of Francine's security in her own preferences, in fact, meant that Ralph's suggestions of things they might do were often overridden, and he had begun to suspect that her early willingness to investigate his cultural activities was merely ceremonial. She had beaten him at the negotiating table, he had to admit, with the luring inference that she might be willing to change, but having secured his interest the hint of compromise disappeared. His only manoeuvres were those of indifference, and he was surprised to discover how much of it her vanity could withstand.

'Why?' she had replied, creasing her forehead in the mildly irritating demonstration of incomprehension she gave him when he said things she didn't understand. He perceived the reprimand for obtuseness contained within this expression, and knew that she really didn't see what he meant. Her face told him that he would have to be much clearer, clearer than perhaps he could be and certainly more cruel, if he wanted to make himself understood.

'Why do you want to be on your own?' she repeated.

He realized that she merely considered him boring, a consideration which possibly troubled her as much as his own misgivings. The spirit of reform had left him after that, and Ralph began to wonder if the problem was really his own. The way in which Francine presented herself to him as if with the expectation that he would manufacture substance, would perform tricks like a man sawing at a spangled woman in a box, cultivated in him the suspicion that what he was witnessing was merely the spectacle of his own inadequacies.

Through her he saw the lives of strangers, heard their footsteps echo through the halls of her heart, watched their ghosts slip inadvertently from her lips as she mentioned them, the advertising executive with the sports car, the local nightclub owner, the married manager, even the geography teacher at school, for Heaven's sake; these men whose keys had fitted the mysterious lock with which Ralph daily wrestled, amongst whose furnishings he was expected to make himself at home, these dreadful characters whom he could not but feel it was ordained for him never to encounter, suddenly sharing with him the most galling intimacy! They hung about him like an ill-fitting second-hand coat, a dark path around the collar, pouches at the elbows, a roll of old mints discovered in a pocket. He was repelled by their proximity. He had loathed Belinda's old boyfriends too, of course, but in a more brotherly manner: they were more perfect versions of himself, with whom nevertheless he felt a certain kinship, a loose matching of identities which left his essence undisturbed while jealously could torment his surface. His relation to Francine's redundant men was altogether more troubling, for he could not see what it was that united them. They made a shiftless, uncomfortable group, a band of brigands amongst whom one had to watch one's back, their common principle not love, but weakness.

He had seen Stephen recently, for the first time in weeks, and his familiarity had made an exhibition of Ralph's secret changes, retrieving them from the obscurity of his suffocating heart and putting them on prominent display. They had met in a pub near Stephen's flat in Notting Hill Gate with the intention of having Sunday lunch; an arrangement which Stephen always suggested, making it sound so appealing, so proper, but for which history could make hazardous claims, coming as it did so soon after the night which traditionally saw the eruption of Stephen's worst excesses. Ralph had often sat for half an hour in the pub waiting for him to appear, and would berate himself for remembering the last such interlude, and the resolutions he had made during it, only when immersed in the next. He supposed that in other circumstances he might have been pricked to deny his company to someone so careless of it, but he knew that it was not awe or even ineffectualness which delivered him time and again to Stephen's rudeness. Rather, he saw in Stephen's recurrent request for the assignation a need for someone to be waiting for him on a Sunday afternoon, a forecast of continuation which, when he awoke on Sunday morning, he could use to ward off whatever obsolescence lingered from the night before. That was Ralph's suspicion, in any case, although whether the person equally needed to be him was less a matter for certainty. These days Ralph brought the newspapers to the pub and read them almost contentedly until Stephen turned up.

It had come as a surprise, then, to be met on his arrival by the sight of Stephen sitting on a stool at the bar reading a book. He looked almost dapper, in an old-fashioned tweed jacket with a pale shirt undone at the collar beneath and loose trousers of some soft material. Ralph glimpsed the back of his neck bent over his book as he approached. It was pale and more slender than he remembered, a bare stalk which embarrassed him but which for a moment he almost wanted to touch.

'Good God,' he said humorously, standing next to Stephen's stool. An inappropriate feeling of love lodged fluttering in his throat.

Stephen's eyes stayed on his book for a second too long, and Ralph remembered how he had used to read like that when they were at school, striking a contemplative pose and ignoring anyone who approached him, including teachers, until he had finished a particular page or chapter. His bouts of reading usually occurred directly after the execution of some misdemeanour or other, and Ralph had come to suspect that Stephen's erudition was merely a dramatic device for the production of high contrast, a baroque detail of the measured eclecticism with which he created himself.

'Afternoon,' he said finally, snapping the book closed without, Ralph noticed, marking the page. 'You're looking very chipper.'

'Likewise,' said Ralph. 'I hardly recognized you when I came in. What's going on?'

'I will brook no interrogations,' said Stephen briskly. 'Your absence has been noted.'

'Sorry. I've been busy.'

'I *know*.'

'What do you mean?' Ralph's voice sounded fluting and nervous, like a girl's.

'Oh, calm down.' Stephen cackled with laughter. 'I'm merely – *surmising* from your failure to return my calls and your shining pelt that you've been—'

'Do you want a drink?'

'—hard at it. Right you are.'

Stephen raised his eyebrows and smiled. Ralph turned to the bar and fumbled in his pockets for money. For a moment his thoughts were in darkness, but he could feel their predatory movements.

'What've you been up to?' he said. He kept his face turned away, his eyes following the ministry of the barman. He could feel the heat of Stephen's examination beside him.

'Oh, working, same old crap. The magazine menstruates monthly. And I'm being punished for a little – cock-up from last month.' He seemed willing to offer an explanation but Ralph, shying from involvement with his complications, didn't ask him for one. 'So this month it's *cars* of all things, talking to morons about the potency of their Porsches. Loaded, every last one of them. Sticks in my craw, old boy.' He sighed and then laughed. 'I've got a good one for you, though. This bloke, this real Home Counties Kev, said to me, you'll love this, he says, "Look, mate—"' Stephen lowered his voice in imitation, gruffly conspiratorial. '"Look, mate, I know it cost a lot, but it's paid for itself in twat, see?" In twat! Glorious!'

'That's funny,' said Ralph. He turned to give Stephen his drink and met his eye.

'And yourself?' said Stephen.

The pub was filling up, and in the warm, rising clamour of voices, the furniture of bodies from whose mouths brazen laughter burst in white plumes of cigarette smoke, Ralph felt his painful singularity begin mildly to disperse. He knew he shouldn't discuss Francine, but Stephen's almost involuntary skill at interrogation meant that only physical escape would make a certainty of his intentions. From the bruised and tender distance of Ralph's curtained intimacies, Stephen seemed more abrasive than ever, and although the sight of his friend pressed upon him a chilly consciousness of his recent loneliness, he feared the confessional impulse which was every moment mounting within him.

'Oh, not much. Work, I suppose. Nothing much, really.'

Stephen's face betrayed a fleeting impatience and he jigged slightly on his stool as if in encouragement of social momentum.

'Met anyone new?' he chirped hopefully.

The unexpected appearance of Roz's terrible question filled Ralph with a sudden private mirth, and before he could stop himself he heard a ghastly laugh rush from his lips. Stephen looked at him in surprise, and, really only to cover his moment of awkwardness, Ralph suddenly found himself prepared to admit everything.

'I've been seeing Francine,' he said loudly, turning to face the room. 'Shall we sit down?'

'Who?' said Stephen. He picked up his glass and followed Ralph to a table, hovering avidly behind him like a reporter.

'Francine.' Ralph felt his brief flash of euphoria subside. 'The girl we met at Alf's.'

'The secretary?' Stephen sat down, as if in shock. His face was a cartoon of astonishment. He began to laugh, shaking his head. 'You're joking. I don't believe it.'

'Why not?'

'I don't believe it.' Stephen paused for a moment and then yelped again with laughter. One or two people turned their heads. 'I just don't believe it.'

'Well, it's true.'

'Francine!' His disbelief dissipated into a wide smile. 'You're a bloody quiet one. I wouldn't have thought she was your tipple, not in a million years.'

'I'd rather not talk about it.' Ralph picked up his glass. His hand was shaking.

'What's she like?' said Stephen, grinning.

'What do you mean, *what's she like*? Is that all you think it is?'

'Well, what is it, then? She's a—' He gestured mountainously from his chest with his hands and then looked exaggeratedly contrite. 'She's a nice girl.'

'She's not stupid, if that's what you mean.'

'Of course she's not.'

Stephen leaned forward and fixed him with a serious look, his eyebrows mockingly furrowed. Ralph shrugged and stared at his hands. They lay on the table, waxy and nerveless, instruments of indifference. The articulation of his secret had illuminated in its very first hateful exposure a veiled background of half-denied truths. In that moment Ralph knew his own misery, recognized it beyond doubt.

'I don't know what's wrong with me,' he said dully. 'I can't seem to get out of it.'

The residue of mirth drained from Stephen's cheeks and Ralph was almost gratified to see a glint of sobriety in his eyes. It was difficult to slay his good humour, and there was a strange pleasure to be derived from being the proprietor of a situation serious enough to achieve it.

'You prat,' he said, more kindly. 'What are you on about?'

'She won't – I don't really understand it. I don't know what to do.'

'She won't what? Bugger off?'

Ralph nodded.

'When it first started, I thought she understood it was just a temporary thing. You know, a one-off.'

'One-off!' Stephen barked with laughter.

'You know what I mean,' said Ralph irritably.

'All right, all right. *Une fois.*' He laughed again. '*De temps en temps.*'

'I mean, you can't just *tell* someone, can you? I thought I made it as clear as it could be.' Ralph shook his head. 'She came round for dinner and it was quite friendly, but we didn't exactly hit it off, for God's sake. I was actually surprised when she *offered* . . .'

There was a pause, and in it the two of them reached for their glasses.

'Consummation?'

'Yes.'

'So what was it like?'

'I don't remember,' said Ralph stubbornly. 'I was drunk.'

'And since then?'

'All right, I suppose.'

'Fussy,' said Stephen, raising his eyebrows.

'No – well, yes, in a way, except that I don't really care about all that. I mean, I do care, I want to care, but then she'll say something and I just—'

'Don't give a shit?'

'If I could see what was in it for her then at least there'd be something to, you know, get to grips with, but she doesn't even seem to like me very much.' As he said it, Ralph realized that it was true, that it was the most bewildering thing of all. His predicament seemed suddenly more inescapable than ever. Stephen's face before him was perplexed. 'That's it, really. She doesn't actually like me.'

There was silence, which the noise around them at first amplified and then engulfed. Stephen drained his glass, his head tipped back, his throat pumping.

'Another?' he said, standing up with his fingers on Ralph's glass.

'Thanks.'

While he was gone Ralph waited anxiously, as if his absence were some kind of judgemental interlude from which he would return with a result.

'Things have been pretty sweet lately,' said Stephen when he returned, setting the brimming glasses carefully on the table and sitting down. He stretched contentedly and gave a grinning yawn.

'That's good,' said Ralph. He felt the jolt keenly, the brutal message that Stephen found him tiresome. A feeling of dislike for himself gathered and sluiced coldly over him. 'Tell me what's been happening.'

'The pursuit of pleasure,' said Stephen vaguely. 'Grotesque but successful. For the time being, anyway.'

'What was that problem you mentioned at work?' said Ralph, driving back his growing awkwardness with ingratiation. He felt peeled and exposed. 'Nothing serious, I hope?'

'Oh, that. No, not really. They should have seen it coming. They sent me off to do a piece on *girls' boarding schools*. Can you imagine?' He laughed. 'So I roved for a week through the groves of girlhood, and my God, there's some talent there, old boy. Nothing like those speccy dogs they used to recruit from the local brain-bin for our end of term disco.'

'So what happened?' interjected Ralph. His voice sounded false with dread.

'What do you think? One of them took a fancy to me, I invited her up for the weekend, and next thing the head-mistress dobs me in to the magazine. Slapped hands all round.'

'How old was she?'

'Fifteen. Is.'

'You're still seeing her?'

'Doing the school run, as they say. Very hush-hush, though. She's an enterprising girl.'

'Right,' said Ralph despairingly.

Afterwards, they walked through the cold, electric sunlight down the Portobello Road towards Stephen's flat. The light made Ralph feel fatigued, blinding him, blanching life from his skin. Stephen suddenly extended an arm and patted his shoulder jovially.

'You'll be all right,' he said, looking into the distance like an explorer and wrinkling his eyes.

Ralph felt duly comforted. Stephen always provided him with curious remedies for the injury of his friendship. The bare assertion of his loyalty, their odd bond which had gathered so little to it over the years, was often the only thing which could palliate the pain which Stephen sometimes brought with him. Despite all that they had shared, Stephen still wrought in Ralph a unique discomfort, a feeling of terrible confinement within himself. He wondered now if that was how families felt, all that trapping knowledge, that looming history. Stephen knew too much about his past to believe in the secret alchemy of personal change. In his eyes he, Ralph, could never be more than the sum of Stephen's knowledge, could never escape the arithmetic of those redundant selves and conjure himself from the air.

'Maybe.'

'Why can't you just enjoy it?' cried Stephen, exasperated. 'You're a lucky sod. Just enjoy it!'

'I can't. I'm not like that.'

'Then tell her to fuck off!'

Stephen broke suddenly from his side and Ralph watched him run ahead. He began skipping and leaping wildly on the pavement, waving his arms above his head in a sudden deluge of irradiation, while the cackle of his laughter made its contorted flight back to Ralph's unhappy ears.

Eleven

Francine's flat was irrefutably located at the western end of Mill Lane, and much as she might try to clothe the fact in whimsically stated preferences for longer walks to leafier branches of transportation, the Tube station at Kilburn was undeniably her most expeditious point of contact with the outside world. On the occasions – really only once or twice, in fact, and more towards the beginning of things – on which Ralph had come to stay, she had directed him to the longer route, believing that her lair was better approached from the more seductive angle of West Hampstead. He had taken matters into his own hands, of course, by consulting a map, and as seemed often to be the case these days Francine had found her persuasive version of things overridden by the more logical conclusions of research. He had been so serious about it, showing her the map on his arrival and drawing the route with his finger as if she had no idea where the Tube station was, and she was forced to pretend that she hadn't in order to keep the tedious conversation brief.

'Actually, I might even have gone a long way round myself,' he had said, stern with puzzlement. 'Now that I look at it, this way's probably quicker.'

While he spoke she had remembered another conversation, with his friend Stephen at the party, and it had kindled in her a flicker of pleasure and irritation. He had asked her where she lived and when she said West Hampstead he had laughed.

'That's Kilburn to the likes of me,' he had said, winking at her conspiratorially so that she had laughed too.

She preferred to stay at Camden anyway, for the dawning of truth over her own home had illuminated other things alongside its unpleasant location to place it irremediably into disfavour. These days the flat didn't seem nearly as nice as Ralph's, and even the masculine flavour of his bathroom – the only thing which, in the early days, had made her long to be back amongst her impedimenta – had been sweetened with the transportation of a half share of her abundant bottles and jars to its shelves. Ralph evidently hadn't understood the rationale behind the relocation of her things – including several key elements of her wardrobe – and kept asking her if it was really necessary. ·

'It's not like you'll be staying here that often,' he had said. 'And what will you do on the nights when you're at home?'

She had explained to him, faintly touched by his concern, that what he saw was merely an emergency consignment of the greater stockade which remained in West Hampstead, and besides, as Janice had said when Francine told her of their difficulties, the proper maintenance of a beauty routine constituted an effort from which both parties benefited. Francine was surprised to suspect that Janice didn't think much of Ralph, although on the few occasions they had met she had certainly made a point of giving the opposite impression. She would drift around the flat in a silk robe when Ralph was there, asking him if he wanted anything and putting her hand on his arm. Once, Francine had been disturbed to notice that Janice's robe had come loose at the front, and when she bent over Ralph to give him a cup of coffee it became clear that she wasn't wearing anything underneath. Ralph had looked uncomfortable, but his eyes had flown through the gap just the same, and Francine had decided there and then to reduce their visits to West Hampstead. It was Ralph, in fact, who ensured her continuing appearances at home with his frequent appointments with himself. Two or three times a week he would declare that he needed to be 'on his own', and Francine, at first thinking that the request referred to a fashionable occupation of which she had been unaware, and only later seeing the slight it made against her company, was eventually forced to take matters into her own hands. She pre-empted him with arrangements of her own, both fictitious and concrete, which meant that she was unable to see him as often as he didn't want to see her.

Things weren't perhaps going as well as she had hoped, and feeling increasingly certain that Ralph was harbouring one or two criticisms – whose presence she caught leaking through his manner, even if she couldn't exactly identify their source – of her, she permitted herself some grudges of her own. He was so boring, never wanting to go out except to see films, and even then only films in which nothing much seemed to happen either and of which the girls at work had never heard. He was always reading, too, even though she had been brought up to think that it was rude to read when there was someone else in the room. She had told him that once, enjoying the thought of how he would react to her knowing more about manners than he did.

'Why is it rude?' he had said, sounding more interested than perturbed. He hadn't even put down his book when she said it, just lowered it a couple of inches so that he could see her.

'It just is. It's bad manners.'

'What, like burping?' He began to laugh. 'Or picking one's nose?'

'It's not like you have to do it,' she had replied, disgruntled. 'You're not revising for an exam or anything.'

Her aversions, though, were the product of slightly unnatural impulses: it was easy to cultivate indifference in an atmosphere of intense interest, but the business was thwarted by unfriendly conditions and Francine found her stratagems ailing and refusing to yield. She would make accusations of his dullness or his unwillingness to take her out, or give displays of restlessness in the evenings, to which he would respond unnervingly.

'Feel free to go out if you're bored,' he would say, rooting himself more firmly behind his newspaper. 'I won't mind at all.'

The proliferation of her freedom, the suggestion that it could be returned to her at any time, undeniably cheapened the commodity. It was hard to hold Ralph accountable for the fact that he rarely went out, that he didn't particularly like to spend money, and that he didn't come accompanied by a glittering entourage of friends, when he seemed willingly to accept the charge. What was easier was to suspect that he had conspired to give the impression of his glamour – his elegant flat, his educated manner, even his invitation to the party at which she had met him, where her own presence had been importunate; all of this had suggested the existence of greater things, a whole world of which this was merely the residue! – and, easier still, that this now-punctured illusion rendered his ability to resist her a sign not of the refinement of his tastes but of their mediocrity. This was her most substantial complaint – the fact that Ralph didn't appear to be infatuated with her – and it was also the most difficult to lodge. The decline of his character in the light of his failure to find her enchanting was inevitable, but her own disaffection offered little hope for progress against the current of his. Her self-love would occasionally rally from his blows and return with zealous contempt for its injury; but eventually she would subside into paralysis, the helplessness of realizing that, being apparently unable to attain what she wanted, she might have to settle for what was being offered.

Leaving Ralph's flat sometimes in the mornings, she would catch people looking at her as she walked to the Tube station and would touch her face secretly with her fingers or strain to get a glimpse of it in passing shop windows, sure that some deformity must be drawing their attention. It was often several hours before the gloom of Ralph's indifference dispersed and Francine realized that the glare from which she shrank was nothing but the friendly sun of admiration. Even the mirror seemed to have lost something of its magic, and Francine would wonder with a lurch of bereavement if her most companionable and delighting ally – herself – was gone for ever.

'He's dark,' concluded Janice, when Francine revealed to her something of her troubles. 'I knew it from the start. He's crying inside. Look out for post-nasal drip – it's supposed to be a sign of life-sorrow.'

Francine tried to enjoy the approval of those in her path, gleaning from it the confirmation of Ralph's stupidity, and she had recently had the idea that when next she became the subject of concerted advances, her acceptance of them would provide the final triumph. Sitting at her desk, though, she would feel a yawning emptiness in her thoughts when she tried to consider her possibilities and would long for the return of their once-bright clutter. In these moments she could take no pleasure from the cheerful lust of the men who came into the office or the longing eyes which met her when she went out to buy her sandwich. She had lost the taste for her own imagination and it was suddenly hard to believe in the adventures it haltingly enacted. It was not love for Ralph, she was sure, which depressed her. She had never supposed herself to be in love with anybody, although she was prepared to accept that they might be in love with her. No, it was the suspicion, which daily gathered more evidence to it, that in Ralph's eyes she lacked something which was dragging her with unjust fingers down into its pit. Why she didn't run from it, loosen its grip with a minute's denial that she cared what he thought, was a question she heard only faintly. Her motives were listless things, grown diffident from her failure to examine them, and while once she had enjoyed the recumbent ease with which she could drift along with only the force of others' desires to fuel her, she now found herself unable consequently to propel herself away from danger. She had finished affairs certainly, in the past, but it had always been easy: someone new had arrived to rescue her, or she had merely woken one day to find herself liberated by boredom or the facility of change. The infliction of pain, besides, was often a source of pleasure, reflecting as nothing else could the real depth and accuracy of her penetration, and she had found that the pinnacle of a man's interest could be recognized by her own sudden natural impulse to flight once she had arrived at it.

Had Ralph been repellent to her in the way so many other men now were, she might have found it easier to escape from him; but her inability to understand him grounded her, and the more he eluded her faculties, the more resolved she became to better him. He had somehow succeeded in belittling those past conquests of which she had once been so proud, although she hadn't told him much about them. It was in her own thoughts that she judged them, shrank from their coarseness or their stupidity, pitied the ease with which she had mastered them. He had raised a standard to which he evidently had no interest in conforming, made her dissatisfied with what she had, and yet refused to palliate her new appetites. As much as she tried to satisfy herself with thoughts of his dullness, his stiff manner, his unfashionable pursuits, the memory of his face would occasionally fill her thoughts when they were apart and she would feel a contraction in her chest which, like hunger, would direct her to seek him out. She liked to look at his face, in fact, and sometimes would forget herself for several minutes whilst looking. It seemed odd to her to do that, and the naked sensation it gave her revealed what appeared to be glimpses of her own worthlessness. She had confided to Janice that she and Ralph didn't speak the same language, and it was true. His sensibility felt awkward in her mouth when she tried it, and he didn't seem to understand the meaning of anything she said, either.

Lately she had begun to feel a deeper, more pressing anxiety which occasionally drew itself through her stomach in a slender, nervous thread. She had come home one night to find Janice reclining on the sofa with a hot-water bottle clutched in her arms, regarding her midriff with a look of pained tenderness.

'Are you ill?' said Francine. Janice's ailments were frequent and vague, but their interpretation nevertheless dramatic. She would complain of energy blocks and decentralization, mysterious agues for which lengthy meditations on their probable causes was often the only cure.

'I'm coming on,' said Janice dully.

Francine had only ever heard her mother use that expression, and the moment was a confusing one, suggesting as it did unthought of affiliations between people she had considered unconnected. In that second of disjointedness, that temporary blank, an idea insinuated itself in Francine's mind. She stared at Janice, wondering how so large a piece of her, as dependable and unexamined as an arm or leg, could have gone missing without her noticing. She stood silently, all her efforts bent on the attempt to remember the last time she had seen her own blood, to track down recent scenes of its inconveniences and look at them afresh for evidence. Before long she had located a few minutes in a ladies' toilet somewhere, caught by surprise and pushing coins into a dispenser. Where had it been? It certainly wasn't Lancing & Louche, for she remembered looking in a small mirror afterwards which couldn't be mistaken for the opulent wall of glass at the office.

'You could make some tea,' said Janice irritably from the sofa. 'I can't get up.'

Francine went to the kitchen. The toilet had been at Mr Harris's office. She had been surprised to find a dispenser there, although the only thing it provided was a giant white slab, an ancient relic like a mammoth's tooth. She tried to number the weeks in her mind by means of their highlights, but they became blurred and resistant to her arithmetic and eventually she reached for her diary. The intractable symmetry of the pages caused her heart to clench with fear as she leafed backwards in search of Mr Harris. It was impossible that so much time should have passed, and yet the entries she glimpsed as she retreated week by week seemed horrifyingly distant and unrelated to her, as if they described the life of another person. Finally she found the Monday on which she had started with Mr Harris, and as she saw it remembered that her crisis had occurred on the second day of working there. She retraced her steps to the present moment, counting the weeks. There were just over six of them, and as they sprang up around her she felt the chill of their sudden shadow.

'Francine!' called Janice feebly from the sitting-room. 'Fran*cine*!'

Francine stood in the doorway. The thought that she could be pregnant didn't seem to have adhered to her. She felt it prowling loosed around the flat, and she had a strong desire to hide in the hope that it might forget her.

'What's the matter?' said Janice. She sat up slightly, her senses pricked for excitement.

'I think I'm pregnant,' said Francine. The idea seemed even more remote now that she'd said it.

'I knew you were going to say that!' shrieked Janice. She swung her legs off the sofa. 'I knew it! Isn't that weird? That's my sixth sense – just before you said it I knew what you were going to say!'

'Really?' said Francine.

'God, weird.' Janice collapsed back on to the sofa. 'That's the second time that's happened to me recently.'

'It's been six weeks,' said Francine. Her revelation didn't appear to have made any impact, and she wondered if she had really said it. An unfamiliar need to be alone tugged at her, but the nervous bustle of her thoughts insisted on further attempts at socializing.

'Sorry, I'm just in shock,' said Janice. She breathed deeply, as if hoping to overcome her fascination with her own clairvoyance. 'How late are you?'

'Six weeks,' repeated Francine.

'Since it should have started?'

'No, no, since the last one.'

'Oh, that's not so bad. Are you regular?'

'Yes.'

'It's anxiety,' diagnosed Janice. 'Did you forget to take a pill or something? Often worrying about that can do it. I knew a girl that happened to. She—'

'I'm not on the pill, actually,' said Francine.

When she was younger, Francine's mother had forcibly accompanied her to a doctor's surgery and come away triumphant with several foil packets of tiny pills which she directed Francine to take.

'I know you're a good girl,' she had said comfortingly in the car on the way there. 'But boys your age have hormones. It gives them bad skin and worse ideas. Tell the doctor you've got cramps.'

Within weeks Francine's flesh had fattened alarmingly, and she had secretly stopped taking the pills, removing one each day from the foil and dropping it down the plug hole when she brushed her teeth so that Maxine wouldn't find out. Remembering the terror with which she had watched herself inflate before the mirror, the well-composed lines of her figure blurring, she had never tried them again; and she had learned from that same reassuringly truthful oracle that she was lucky. The passing of time, undisrupted by misfortune, monthly confirmed the news. Even treading the high-wire of personal risk Francine had felt no fear, for the aggregate of her impregnability grew with each proof of it. She had, she was sure, cultivated a certain immunity, for which indifference provided frequent boosts. The physical intrusion which was often the price of her pleasures – a pay-off for the attention, infatuation, and supplication which preceded it – was a distant thing, a remittance calculated according to the principles of fair exchange. The scope of invasion was limited to areas of public access and in the privacy of her own thoughts, where she could wander freely amongst a range of other subjects, the trespass usually didn't trouble her. She didn't see why she should be expected to enjoy it, for the privilege was not hers but theirs. She had always felt herself to be most untouchable when being touched, and although of course she preferred the presence of a barrier between that suspect male flesh – who knew where it had been? – and her own, it was often an effort to remember in her detachment to insist on it. Ralph, however, had protected himself so vehemently as almost to give offence, and Francine understood enough about irony to recognize that perhaps she had become the victim of it.

'Well, it's all in the mind, anyway,' said Janice briskly. 'Everything that happens in your body is under your control. I mean, maybe you're feeling that you want a bit more attention, Francine, or a bit more security, and this is your body's way of telling you. You have to listen to it. Just try and relax. Try and visualize' – she gestured dramatically with her hands – 'visualize the blood coming, pouring out. I can teach you some meditation techniques. They're really effective.'

Francine gleaned some comfort from Janice's advice, and as her inability to visualize the torrent of reassurance which any day must visit her was matched by a curious blank shielding her efforts to foresee what would happen if it didn't, a neutral mood settled upon her which permitted several days to pass without much trouble. It was surprisingly easy to forget the threat which shadowed her. Had she seen Ralph it might have taken on a clearer, more imminent form, but a faintly sinister calm beset her whenever she thought of calling him and it barely troubled her to notice that he did not interrupt her silence. She had seldom been less conscious, and had a cure for anxiety been what was required Francine felt she had surely effected it.

It was only when she was walking home from the Tube station on Thursday night, towards one of the many suddenly empty evenings she had lately endured, that a piercing sense of her own loneliness visited her and opened with it the tightly barred gates of fear. An overcast sky understudied a precipitant darkness, and a harrying wind struck up while she walked, pulling at her clothes as if in an effort to attract her attention to a nearby danger. As she passed the petrified estate which silently crowded the road, large drops of rain began to hurl themselves at her like spit, and thus besieged Francine felt a bloated wave of self-pity surge forcefully through her and brim at her eyes. In the vacuum which followed it, an irresolvable panic construed itself, as if she had been caught in the sights of a weapon. The troubled sky puppeted the drama of her exposure, and for the first time Francine felt herself to be without shelter, cornered by facts she could not outwit. At lunch-time, still in her mood of slippery certainty, she had gone to a pharmacy and bought a small kit, the allure of whose pastel-packaged chemistry had at the time appealed to her as gentle. Now, with it unopened in her bag, it seemed impossible that so slight a device could still the cauldron of terror which had begun to boil within her.

When she got home, however, her tranquillity resurfaced from the tumult of her fears and she felt the tide of inevitability driven back once more by the magic of possibilities. She laid her bag carelessly on the kitchen table and went to run a bath. Submerged in warm water, she felt rapt in ignorance, and the elasticity of unknowing gave her a momentary sense of returned power. For a while she felt she could exist for ever in the current void, could make it habitable enough, but as the water cooled the merciless progress of time dragged her once more in its wake. She delayed her ministrations, drifting aimlessly to the bedroom and then the sitting-room in a vague pretence of occupation, but when finally she came to open the packet she felt raw and wet with fright. The execution of the test constituted a mild distraction from itself, and as Francine performed it she found herself forgetting the pressing intimacy of its conclusions. The instructions informed her that the interval of its diagnosis might be lengthy, and so when it began immediately to metamorphose before her eyes, she found herself unprepared for the translation of its results. Its filter had turned a bright and unmistakable pink, and her heart thudded like a drum as she scanned the leaflet for meaning. For a moment she could make no sense of it, and when finally she located the interpretation a malfunction of understanding caused the words to inform her that the test had been negative. Seconds later, reading it again, she gained the opposite impression. A terrible stupidity webbed her thoughts, as sticky as tar. She breathed deeply, trying to regain control over the insurrection of her powers of comprehension, and then allowed her eyes to travel slowly along the lines, enacting every sentence. The colour pink indicated that she was pregnant. She considered this, trying to find some concrete quality in the words which might hold down their meaning. They slipped and rose like balloons before her. She repeated them aloud, and it was then that a cold blade of acceptance penetrated her heart. She threw the leaflet away and wrapped the kit in the paper bag from the pharmacy. In her room, she opened a drawer and placed the bag in it.

Janice was out and had not said when she would be back. Francine went to the sitting-room and sat down, waiting for some direction to indicate where the rest of the evening might go. Once or twice she thought she would turn on the television or open a magazine, but the flicker of energy generated by the idea was inadequate to make her body perform it. Besides, the time was passing quite quickly as it was, and before long she would be able to go to bed. After a while, she had an odd sensation of looking at herself sitting on the sofa as if she were somebody else on the other side of the room. The image was unpleasant and she struck about, trying to find something on which she could fix her eyes. Janice kept a poster on the sitting-room wall, a blown-up photograph of a chimpanzee, and Francine looked at it for what seemed like the first time. Its hairy eyes held her until she was overpowered and for a while she disappeared, absorbed into its kindly, old man's face. An explosion of exhaust from the road startled her and she wondered if she had been sleeping. She looked at her watch. It was ten o'clock. She picked up the telephone and dialled Ralph's number.

Twelve

'Oi, it's Friday night!' called Neil from the door of the office. 'Haven't you got a home to go to, mate?'

He was wearing an overcoat which had a strip of fur around the collar. Its attempted projection of prosperity had somehow mutinied to make Neil look even shiftier than usual and Ralph felt a smile pull at his lips.

'Soon,' he said. 'I'm going soon. I just want to finish something.'

'Suit yourself,' said Neil.

He waved his hand as if across a great distance and stepped awkwardly back into the corridor while still facing the room, as though worried that some physical attack might be launched on him if he turned his back, to complement the psychological assault already being perpetrated. Ralph stretched pleasantly and looked at his watch. It was seven o'clock, later than either he or Neil had ever stayed before. Although he had clearly finished his day's work Neil had lingered stolidly in what Ralph understood to be the spirit of competition, shielding with a clumsy, subversive hand the newspaper he was reading at his desk, as innocent and obvious as a child. From the corner of his eye Ralph had seen the broad blank of Neil's face turn regularly on its axis in nervous observation and had rather enjoyed the clockwork motion with which he looked, paused, and then lifted his wrist to glance incomprehendingly at his watch. Finally, with a raucous and guttural clearing of the throat, Neil had risen from his desk in defeat. After he had gone Ralph felt rather guilty at keeping him, for in truth he didn't have much to do and in any case had no interest in making a show of his industry. He was merely compelled by a new access of energy which, although it had been generated to drive a specific part of his life into action, seemed also to infuse the rest of it with secondary force.

In the days since his afternoon with Stephen a new resolve had taken him in its grip, and he felt an earnest zeal at the thought of purging shadowy corners of the habits which had been allowed to gather there unseen. In the flurry of his activity he had not yet had pause to consider what actually had been achieved by it, and although he dimly knew that the most disorderly part of himself remained untackled, the atmosphere of regeneration often gave him the mistaken impression that the opposite was true. Francine's disappearance over the recent days deepened his sense of liberation, and a residual cowardice suggested to him that he might be spared a detailed confrontation with her merely by upholding his end of the silence.

He had stayed gradually later at the office every evening, often achieving little but a pleasant, unimplicated solitude as darkness fell beyond the windows, and the freer nature of his journey home once the clamouring rush-hour crowds had dispersed permitted him to see himself more clearly than he had for weeks. Normally recalcitrant in matters of social contact, he had recently telephoned one or two flagging friends and had spent enjoyable evenings in the pub rejuvenating their interest. His later hours at the office meant that he could travel directly to these assignations after work, and he had spent little time alone at his flat. Coming home and going directly to bed, he would occasionally feel a mild and inappropriate guilt, as if he were attempting to smuggle himself into his room unseen by some vigilant authority. It seemed then, especially if he returned in a state of drunkenness, that his flat had allied itself with Francine and was awaiting him accusatorily. In those muddled hours he had even felt once or twice as if he missed her.

Nevertheless, her telephone call late on Thursday evening had still taken him unpleasantly by surprise, particularly as his presence at home had failed to represent the trend of his many recent absences. Being found thus, he had suddenly felt unkind for the fact that he hadn't communicated to her his change of heart. She had sounded different to him on the telephone, her voice spare with intent and acceptance, which informed him beyond doubt that at least she had read his misconduct correctly and was demanding a meeting merely to finalize its terms. She had wanted to meet the next evening, and Ralph, glad again to have reinforced his life with activity and thus protected himself from things he didn't want to do, had said that he couldn't.

'Why not?'

'I'm busy. I'm going out with some friends.'

'You'll have to tell them you can't come.'

'I can't do that,' said Ralph gently. The swingeing ferocity of her demands, in trying to grip him, merely knocked him further from acquiescence. 'It's too little notice. It's all been arranged.'

He had insisted on meeting her instead on Saturday afternoon, convinced by a sudden access of inherited wisdom that, while the inception of such romances belonged to the soft, veiling influence of the night, their termination was best performed in broad daylight. She had reluctantly agreed and the conversation came swiftly to an end.

Thinking about it now Ralph felt inexplicably sad, and a

sudden consciousness of his loneliness in the empty office worsened his condition. Even through the spreading miasma of emotion, however, he could still recognize that his mistake had been at the beginning, in taking up with Francine at all, and that the palliative for his pains – the sweet oblivion of inaction, the peculiar dreaminess of lies; in short, the ease of doing nothing – which was at that moment suggesting itself would inflame rather than cure them. Once he had finished things for good, he would feel better. He *did* feel better, even with the flogged form of the dreadful past few weeks still on his hands. Soon he would be rid of it. The thought that he had in some way duped Francine dimmed slightly the honest allure of his future freedom. She had sounded so hurt on the telephone. It would be even worse on Saturday. For a moment he ached sentimentally for her, and then hardened as he remembered how he had learned to inflict pain – from experience! Everyone got hurt at some point. Why should she be spared? He looked at his watch and saw that half an hour had passed. He was late. He put on his coat and left the office.

It was past midnight by the time he got home, and as he unlocked the door to his flat he had an odd sense of a menacing delegation rising to greet him from the dark, a group of troubles whom he had kept waiting during his forgetful hours away. He was tired and he carried his sense of unease with him to bed, hoping to dissolve it with sleep. As he lay down, however, a horrible alertness visited him: every thought in his head seemed to ignite and rage until his mind was a furnace, and he lay awake in its uncomfortable heat, often unsure whether he was conscious or dreaming. He hadn't lain thus since he was a child, and he was surprised to see how much shorter the night was now, its later hours, which once had filled him with terror, made familiar to him at parties and in late-night conversations. When the clock beside his bed began to approach three, he felt the swelling tide of sleep finally rise in him, and when he awoke it was almost with a feeling of excitement for the day ahead. As he bathed and dressed, the false promise of his arrangement with Francine continued to trick him, sending stabs of inarticulate anticipation through his stomach from which, seconds later, came more conscious trickles of dread. It was still too early to leave by the time he had readied himself, and he sat aimlessly in the sitting-room with a book, as if he were waiting at an airport. He hadn't wanted Francine to come to the flat, and the ethereal but none the less obstructive presence of Janice had ruled out a visit to West Hampstead, so in the end Ralph had suggested a walk in Regent's Park; a place to which he rarely went, but whose foreignness was, he felt, countermanded by the advantages of the open air. It was the least intimate of settings, and the possibilities for escape from it were unlimited. He had calculated it would take him fifteen minutes to make the journey, and he ruled his impulses sternly until the appointed time for departure so as to blockade all possible diversions.

He saw her as he came up Prince Albert Road, standing on the pavement by the entrance to the Outer Circle beside a pedestrian crossing. She was looking across the road, her posture held in that attitude of vacant stillness which he could never decide signified poise or inertia, and as he approached he saw several cars slow down to permit her to cross, their headlights empty as leering eyes, and then buck irritably on as she remained immobile. He proceeded towards the pedestrian crossing himself, but a sudden stream of traffic prevented him from going over. As he stood there stupidly, she caught sight of him and he saw her face change oddly with a kind of backstage movement, like a mask behind which a living face had briefly appeared. Seconds later she looked away again, as if pretending she hadn't seen him, and as he waited to cross the road he found himself struck again by her beauty, by its precarious quality of aloofness which could move him either to worship or indifference. From a distance he noticed a new fragility in her features, accentuated by the black coat which she had wrapped tightly around her, pinning it with self-embracing arms. He had remembered her as robust and fully coloured, a dominating presence in which only the most obvious things survived, while paler, more delicate effects were lost. Even though only a week had passed since last he had seen her, her face seemed thin and translucent, and as he looked he saw something in it, some evidence of emotion, which hazily informed him that she had changed.

'Just coming!' he shouted awkwardly over the noise of passing cars, as he lunged forward into the road with one cautionary hand raised like a policeman. 'Sorry about that,' he said, reaching the other side. He could hear himself panting, although the exercise had been mild.

'Shall we go?' said Francine quietly, turning to face the park. He glanced at her and saw the perilous thinness of her neck, from which it appeared her bone-china skull might at any moment tumble.

'Right, yes,' he replied, setting off exaggeratedly so that she would know which way they were going. 'Sorry, that was my invisible man routine again back there.' He laughed, but the sound came back unabsorbed from her unresponding face. 'How are you?'

'I'm fine,' said Francine.

She spoke only a trifle too wanly, but it was enough to inform Ralph that she wanted him to know that she wasn't fine at all. Even through the beginnings of perturbation at her unstated crisis, Ralph felt himself withdraw from her, the reaction he always had when the frigid barrier of her self-consciousness rose up between them. A brief anger warmed him for the way in which she overplayed herself, like a second-

158

rate, actor too enamoured with theatre to serve the reality it shadowed: even now, when she had for once affected him merely with the eloquence of a look, her clumsy demands stood up to conduct their loud negotiations. He had forgotten how impenetrable she was, how devoid of any depths into which feelings could sink, any softness to cushion reactions. Her surfaces were hard and extensive, and the little routines she devised were embarrassingly visible to the naked eye.

'Let's go this way,' he said, leading her towards a gate which gave access to the upper part of the park. As they proceeded down a small avenue of trees, the noise of traffic was muffled, and in the sudden silence Ralph realized how still the day was beneath the rigid, toneless grey of the sky. Nothing moved, no leaves flickered, and the thick, paralysed air gave him the impression that time had stopped. Once or twice, when he was younger, he had woken in the dark to a similar stillness, and had lain nervously waiting for some noise or movement to signal that the world had not ground to a halt.

'You're obviously not fine,' he said finally, hating himself for being led so easily away from his purpose. 'Is anything wrong?'

Francine didn't reply, and as her silence wrapped itself around him Ralph felt a strangling panic at his throat. He could feel her coat brushing against him as they walked, and her proximity struck him just then as more impertinent, more inappropriate, than even their sexual closeness had been. Thinking of that, his memories of it were barely visible. It was as if it had never happened, a renegade adventure of bodies, a desertion of consciousness by flesh. It had left no traces in his thoughts. He felt their limbs locked in brutal conversation as they walked, while his mouth – and the realization seemed suddenly awful to him, bothered him more than anything else – had nothing to say to her.

'Francine?' He stopped and faced her, not daring to put a hand on her arm. 'What's wrong?'

Her eyes evaded him, but the sulky fall of her face told him that he was to be presented with a complaint. He groaned silently with the burden of her dissatisfaction, so much heavier now that he was on the brink of shrugging it off, and wondered what was stopping him from just leaving her there and then.

'Why do you care?' she said.

'Of – of course I care,' he replied. He had an odd sensation of not knowing which words were at his lips until he heard them. 'I want us to be friends.'

'I get it!' she said. He heard rather than saw that she was angry, for her face was curiously expressionless, except her mouth, which, loosened from its fine circumference, reminded him for a moment of Roz's. 'Don't worry, I get it!'

'Francine, you don't understand,' he began, seeing his mark but suddenly afraid to drive his point home on it. He felt a frantic urge to retract. 'It's not like that at all, please don't be upset. It's my fault, there's something wrong with *me*—'

'I'm pregnant,' she said loudly over him. 'I'm pregnant.'

She said it again, although he had heard her clearly, and for a moment Ralph didn't feel anything at all. The silence of the park thronged around him like an invisible crowd and everything appeared suddenly rather deadened and remote, eroded until he experienced the most luminous solitude he had ever felt. His skin was very warm. For a delirious few seconds it seemed as if his body was not going to produce a reaction. He gazed curiously at Francine, trying to see her and thus tell himself at least that he would remember this moment for the rest of his life; but it was as if there were nothing beyond him but empty space, while inside him the whole world was contained. Her face was the face of a statue or a portrait in a frame, and as he looked at it he had a feeling of something else trying to communicate with him through it, of having been singled out by a hidden intelligence for the bestowal of some great secret. Significance moved across his thoughts, at large. Moments later it struck him that Francine seemed to be growing impatient, and it was then that he understood what was being expected of him. She was telling him something she thought he should know, returning what belonged to him like a wallet dropped in the street. She expected him to take charge. Faster than he would have thought possible, a torrent of fear tore through and drenched him.

'I'm completely sure,' she said, watching him as nervously as if she were lying. 'I found out yesterday. I did a test.'

Ralph felt an awful laughter well up in him for the way in which she recited her answers, regardless of his failure to question her. Astonishing, inappropriate reactions were beginning to dance in him like broken puppets. Beneath the patina of personal novelty, the well-worn nature of the scene engendered in him an uncontrollable resistance to its clichés. He understood that he must do something, and the only quandary that offered itself up for resolution was his embarrassment at being in the park. Francine stood before him, tense with requirements.

'We'd better go home,' he said, taking her arm and guiding her back to the gate.

On the bus to work on Monday morning, Ralph found himself wishing that the unusually rapid stream of cars which rushed past the vehicle, quickly dividing and re-forming like water flowing around a rock, would tangle and clog to obstruct their progress. The journey constituted the first real opportunity for reflection which he had been permitted – not that he hadn't been able to think in Francine's presence over the weekend, for she had been silently expectant for most of it, but he had known that his meditations would take a different, although unguessable, form once he was alone – but the speed with which he was hurtling towards the Holloway Road gave him an odd sensation of falling, and he found himself gripping his seat with little thought for anything but his survival.

There wasn't that much to think about in any case, he supposed, and even the small freedoms of consciousness which he had so far allowed himself merely reinforced his greater physical imprisonment. He had been called up, and the incontestable nature of his conscription summoned deep mechanisms of acceptance to quell the cunning instincts of evasion. The trajectory of his responsibilities was long, its demarcation unmistakable, and although he had sufficient memory of small desertions in the past to know that the stuff of self-interest was within him, escape from the current crisis required a crime larger than he was able to commit. It was easy, having been so comprehensively caught, then to detect the seeds of a harder salvation in his predicament. It offered a strange security from fear, the potential for absolution from himself, and having recognized the face of his enemy it was but a short step to believing that everything he had ever done – things, indeed, which had been done before he even existed! – had brought this moment upon him.

It seemed to him that Francine had reached the same conclusions, although by a blunter route. They hadn't talked about it much over the weekend – hadn't talked about anything at all, in fact – but her stolid, automatic presence in his flat bespoke intransigent atavisms to which he dared not even suggest modern solutions. He had tried to detect the surface movements of consciousness beneath her veiled expression, but had seen nothing beyond the certain obstinacy of a claimant, a look of stubborn patience which had filled him with apprehension. It had shamed him to wonder, as he had done once or twice with fantastical desperation, if she might at any moment reveal her intention to dismiss him from his duties, but by the end of the weekend it had become clear to him that she saw nothing in the tenuous nature of their experiment with each other which should invalidate its result. Her aspect, in fact, was more accusatory than troubled, and when finally he had asked her, late on Sunday night, what she was going to do, she had fixed him with a look of such disdain – almost of hatred, in fact – that a terrible panic had beaten like wings about his head as he watched her.

'What do you mean, what am *I* going to do?'

Over the course of the weekend Ralph had read a whole lexicon of new expressions in Francine's face, and he wondered if her features would learn them, would progress with them from her pristine prettiness to something more complex.

'I only meant that I wanted it to be your decision,' he had replied. A note of weariness crept into his voice.

'Don't think you're getting out of this!' she shrieked, sitting up in her chair.

'Of course I'm not.' He was horrified, but he forced himself to sit down beside her and place an arm around her shoulders. He was surprised to realize that it almost repelled him to touch her. 'I don't want to get out of it. All I'm saying is that you should choose, and whatever you choose is fine by me.'

The implication of his words was appalling, and for once he was grateful for Francine's lack of expertise in meaning. She pursued him no further, and although Ralph was too frightened to ask her whether she intended to go home, she soon made it clear that she didn't by telling him she was going to bed. He had sat up late on his own, tempted to fall asleep in his chair and pretend in the morning that he had done so by accident. In the end he had dozed for a while, and when he awoke after an hour with a stiff neck he forgot for a moment what he was doing there and endured a few seconds of dreadful confusion. Often, when he took himself by surprise by coming to in this manner, he even found it difficult to remember into which phase of his life he was surfacing; and he sometimes feared that his dreamlike grasp of things could be loosed by one of these sleepy interludes, returning him to the custody of a past he had thought escaped or, worse still, to a future he was attempting to flee. On this occasion he recalled the presence of someone in his bedroom and thought for a while that it was his mother, before the memory of Francine opened a door on reality and let the cold wind of her revelation rush in. He stood up and switched off the lights, and when he entered the bedroom the anonymous huddle of her form beneath the blankets filled him again with confusion. She didn't stir as he lay down on the bed, not bothering to undress, but he heard her say something. It sounded like a name, 'Mark' or 'Mike', but when he said 'What?' she didn't reply and he knew she must be asleep.

The bus stopped and Ralph got off. His head hurt, and fatigue lent the crowded pavement and grey, busy road a ghostly quality which made him walk carefully lest the ground should disappear beneath him. A small boy stood by the door to his office building, and as Ralph approached he turned and stared; not a rude or hostile stare, but more of an innocent, inquisitive look, as if in expectation of something. He hadn't thought much about the notion of a child, but gazing into this boy's dark, open eyes the singularity of what he had engendered broke from a crowd of possibilities and appeared to come and stand by his side. He stopped by the door, close to the boy now, and felt an inexplicable urge to take him inside off the street and perhaps take care of him for the day. The boy was still looking at him, but a woman's shout from further down the pavement turned his head.

'Rick! Rick!'

Ralph saw a young girl thundering towards them, a pram

in front of her. Tails of hair flew about her face and her mouth was an angry rip.

'You come away from there!' she yelled. A stream of passers-by backed up around her and stared. She put out an arm without slowing her progress, as if with the intention of hooking the boy up as she passed. Ralph felt him flinch beside him.

'I thought he was on his own,' he said to the woman.

She stopped and grabbed the boy's hand, yanking him towards her.

'You leave him alone,' she said, thrusting the fist of her face at Ralph. The boy still looked impassively at Ralph, his manacled arm raised above his head. 'You dirty bugger.'

'Really, I think that's quite unnecessary,' said Ralph stiffly, but the woman had already turned and continued her furious progress up the road. As he watched, he saw her let go of the boy's arm for a moment and slap him hard across the backs of his legs, before seizing his hand again. He dangled for a moment, losing his balance, and then scuttled after her.

Roz was at her desk, her finger already clicking, and Ralph could hear the tinny acoustics of warfare buzz from the screen as he sat down.

'Hello,' he said loudly. 'Nice weekend?'

'Hello,' said Roz. Her eyes didn't move.

She had ceased to exchange pleasantries with him since his admission of treachery, and although Ralph had thought at first that the remission of her interest would improve things at the office, the sense of invisibility it forced upon him actually made his days less bearable than ever. He thought of describing for her the scene which had just taken place downstairs, but knew instantly that his sociability was merely a misguided nervous impulse guaranteed to earn a punishing silence.

'How's Frances?' she said suddenly. Her voice was so loud that Ralph started. He looked up and met her eyes. They were guileless, but in his tremulous state he thought he saw a blade of malice glint behind them.

'Francine,' he said. 'She's fine.'

'Oh,' said Roz.

He hadn't asked Francine to stay at his flat that evening and nor had she requested an invitation, but the mute agreement of their new complicity informed him that she would come and he hurried home earlier than his usual time. A few hours away from her had introduced him to the urgency of their situation, and he wondered why they had spoken so little of it over the weekend. He supposed they had each been waiting for the other to formulate an opinion strong enough to begin the business of action and reaction, but beneath the passivity of Francine's aspect he feared the presence of something stronger, a predator which might be stirred by a glimpse of its prey. He had no way of knowing which of his tangled thoughts would prove the bait for her attack, and his diffuseness left him feeling unguarded and afraid.

She rang the doorbell moments after he had let himself in, with an eerie promptness which heightened his hunted spirits. He opened the door and she walked past him without saying anything, but the brief impression he had of her face told him that she looked oddly better than she had done over the weekend. He followed her into the sitting-room and in the stronger light saw that the solidity had returned to her features. He wondered if it signified resolution, and his heart began to pound in his chest.

'How are you feeling?' he said with ridiculous solicitude as she sat down on the sofa.

'OK,' she replied. 'A bit sick, that's all.'

She smiled at him, and he felt a companionable nausea rise up in his throat.

'Francine.' He sat down beside her. 'Look, I don't mean to alarm you, but I think we must decide soon what we're going to do.'

'Do you think you could make me some tea?' she said. Her voice was sweet, but a momentary strain paraded across her features and she laid a hand on her stomach. 'It helps.'

'Of course, sorry,' said Ralph.

He went into the kitchen and leaned against the fridge with his eyes closed. Already he was beginning to feel dangerously detached and he pressed hard on his face with his hands to remind him of the imminence of his predicament. It amazed him that Francine could continue to defeat him when he could see her so clearly, every mechanism on display like the guts of a clock. Worse still, he could also see that he was conspiring with her against himself, promulgating the consciousness of her advantage. She knew that there was no chance of him deserting her, and her knowledge – provided by him! – made her unassailable. There was nothing he could do but wait, in the faint hope that her muddled formulas would end in a passable result for both of them. His helplessness dragged at him, amplifying his first faint identification that morning with the mysterious entity of which Francine had such complete and bewildering charge into a stronger allegiance. It was a mistake, he knew, to start getting ideas about this captured pawn, this knot by which he had been tied, but the power of relation, of bound blood, both frightened and drew him. He felt its absolutes mired in the sinking ground of his dispossession. It hadn't flowered yet into any definable emotion but its sturdy roots and trunk were exerting their pressure inside him. Feeling it there, growing tight in his chest all day, he had had to fight off hourly the temptation of thinking that he was no longer alone.

He carried the scalding tea back into the sitting-room, and, as he lowered it on to the table in front of Francine, was ambushed by a violent image of throwing it at her. He closed his eyes for a moment, and when he next looked up Francine was lapping at the cup contentedly.

'So,' he said again. His persistence reminded him of times when he had dialled a continuously engaged number with little hope of getting through. 'What are we going to do?'

She looked him through a pale shimmer of steam.

'What do you want to do?' she said.

He sensed from her calmness that she had already thought of this exchange and that she didn't really care what he said during it. It occurred to him that she was enjoying the extended interlude of their uncertainty, was perhaps even protracting its entangled hours.

'I don't know,' he said. 'It's not easy. Obviously, we have two choices.' He felt rather foolish putting it so formally, but his longing for something concrete to displace the stifling vagueness of Francine's evasions urged him on. Her look of sweetness had begun to cool into a less yielding expression, and he realized, his understandings coming at him now as fast as flying fists, that she actually saw something romantic in it all which his mention of choices was about to destroy. 'Come on, Francine,' he said, more gently. 'I know it's hard, but we've got to face it. It happens all the time—' He heard the suggestion in his voice and reared away from it, frightened for a moment, before plunging over. 'People do it every day, I promise. There's nothing wrong with it – I know loads of women who've done it. It's easy. It was an accident, that's all. It doesn't mean anything.'

She had turned away from him slightly while he spoke, and her face had found a certain angle from which she was utterly unfamiliar to him. Through this point, this tiny gap of dissociation, rays of alienation and loneliness fanned coldly over him. He wanted desperately to be away from her, for their whole rambling disaster to compress itself into a noxious pellet which he could spit from his mouth. It was only when she turned her head again and met his eyes that he saw the mesh which webbed his limbs and felt the sting of hooks in his tender flesh.

'What do you mean?' she said. Her eyes were full, though whether of ammunition or feeling he could not tell.

'I only mean that it's not such a big thing.' It was an effort to remind himself of how charged she was, how filled with the capacity to hurt him. 'It was a mistake. You shouldn't get too – upset, you know, about getting rid of it.'

To his relief, she didn't say anything. As he watched her, he suddenly felt such a surge of pity that he rose from his chair and went to put his arm around her. The action returned to him his sense of normality, of propriety, and with it came a feeling of acceptance – almost warmth – for the grain of intimacy at the heart of their situation and the common history which wrapped it. He was suddenly convinced of the fact that these things happened all the time, just as he had said, and that their unpleasantness was as controllable as that of an injection or a dental appointment.

'There, there,' he said awkwardly, patting her shoulder. 'There, there, darling.'

'I'm keeping it,' she said.

'What?'

Her form felt so lifeless beneath his arm that her voice seemed separate from it, as if there were someone else in the room who spoke.

'It's mine. I'm keeping it.'

'But you can't!'

She stood up, shrugging his arm from her shoulders.

'I can do what I want.'

*

169

Later, he didn't know what time it was, Ralph lay on the sofa. He was alone, but Francine was still in the flat somewhere – in bed, that was right – and he was drinking far too much considering he had to go to work the next day. He wanted to talk to Stephen but there had been no answer when he'd dialled his number and the machine wasn't on either. Stephen was never there when he wanted him. What was strange was that earlier he had suddenly remembered the telephone number of his parents' old house and had thought he might ring them. When he'd tried, though, all he'd got was a horrible noise. He didn't want to talk to his mother anyway – he hated his mother, actually, he'd decided – but his father would have been all right. He'd talked about things like this with his father before. It had been a long time ago, but he felt sure his father wouldn't have forgotten their conversation, and he'd been drunk himself then, after all, so he'd be a hypocrite if he criticized Ralph for it. He'd have understood, too, about Ralph not liking Francine much, because he'd told Ralph that time that his mother hadn't liked him much either, but she'd married him just the same. Ralph had been his ticket home, he said. His lucky charm. She was the love of his life, he said, and after she'd gone he'd promised himself to look after Ralph, because Ralph was what had brought them together, after all. He had put his big hand on the back of Ralph's neck. Ralph could feel it there now, warm and surprisingly steady.

Thirteen

The wall behind Francine's desk was almost entirely commandeered by disciplined rows of large files, all of them presented in military grey, distinguishable only by a typed label centrally placed on the wide spine. She rarely looked at these files, for they were undisturbed historical annals of past deals, of correspondence long since read and answered, and had been superseded by the more active system on the other side of the office. Now and then, however, her aimless eye drifted over them, and she would search their dry demarcations anew for some drop of interest to relieve the boredom of her desktop. Once, she had chosen one at random – Investments (1984) – and had leafed nonchalantly through it, but her expectation that she would find nothing in its pages to amuse her had been unpleasantly confounded by the strange sensation she had experienced when contemplating the familiar, monochrome vistas of type. The letters and reports were identical in style and substance to those she daily produced, and seeing them thus interred she had received an unsettling impression of her own disposability, and with it a desire to leave in commemoration behind her artefacts which were distinguishable in some way from the remains of those who had gone before.

Her tenure at Lancing & Louche was proving to be the

most enduring of any she had had, and Francine had begun to admire her own stamina enough to believe that she deserved some relief from it. The habit of migration had been soothed rather than broken by the lulling custom of the recent weeks, and the desire for change, like a biological imperative, was manifesting its symptoms despite her attempts logically to resist it. She began to recognize the dissatisfactions which normally heralded the close of one era and the beginning of another, a sudden awareness of the grinding irritations of office life on which she rarely had time to dwell as a general danger owing to the frequency with which she moved on from the scenes of her displeasure. Constant change lent the annoyances of her job the illusion of specificity, and by the time they recurred elsewhere she had forgotten ever meeting them before, nor recognized again the allied hopefulness with which she had craved novelty.

The munificence of her current employers, however, the splendour of their headquarters, the sheer size of their enterprise, conspired to keep her in her place with the suggestion that she had reached a limit of expectation beyond which could only lie decline. Although Francine was too schooled in the facts of her superiority to believe at heart that anything was good enough for her, she was disturbed by the recently indifferent quality of her work and the consequences it might invite. For the first time she found herself wishing that she was able to remain contentedly in one place, and she tried to suppress the evidence of her frustration – a slight carelessness in her manner, an overwhelming lethargy in the face of her duties, a compulsion to leave the office at ever earlier times – as well as images, which were fearful in nature, of what she would do next.

It was hard to concentrate on her job when a malignant consciousness of her greater emergency resided in her so heavy with unacknowledgement that it made the performance of the simplest activity difficult. The thought that she was suffering from some injustice, although its oppressions were barely noticeable, filled her with requirements for sympathy and concern, and looking at the faces brutal with ignorance around her she felt a constant urge to announce her misfortune and thus elicit a dispensation from her responsibilities. At the same time, it was hard to believe that the crisis by which she was officially declared to be gripped would ever come to its logical conclusion. Her faith in her own good fortune was here supported by evidence of a persuasive nature. She didn't feel as if anything had physically happened, had observed no changes in herself which might signal the presence of a serious ailment – although her general grasp of those changes which were appropriate to her diagnosis had led her to suspect them once or twice – and in this unafflicted state it really seemed as if the problem might at any moment just disappear.

Her feelings of suspicion about this mysterious blockage, and her secret hopes for its evaporation, did not lessen her admiration of its power. It was certainly a triumph to be the proprietor of such a weapon, and it was hard, after all the awful things Ralph had done to her, not to feel some pleasure at having him at her mercy; but even with her eyes averted from the future, Francine could see that the shifting, explosive nature of her arsenal required skilful handling. The feeling of emptiness she had experienced when Ralph had made its disposal sound like a matter of course, the work of a moment, had sent her rushing to defend it; but in the delightful discovery that she had the inalienable right to do so, she had glimpsed a certain difficulty. Much as her dislike of criticism had been offended by Ralph's suggestion that they might usefully get rid of something which could be said to be a part of her, her protective stance over what would eventually, hard as it might be to believe, effect her own overthrow resembled something of a trap. It would have been impossible at that point to tell Ralph that her feelings were largely theoretical, and hinged on what his preference inferred of his attachment to her, and even knowing that she had at least secured his attention failed to reassure her. Had he begged her to keep it, it would have been easier, she felt, to consider the possibility of not doing so; but his apparent indifference to the weight of her claims on him left her with the unpleasant responsibility of reminding him of them.

Her life had suddenly become somewhat unrecognizable, and it surprised her, not really able to see how she had got there, to have arrived in so unexpected a place. She barely knew herself in it, and in this unfamiliar state she had a dim consciousness of new structures rising in her overnight, of hasty extensions being added to more established facets. Normally she enjoyed lingering over the design of change, but now she was being pressed for such quick reactions that she had a disagreeable sense of events not turning out as she wanted them. It was clearly Ralph's fault: she had tried to delay any talk of decisions, having yet perceived no outcome which pleased her and certain that one would at any moment present itself, but Ralph had forced her into saying things over which premeditation had given her no control. She had never even thought of such a situation before she found herself in it, and her instincts, used to a gentle life of service at the court of her self-interest, were wild and ineffectual in the field of battle. Her skill at pleasing herself and eliciting flattery, though practised, was being severely tested, but she could conjure up at such short notice no more reserves than those on which she had always depended. Several times she had thought of how pleasant it would be if, after punishing Ralph appropriately with it, their 'accident', as he called it, could just somehow be forgotten about, but this did not appear to be among her alternatives. The forked path of the future led, whichever of its vicious tongues one chose, only to what was undesirable.

Had she been less annoyed about the way their negotiations were going – and less conscious of the fact that this uninvited third party appeared to be elbowing her away from the centre of attention – she might have found it amusing to observe how Ralph danced at her every word as if his limbs had strings attached to them. She had said things merely to see what he would do, delighting at first in the excitement of the game, the height of its stakes; but since it had become clear that he wasn't playing as she had expected him to, she had begun to suspect that the victory she pursued conferred only uncertain advantages. For once, there was nothing to be gained from getting her own way. All this talk of it being her decision – as if there were something she wanted to do! – made her predicament more frightening than ever. She supposed that when she had first told him of it, she had done so with the expectation of better things, a romance of emergency out of which some good might come; but nothing was happening as she had expected it to, and in reaching this false summit of her experiences she had felt the cataclysm of personal change, as a new range of unimagined, impossible ascents opened out above her.

The feeling that she was now far beyond the sphere of her abilities swamped her with the imminence of failure. She had never thought that she would be unhappy, but it was becoming clear that there was a vast world beyond the limits of her own, which her compass had been too occupied with directing her towards things that were to her liking to find: she felt its massive, secretive presence gradually unveiled in the slowly receding mists of her complacency, made out its continents of disappointment, its great seas of doubt. Yet even in the midst of these discoveries she began also to discern a more familiar route, a path which skirted complexity and meandered over care. It was still possible, she suspected, to pass through this new and frightening place with indifference, to tread these greater emotions under foot as she had learned to do lesser ones.

Sometimes, when she caught a certain expression making its hasty exit from Ralph's face, it would occur to her that it was not he but she who had been captured; but like half-formed ice her independence cracked beneath her when she tried it and she would come reluctantly back to him for security. His denial of it made her dependence chafe even more. He had been kind to her, she supposed, but he possessed a certain detachment which suggested that he was observing their drama rather than playing his part in it; and, moreover, that it was failing to excite him. She had spent most of the last week at his flat, returning to her own only once to gather things she needed, but although she had enjoyed an exquisite satisfaction in the exercise of her rights, she had begun to fear lately that even that comfort would be taken from her. The last few times she had arrived Ralph had behaved oddly, as if he didn't know why she was there, opening the door with a weary expression or worse still an attitude of surprise, and once even going out for the evening, leaving her alone in front of the television. For the first time Francine felt herself to be at a loss. She had never required attention so keenly, but could think of no new tactics to secure its satisfaction. If her affliction didn't guarantee Ralph's interest, what would? Sitting in the office one afternoon, it occurred to her that by presenting him with her absence she would deprive him of the opportunity to act as if she was a burden on him. The only ingenuity available to her was that of not telling Ralph what she was doing, and having no more sophisticated instrument with which to inflict pain, she was forced to content herself with it.

*

'But what does *he* want?' said Janice, the passion of her question undimmed by repetition. She attempted to wave one hand in order to lend it new force, but the dinner plate displaying two crackers, a slice of cheese, and a small mound of peanuts which was balanced on the arm of the sofa tipped dramatically and she withdrew her hand to steady it.

'I don't know,' said Francine again. Her reply seemed to her each time more profound. She hadn't thought much about what Ralph wanted, and now that Janice had got her on to the subject she longed to see him so that she could ask him herself. 'He says he's happy with whatever I choose to do.'

'But what does that *mean*?' Janice thumped the sofa triumphantly with her other hand. 'What does it *actually mean*?'

'I don't know,' said Francine, mystified.

She had not spent such an enjoyable evening for some time. It was so nice to be able to talk things through. Ralph never wanted to talk about anything – or at least not in any detail – but Janice seemed to understand the importance of circling a subject without needing to gain by the arrival at any conclusion. It amused her to think of how clever Ralph thought he was, when really he didn't know anything about conversation – the *art* of conversation, she believed it was called – at all. She lit a cigarette and exhaled with conspicuous elegance. She hadn't felt able to smoke recently in Ralph's presence, unsure of what he might infer from such a gesture and conscious that it would perhaps not be to her advantage, but now it seemed the perfect adjunct to her liberation from his strictures.

'God!' Janice sighed and fell back onto the sofa. She took a cigarette from Francine's packet and lit it in a gesture of solidarity. 'God, that's so – typical!'

'I think he just doesn't want to pressurize me,' said Francine, reconsidering Ralph's reluctance to interfere as a matter for pride.

'Don't defend him, Francine. It's his problem too, you know. If he thinks he can just walk away, then' – Janice's pronouncement hung dangerously between them – 'then he's wrong.'

'Oh, I'm sure—'

'A lot of men, Francine,' continued Janice, raising her hand, in which the cigarette smouldered ominously, against interruption, 'a *lot* of men think they can make a problem like this just disappear. They think, "Well, she can go in in the morning, out by lunchtime – and *Bob's your uncle*," ' she added darkly. 'Often they don't even pay for a private clinic.'

'Is that how long it takes?' Francine was astounded. 'Just a morning?'

'The emotional work takes much longer,' said Janice.

'How do they do it?'

'Suction.' She demonstrated with her hands, while making a sucking noise through her lips.

'Does it hurt?'

'They knock you out,' said Janice brightly, as willing now to argue the facility of the process as she had been moments earlier to demonstrate its duresses. 'It's really easy. You just go home afterwards and carry on as if nothing had happened. A friend of mine did it recently. She went straight from the hospital to the pub.'

Francine digested this news in amazement. At school, there had been a girl called Roxy who had disappeared one day in a cloud of rumour that she had got herself pregnant and had come back for the new term grey faced and alone. She had been quite a popular girl, Francine remembered, but after that no one had paid any attention to her, except to follow her through the corridors imitating the hilarious way in which she hung her head, her fringe grown long over her eyes. Francine's mother heard of the incident and told Francine not to talk to Roxy, even though she had come to their house once or twice after school.

'I knew that girl would never come to any good,' she said, nodding her head. 'She was always over-developed.'

Francine had certainly worried at the time about Roxy's misfortune, for, not quite understanding how this unpleasant fate had been visited on her, she feared becoming its victim herself. She took her mother's advice and avoided Roxy's contagion, and even later, when Francine used to see her sometimes at the newsagent's where she worked, her bulky form and the continual rash of spots on her forehead occasioned by her drooping fringe still seemed to suggest the marks of her shame. Francine hadn't really kept in touch with anyone from school after she'd left, but she knew that quite a few of the other girls had had babies. When she saw them lumbering along the street with their squalling charges, she regarded their soft stomachs and angry maternal faces with pity and a certain contempt; but she never felt the dark fear and revulsion that belonged to Roxy. At least these girls *had* something. Roxy was alone, and her loneliness was to Francine the most terrible evidence of her punishment.

'Straight to the pub with her boyfriend,' said Janice. She smiled at the memory. 'I met up with them later. They were completely pissed. We had a good laugh.'

'How do you arrange it?'

'You just phone a clinic. I can phone if you want, I've got a number. I'll go with you if he won't. He doesn't even have to know what you're doing.' She paused for a moment, her brows furrowed with decision. 'Are you sure it's what you want, Francine? We don't have to do anything against your will.'

'No,' said Francine, confused.

They looked at each other across the cosy room.

'Look at us!' burst out Janice suddenly, laughing.

Francine laughed too, overwhelmed with warm feelings for her friend. Janice was so supportive and easy to get along with – she wondered why she had ever thought otherwise – and she always seemed to have the answer for everything. She had such nice clothes, too, silky, expensive things. Francine wished that she could work in retail. It was so much more glamorous than secretarial. She wondered if Janice would put in a word for her at the boutique. The telephone rang, making them both start, and Francine jumped to her feet.

'I'll get it!' she said, keen to reach the phone before Janice, in case it was Ralph. Janice always spoke to Ralph on the phone in that whispering voice she put on when she was talking to her own boyfriends.

'It's probably him,' warned Janice.

'Hello?'

'Can I speak to Francine?' said Ralph.

'Yes, it's me.' She felt aggrieved that he did not recognize her voice, and her excitement at the sound of his, along with all the pleasant contrivances of the past hour which had made things seem so much better, disappeared. 'What do you want?'

'What's wrong?' he said. His voice was surprised.

'Nothing's wrong.'

Janice rolled her eyes on the sofa.

'You sounded a bit upset, that's all. I was wondering why you didn't come round tonight. I thought something might have happened to you.'

'I'm fine. I just wanted to be on my own.' The phrase sounded triumphant to Francine. She looked at Janice, but she had leaned back and closed her eyes, as if she were asleep. 'I am allowed to be on my own, aren't I?'

'Of course you are. You might have told me what you were doing, though. I was worried.'

'You don't own me,' said Francine. 'I can do what I want.'

Ralph was silent for several seconds and her heart quickened with the delivery of provocation as she awaited his reply.

'So you keep telling me,' he said finally. Something crackled dangerously in his voice and a wave of apprehension rose in her stomach at the sound. She sensed that he was not going to respond to her challenge in the manner she might have wished. 'But in case you hadn't noticed, we seem to be stuck with each other, so why don't you just stop messing around and start acting like a decent person?' The last words were delivered at a shout, and a tremble of awe warmed her at the emotional force of their interchange. 'Now, if you want to sit around with your – your *bitch* of a flatmate talking about how awful I am, then that's fine, but don't come round tomorrow expecting sympathy!' He paused, out of breath. 'OK?'

Francine was surprised to feel the prickle of tears at her eyes, and having no better weapon to hand, she seized on them, forcing them out with sobs loud enough to inform Ralph on the other end of her distress. Janice looked up, suddenly alert, her face a picture of outrage. She made slamming signals with her hand which suggested that Francine should put the phone down.

'Francine?' said Ralph nervously. 'Francine, I'm sorry. Please don't cry. I'm sorry about that. I'm just tired, that's all.'

'That's OK,' said Francine, sniffing softly.

Janice shook her head dramatically.

'Come round on Thursday. Can you do that? We'll have a good talk. Everything will be fine, I promise. Will you come?'

'I – I'm not sure,' she demurred. 'You frightened me.'

'Oh, for God's sake—'

She could hear impatience rising again in his voice, and knew that an aspect of surrender was her only refuge.

'What time shall I come?' she said weakly.

Janice put a despairing hand to her forehead.

'Whenever you like. No, come at about seven. I won't be able to get away much before that.' He paused. 'I'll see you, then.' ·

'See you,' said Francine.

Fourteen

Ralph sat at his desk and looked out of the window at the sky, where swift, muscled clouds were chasing the sun, intermittently cloaking the nervous glare of the Holloway Road with their grey pallor. He was finding it difficult to work, although only a few minutes ago Neil had visited his desk, straightening his sportive mustard-yellow tie to signal the imminent assertion of his authority.

'Watch at the mender's?' he had said jovially, gripping the back of Ralph's chair with his large hands and leaning close to his ear.

'I beg your pardon?'

He had shrunk from the sudden assault of Neil's breath, which was warm and bitter with coffee. His physical proximity, only an hour or so after Ralph had reluctantly emerged from the clean, tight bud of sleep, was ripe with odours. Seeing Ralph flinch, Neil drew back stiffly.

'You're late again, mate,' he said, cold with offence. 'We start business here at nine o'clock sharp and not even flipping royalty comes in at half-past.'

'Sorry,' said Ralph. Roz was staring at him, her face empty as a plate. 'I got stuck in traffic. I'll leave home earlier tomorrow.'

'If you would,' said Neil. He observed a calculated pause

before delivering his final blow. 'Pull your finger out, mate. All right?'

Ralph didn't reply and Neil walked back to his desk, his retreating shoulders awkward with importance. Roz continued to stare. Ralph could feel her drifting at the periphery of his vision like a moon.

'I went to my grandad's last night,' she said suddenly.

He looked at her in astonishment. His life seemed to have taken on an atmosphere of unreality in which he had been rendered powerless.

'Really?' he said.

'We sorted out his attic.' She nodded. 'It was a right mess.'

'He must have been pleased,' said Ralph. He held her gaze for a minute longer and then directed his eyes deliberately back to his work.

'He's dead,' said Roz.

'Oh, I'm sorry.'

'I saved something for you. Do you want it?'

Ralph felt hot with desperation. His throat was tight. He stared at her helplessly.

'What is it?' he said.

'Magazines,' replied Roz. 'I got a whole box full.'

'What sort of magazines?' He tried to sound interested and alert, but thoughts of a fingered pile of obscenities, rancid with second-hand loneliness, made his voice unsteady.

'Cars. Do you want them?'

'Oh – OK.' Relief made him biddable. 'Thanks very much, Roz.'

'I'll bring them in tomorrow,' she said.

The desire to avoid any further communications on the subject infused Ralph with application. He bent over his work, willing it to occupy him, as hungry for its oblivion as an insomniac begging for sleep. Gradually he was absorbed, and by lunchtime he had completed his whole day's ration of copy. He put it on Neil's desk.

'I've finished,' he said ridiculously.

Neil looked at him and suddenly emitted a high-pitched laugh.

'Got your knickers in a twist, did I?' he said. 'It's that posh school you went to, old boy. Next time I'll give you a good caning and me and Roz can take the day off. Ha, ha!' He bent over his desk, convulsed with humour.

Ralph left the office to go shopping. Francine was coming that night, and the thought of buying delicacies for her made him feel less guilty for the fact that he recoiled from the prospect of her arrival. He imagined arranging things on plates, sentimental offerings behind which he could disguise himself and skirt the void of his affection for her, frightened of what might happen if he tripped and fell into it. It had been good spending a night away from her. He had slept deeply, marinated for hours in the dreamless essence of himself, and when he woke it had been just as he had feared: incandescent with autonomy, he couldn't even stand the thought of her. He had tried to warn her of that on the phone, the fragility of their concord, the risk she ran by taking even a small step back that he would see her too clearly. Sometimes he felt that it would require only a breath to extinguish his guttering feelings for her completely. As he joined the shabby flow of people drifting along the littered pavement outside the building, he grew fascinated by the sudden sense of his own hollowness, his transparency; so much so that within minutes he had collided painfully with a man coming the other way. Stammering his apologies, he felt the blood burn again in his skin and he walked on towards the shops, clumsy now with physical solidity as an ache glowed in his shoulder.

He supposed it didn't matter what he felt, in any case. He

had recently begun to think, as he had done when he was younger, that unhappiness could be conquered merely by the denial of its rights, the dissolution of its property: it had no claims outside those which he permitted it, manifested itself in no physical way, and simply by declaring that the part of himself in which it lived did not exist, he felt sure he could actually make it disappear. He had always drawn a strange comfort from thinking that it didn't really matter what happened to him. It was interesting to see how just the idea of it could cancel out fear. The problem with fear, though, he realized, was that it was hard to kill at the root. It had ways of springing again to life just as one turned one's back on its slain form, breeding at the blink of an eye into multitudes. He felt it now, gnawing at the membrane of his sleep, penetrating the glassy, muted morning. Thinking of Francine, his skin suddenly prickled as if it were about to burst into boils.

He reached the bank and anchored himself at the end of a long queue. Ahead of him people stood mired in different postures, an alphabet of inertia. Watching them, Ralph considered the fact that in each of them a torrent of consciousness bubbled or raged, or was perhaps still, and for a while the bank was so quiet that he imagined he could hear their thoughts.

'I keep telling them, but no one listens to me, of course,' said a woman loudly in front of him. She was well spoken and he could see the shiny black haunch of a handbag protruding from beneath her elbow. The back of her head was level with Ralph's eyes, and her chalky scalp was visible through the erosion of brittle hair. 'It's so easy, isn't it, if you think about it?'

There was a brief silence and Ralph suddenly realized that the woman was alone. Several people in the queue turned round and then quickly looked away, their faces thick with embarrassment.

'You go out at night and just put them somewhere quiet, under a tree or behind a hedge, and if it's a cold night they'll be gone by morning.' She paused and turned to Ralph. Her face was bloodless and grainy with powder, but her eyes were alive, trapped in pincers of wrinkles. She smiled, showing him hoary teeth. 'Girls always did it when I was younger. Just put them in a basket and they'll be quite comfortable. It won't hurt them at all. They just – drift away!' She gestured lightly with her hand and leaned towards him confidentially. 'It must be a cold night, you understand. And it's so much better for them in the end.'

The queue shuffled disparately forward and a girl further up caught Ralph's eye and giggled.

'I'm quite, quite against cruelty, you know,' said the woman, turning again to Ralph. 'Quite against it.'

He smiled at her briefly and then looked down at his shoes, praying that she would be quiet.

'A little gas would do,' she said, this time to the man in front of her.

'All right, love,' he replied gruffly. 'Give it a rest.'

Ralph got his money and left the bank quickly. In the air-conditioned avenues of the supermarket next door he felt better, and as he plucked things from shelves and put them in his trolley the growing pile of what he had chosen reassured him. Minutes later, staring at rows of tins, it all seemed rather burdensome and unnecessary and he considered the possibility of abandoning his botched selection and leaving unencumbered. The difficulty of escaping the intestine of the supermarket by any means other than natural ejection through a till discouraged him from this plan, and he trudged once more along its lulling passages. He hesitated over cheeses, wondering what to make. Beyond his considered forecast of dinner, a legion of unpredictabilities massed. He grabbed the nearest thing to hand and tossed it into the now-heavy trolley. When he pushed it, the freight of his anxieties seemed to trundle along with them.

Joining the end of the queue for a till the din of his consciousness grew louder. His situation cried out for his attention and yet, like a fight come upon in the street or the random witnessing of some injustice, he feared the consequences of his involvement with it. Things were clearly outside of his control; how much easier to wait it out than to wade in with flailing feelings and possibly achieve nothing but self-injury. Being with Francine reminded him of films he had seen in which men were trapped with ticking bombs and were forced to defuse them by blind instinct alone. He knew he should feel sorry for her, of course – it was she, after all, who housed this horror – and yet she confounded his sympathy just as she always had. Their bitter exchange haunted him, a silent presence which had grown more menacing over the past few days with each failure to acknowledge it. Now, whenever he thought of broaching it, the subject seemed to have grown too vast and unassailable and he backed off.

He watched the bright hills of food travelling along the conveyor belt ahead of him, dismantled at the end by industrious hands. If he were honest, he was horrified by the vacuity of it all. He had always assumed that somewhere in him was lodged a compass of certain feelings, a device which would direct him in times of crisis to the points of some fitted morality which he had never really tested but which, like the nameless components of an engine, he had taken for granted all along as being there. His reactions now seemed to him like postures, emissaries of selfishness locked in endless conference to settle distant fates. It terrified him to think, remembering that night, that Francine might have more of the stuff of nature – of life – in her than he himself did. When the words fell from his lips, all his talk of accidents and women he knew, they had felt as dry and nerveless as shavings carved from a block of wood. In fact he only knew one woman – Belinda – and remembering *that* made him feel as if he had died some time ago and only just noticed.

'My God!' he had said softly when she'd told him; told him quite casually, only when it came up in conversation. He had felt a peculiar desire to envelop her scoured body with his own and fill it with life.

'It was nothing,' she had replied. 'It was a long time ago.'

She might even have shrugged, he couldn't remember; but what had struck him was how surprised she had seemed by his reaction. Nervously, wanting to love her, he had concluded that this must be the first time he had seen her lying. She obviously still felt very unhappy about it, perhaps even ashamed. He had ached with sorrow for her, his thoughts weeping, but even so a thread of dissociation had wormed its way doubtfully through him.

Now, of course, he felt that he understood her indifference; and yet, had he not detected some failure in her, some unpleasant hardness, a discovery by which he could now judge himself? Loading his shiny packets of food on to the conveyor belt, he wondered what had happened to his blood, his heart, his burning, joyful nerves: all dried up, broken, rusty, abandoned like derelict implements in some forgotten corner of a house.

That evening Ralph stood in the kitchen and stirred a cheese sauce. He had been late getting home in the end, unable somehow to leave the office, and Francine had been waiting on the doorstep shaking with cold.

'I've bought things!' he had cried hopefully, showing her the loaded panniers with which he had struggled back from the Tube station.

She hadn't replied, and his instant conviction for neglect

had removed his freedom to create the new atmosphere between them on which he had decided. Now she sat forbiddingly in the other room with a blanket she had ordered him to fetch, while he made the dinner he had wanted to present as a gift but which had suddenly become a minimum requirement. She was watching television, and the sound of its imperturbable voices made him feel excluded and horribly free. He imagined himself leaving the flat beneath the cover of its noise and going somewhere else. The sauce began to heave and he turned down the flame, his forehead flushing. He remembered the first time she had come to his flat, when he had had an eerie, premonitory sense of her entrenchment. Thinking of that evening, it seemed curious to him that he had not foreseen that his life would become locked to hers, known that those hours were the last in which he would be himself. For a moment he imagined that he was back there now, alone in the kitchen while Francine waited in the next room. The illusion was surprisingly easy to substantiate. He felt light with the unravelling of the past few weeks, a quite blissful feeling actually, awoken from them as if from a frightening dream, and he stayed still, not wanting to jolt himself.

'Is it nearly ready?'

He started round. Francine stood in the doorway, watching him. He fancied her unnerved, as if she had seen his thoughts like ghosts, and he smiled awkwardly to cover his feeling of having been caught. Her expression was more obviously assumed than usual and there was something uncertain and self-critical in her posture, a rare failure of projection which aroused in him a sudden and unexpected affection. He felt rather sorry for her, for he sensed that for once her inability to comprehend certain things irked her. He saw her straining to master the situation, but like blindness her lack was so fatal, so complete, that it rendered a whole world – even the description of that world! – obsolete. There were things she would never learn, for she had somehow evolved, he knew, without the proper instruments of feeling and thought. He had used to think that those tools must lie dormant in her somewhere, awaiting discovery, but now he regarded it almost as a biological impossibility that she would ever understand him.

'Soon,' he said kindly, like a mother. He considered putting an arm around her. 'Have you warmed up a bit?'

She didn't reply, catching a dark strand of hair and twirling it amongst her fingers. Her face was lowered, absorbed in something at which he did not want to guess, and he felt the sudden tug of her inescapability. It lay like a leash about his neck, forgettable sometimes, but always tightening when he strained at it.

'We'll have supper and then you can go to bed,' he said. A feeling of despair martyred him. 'I'll move the television into the bedroom if you like.'

'I don't want to go to bed! I want to talk! You said we'd talk.'

'All right,' he said. His sympathy knocked aside, sent carelessly scurrying like a leaf as her words sped unstoppably along the immutable grooves of habit, he felt unutterably weary. 'Go and sit down. I'll be there in a minute.'

It had only just started to rain, but the sudden outburst was so fierce that long, glassy streaks were already pouring down the window-pane, vainly carving their writhing currents on its surface. Ralph watched the mesmeric patterns of flow, his heart quieted by this generosity of water, its sympathy with him. Francine sat on the other side of the table. She too, he felt, was becalmed by the rain, and a rare harmony was growing between them; not of concupiscence, Heaven knew, but a fragile accord which seemed to have arisen from a silent admission of shared trouble. He had cleared away the wreckage of dinner and had lit candles, not through any desire to set a scene, but rather in honour of this sudden deluge of softness from which he wished to gain nothing but an interlude of peace between their noisy acts. Francine's face opposite him was unusually unconscious, for once not busy with intentions; rather solemn and pale, in fact. Her features seemed more real to him like that, and he studied the miraculous way in which their lines composed beauty. He wondered, as he had done countless times before, how the genius of her design could merely be a felicity of surfaces, a lucky stroke from the hand of an inferior artist. He had used to think, of course, that such a face must have emanated from the heart, and even though he had since seen the rougher clay beneath its glaze, its riddle still had the power to beguile him.

'Do you ever wish you had brothers and sisters?' he said, suddenly wanting to hear her speak.

She looked bemused by his question, and he almost laughed aloud at how much impossibility was written in that sulky, incomprehending glance, what a bitter death it would be to live beneath it.

'I don't know,' she said finally.

'I used to be desperate for them,' he said gaily. 'I used to invent them, in fact.'

'I suppose I used to do that,' said Francine. She appeared surprised at the memory. 'I don't really remember.'

'What are your parents like?' said Ralph.

'My mum and dad? Why do you want to know?'

'Oh – just interested, that's all.'

'They're normal.' She sounded slightly affronted, as if his interest in her parents were unnatural.

'Do you look like them?'

'No. My dad's got a beard.'

Ralph began to laugh encouragingly, thinking her reply hilarious, but she looked at him so strangely that he stopped.

'What about your mother?'

'What, you mean what does she look like? I don't really know. Normal, I suppose.'

'Do you see them often?' he persisted.

'Oh, they're boring.' She dismissed them with a wave of the hand. 'They never do anything, except my mum goes to aerobics and my dad has his night out at the pub every Thursday. It's not exactly exciting. They always say they'll come up, but they never do.' She sighed. 'They don't understand why I live in London.'

'Why *do* you live here?' said Ralph.

He didn't really know why he had asked the question, but he suddenly found himself wanting its answer. Francine's eyebrows furrowed, as if she were trying to decide whether he was joking.

'Everyone lives here,' she said.

They were silent for a while and Ralph noticed that the rain had stopped. In its hush he felt again their hopelessness, and the panic which had momentarily been driven away burst back into his thoughts. As he bore it once more he realized how much he longed to be clear of their endless, muddled communications, their intimate bureaucracy before which he knew his own poverty and powerlessness, to rise above it and gulp down drafts of honesty and sense. He felt his anchor lodged in rock, jammed deep down in the blackest and most inaccessible cave of fear. He had to get out of this – he had to! He caught Francine's eye and she gave him an unnerving look, a look which seemed to have rounded up his thoughts and calmly admonished him for them. He saw her confidence, the fastness of her locks. Surely he could outwit her! He reasoned with himself while panicked seconds passed. He was beginning at least to understand with what force Francine's reactions held sway over her initiatives. She required the greatest delicacy in her handling, and although at that moment he was gripped by a violent urge to rip that part of himself she owned from within her, the fortresses of her flesh, he knew, could only be negotiated by cunning.

'Do you want anything?' he said, half standing in anticipation of a pretext to go to the kitchen and be alone.

'You know what I want.' She looked rather pleased with her own reply, as if she had been awaiting a cue to deliver it. Ralph sat down again. His head began abruptly to ache. 'I want to talk,' she added after a pause, which she had evidently expected him to fill.

'What about?'

He looked at her with what he judged to be an expression of polite interest. He knew he was being cruel, but at that moment it seemed like the only liberty he had.

'God!' She implored the ceiling with her eyes. 'That's so *typical*.'

'Sorry.'

'I mean, you act like this is just my problem. It's like you don't even care.'

'I'm sorry.'

'It's like you want to pretend it's not happening. You never even want to *talk* about it!'

'Well, what is there to talk about?' said Ralph. He realized amazedly that his behaviour had been aptly surmised. 'I was just trying to be nice. I didn't know you wanted to talk about it any more. You gave me the impression that you'd decided everything.'

'I'm allowed to change my mind, aren't I?' she said. 'It's not against the law, is it?'

She stared at him provocatively, a vague smile twisting her lips, and for the first time, without really expecting it, he experienced such a wrench of resistance that his skin abruptly flamed and his heart seemed to fly from his chest. For a moment he could not ascertain what it meant: it was as if he had been told that he would suffer pain, and then been made to wait so long for it that when it came, it felt not like pain at all but reassurance.

'*Have* you changed your mind?'

'Maybe.' She fiddled with something on the table. 'I don't know.'

He opened his mouth but found that he didn't have anything to say. Something strained at the locks and bolts of his thoughts and grew frantic, pounding at its walls. He fought it back, panicked by the things he might feel if he let it out. It wasn't up to him! It had nothing to do with him, none of it! Disturbance sang through his veins, and with it every part of him seemed to find its note, loud as the keys of a piano. He chorused silently his own despair. Francine was watching him now, waiting to see what he would do. He saw himself quite clearly lunging across the table and clawing at her plump cheeks with his blunt, innocuous fingers.

'What do you mean?' he said nervously. 'You must know what you mean.'

He met her gaze, willing her to let him go, but her sharp eyes pricked his swollen, dreamy detachment and he felt its poisons rush over him. He understood then that she wanted to *hurt* him, to draw him out and show him his own helplessness. What had he done? Why was he being punished so? As he wondered, everything – Francine, the germ she carried, the room itself – seemed to gather against him and accuse him of his own significance.

'I don't know,' she said obstinately. 'How should I know? It's too complicated. How do you expect me to just decide?'

'I don't.' He was surprised to feel tears leap to his eyes. 'I thought you had.'

'That's just so *pathetic*,' she spat. 'I mean, you act like it's just nothing, you know, like it's my decision and it doesn't have anything to do with you.'

He saw to his amazement that she hadn't really thought about it at all, that she just said things to engage him; that all the time he had thought her to be moving in a particular direction, however obliquely, she had only been spinning threads around him, a web in which he now knew himself to be caught. Their predicament rose before him, new again, as raw as an untended wound.

'I—' He felt all at once terribly confused and his voice sounded thin, as if he were forcing it through something dense. 'I don't know,' he said weakly. He dragged his eyes to her face. 'I just can't seem to believe in it.'

As he said it, he suddenly knew that at last he had jumped and that something would now happen. He watched Francine as he fell airily away from her, and she appeared to grow so hard before his eyes that he wondered if she might break like a glass bottle if she fell with him.

'What's that supposed to mean?' she said finally. Her voice sounded harsh and deliberate, retaliating for his obscurity with belligerence.

'I don't think you can either! I don't think you've actually *realized* that you're going to have a baby. A baby.' He said it again, understanding that he hadn't really known it until that moment. His acceptance of it came in a rush, whole, as if he had solved a mathematical enigma, and he felt the knowledge begin to function in him as efficiently as a machine.

'You don't know anything!' said Francine. Her words rattled like dice, looking randomly for victory. Ralph realized that he was frightening her, and the sense of returned power, its possibilities, aroused him. 'You don't know what it's like.'

'Go on, then. Tell me. Tell me what it's like.'

She settled back in her seat, confident again, and examined her fingers with studied self-deprecation.

'What do you want to know?' she said, more sweetly.

'I want to know why you've decided not to keep it.' He felt utterly unlike himself, and he trusted his new incarnation, loved the sound of his voice. 'Tell me what's going on in your mind. I want to know how you made the decision.'

Her eyes brightened at his mistake.

'I didn't say I'd decided, in case you'd forgotten. I only said I might have changed my mind.'

She straightened in her chair and looked at him defiantly. His hatred for her snapped its leash and leapt unbounded at her throat.

'But what if I said that *I* wanted you to have it?'

Ralph heard the air gasp. A silence teetered between them. Francine looked down at her hands again, and when her eyes returned to him they had assumed a new softness.

'Do you?' she said.

He almost laughed aloud as he realized that she was actually *flirting* with him. A smile strained at his lips and seeing it, she coyly fiddled with something on the table.

'I'm not talking about us,' he said, surprised to hear the gentleness in his voice. It felt wonderful to say what he was saying. His life flowered before him, a future filled with a person he now knew he could be. 'I'm talking about what's the right thing to do.'

'I can't do it on my own!' she said, thumping the table wildly with her fist. She appeared to have shrunk before his eyes, her words coming in enraged squeaks. 'It's your responsibility too!'

'I know it is.' He paused and then said what all at once seemed perfectly natural. 'What I'm suggesting is that *I* look after it.'

His meaning launched itself, rose, drifted between them.

Ralph watched it anxiously, wondering whether it would work, whether it were plausible and true, a thing that could be said.

'It makes sense when you really think about it,' he continued hurriedly. 'I can provide financial support and' – he felt himself growing horribly ridiculous, his confidence draining – 'and take full responsibility for it, and you can get on with your life as if nothing had happened, if you want.'

Francine was so still that it seemed impossible that she would ever again come to life. His words echoed around her as if in an empty room. Ralph prayed for her to speak, to clothe the nakedness of what he had said.

'Without me?' she said finally.

'Yes.' Her comprehension fuelled him for his last leap. 'I – I don't love you. You must know that.'

It seemed odd to him that he should suddenly have found the means to tell her that which, in the uncomplicated weeks before all of this happened, had been so impossible to pronounce. He was astonished by his own courage, which he seemed to have found lying idle in him as if it had been there all along; an ungainly tool whose beauty he had discovered only in its use. Now that he had it, he could see with one frenzied examination that his life was broken and that he could repair it all. Already he had built a firm platform of righteousness, and from it he steadily viewed the range of what he could do, whole reaches of himself he had never explored. It was as if he had laboured all this time in a dark, unfavoured comer, scratching life from a soil so blighted that it multiplied his efforts far beyond its yield; while all along a whole kingdom had been in his possession to which only truth gave entrance. He had never felt more certain of his recognition of this key, more expert in his ability to pluck it from amongst its thousand glittering imitations.

'I want to go home,' said Francine suddenly.

She stood up, pushing her chair. It fell back, thudding to the floor like an executed man.

'Francine—'

'Leave me alone.'

She looked straight at him, drawing her eyes like knives. His heart flailed in his chest.

'Please stay. We've got to talk – please!'

She picked up her coat and bag and left the room before he could even stand up. He heard her open the front door and he waited a few seconds, praying for her to slam it. The soft and distant click signalled his condemnation.

'What's this?' said Ralph, gesturing helplessly at a large cardboard box which sat on the top of his desk. He put his arms around it to lift it to the floor, buckling beneath the weight, and straightened up to find a dusty embrace imprinted on the front of his shirt. 'Oh, damn it!' he said irritably, brushing himself down. 'Roz, who the bloody hell put this here? My desk is not a dumping ground for boxes of rubbish.'

'It's them magazines you wanted,' said Roz. Her eyes were fixed on her computer screen, but they jumped from side to side in an effort not to look up. 'I brought them in.'

'Oh.' Ralph sat down and bent guiltily over the box. 'That's very kind of you. Did you carry them up on your own? They're very heavy.'

'It was all right,' shrugged Roz. He opened the box and took a magazine from the top of the pile. There were hundreds of them, all with the title *Auto Week* emblazoned across their tattered covers in red. He put the magazine on his desk and regarded it with polite interest. On the front was a photograph of a stationary car. A woman in a swimming costume lay on her back on the bonnet, as if the car had just hit her. She looked rather like Francine. He looked at the date, and saw that the magazine was almost fifteen years old.

'Thanks very much, Roz,' he said loudly. 'I shall enjoy reading these.'

Roz was silent, but he saw a noisy blush begin to march across her cheeks. She sat still for a moment, as if waiting for something, and then began to tap at her keyboard. Ralph pushed the magazine discreetly to one side and stared at his empty desktop. He was tired, his limbs heavy with the residue of a fractious night filled with flickering half-dreams in which he had been visited hourly by the horrible succubus of fear. He had woken feeling smothered and his thoughts still sounded tinny and distant, like a radio playing in another room. Having no alternative, he had put on his life again like a set of old, grubby clothes, hating their smell and feel the more for having removed them. Now and again a fierce pain of recollection stabbed at his chest as memories of the night before struggled free of his attempt to suppress them.

'How do you spell inflation?' said Roz.

She was typing avidly, staring at the screen and sighing as she jabbed a finger at the keyboard to annihilate a word. Ralph watched her, faintly distracted by the rare sight of her industry. She pressed a button and then turned to gaze expectantly at the printer. It began to whirr, disgorging a single white sheet. She picked it up and turned back to her desk, mouthing the words and nodding her head as she read. Then, to Ralph's surprise, she got up and walked in a half circle to his side of the desk, placing it squarely before him.

'What's this?' he said.

She didn't reply and he looked at the sheet of paper. It was a formal office memorandum, addressed to him, from Roz L. Corby. It was headed 'Re: Sale of Magazines'. Ralph looked up, but Roz had disappeared. He turned back to the sheet of paper.

'With regards to the copies of *Auto Week* which I delivered to you this morning, I would like to remind you of the matter of payment for these magazines. The charge will be as is on the cover, which when you consider the matter of inflation is less than you would pay for them these days!'

It was signed, 'yours sincerely, Roz L. Corby'. Ralph put his head in his hands and began to laugh.

Fifteen

'Can I talk to Gary?' demanded an American voice.

It was mid-afternoon, a time of lassitude and meetings, and the office was half-empty.

'He's not here,' snapped Francine, who found interruptions of languor even more irritating than those of occupation. 'Call back later.'

Lorraine looked up from the neighbouring desk, her fingers petrified in the air above her keyboard. Francine felt her gaze loiter and then wander away.

'I see,' said the man sternly. 'And what's your name, little lady?'

'Francine Snaith.'

Lorraine's eyes were on her again, avid now with interest.

'Well, Francine, do you always talk to your boss's clients that way? Because if you do, I think he should know about it.'

'Sorry,' said Francine sourly.

'You don't sound too sorry,' said the man. 'What's going on, Francine?'

'I'm busy,' Francine replied. 'I haven't got all day.'

'Well, if you can find the time in your schedule, tell Gary that Harry Rosenthal wants to talk with him.'

'Who was that?' said Lorraine excitably when Francine put the phone down.

'Harry Rosenthal,' said Francine coolly. She could feel her legs shaking beneath her desk.

'Mr *Rosenthal?*'

Lorraine raised her eyebrows in pencilled astonishment and turned reluctantly back to her work, looking as if she were about to burst with the import of what she had just witnessed. Francine could see her shaking her head as she typed. She got up and made herself some coffee without offering to make any for Lorraine. It was still only three o'clock, but Francine was already straining with an almost uncontainable desire to leave the office. Mr Lancing was out for the afternoon and wouldn't come in until the next morning, but Lorraine was watching her now, glancing vigilantly up from her screen every few minutes with the mistrustful aspect of a security guard. It would be impossible for her to leave unnoticed, and she had already gone home twice in the middle of the afternoon during the past week under the cover of illness and didn't dare try it again. There were only two hours to wait before she could walk away free. Surely she could make them pass? She forced herself back into her chair and cast about for something to do. A tape recorded by Mr Lancing earlier in the day lay on her desk, awaiting transcription. Francine considered the possibility of typing it up, and felt her frame go limp at the prospect of something so laborious. Now that her sense of duty had run dry, she required not industry but entertainment to propel her through the long minutes. It had proved impossible, since that shrouded moment in which she had ceased to be interested in Lancing & Louche, to tame herself again into the habits of work, and her belief that she needed a change permitted the impulses of disruption to rule her in their stead. How could she be expected to carry on, when everything about the place now bored her? She needed excitement, variety! People didn't look up any more when she came into the office – even Mr

Louche no longer loitered at her desk – and Francine knew that, once extinguished, the quality of novelty could not be revived. Occasionally, faint warnings of a danger up ahead reached her ears, and when she heard them unpleasant anxieties crept across her thoughts. The agency would be angry with her if she lost this job. What if she didn't find anything else? What if, when she dug into her resources, she found their seams exhausted, the future used up, all her luck gone? The idea was enough to induce panic, and Francine would try to struggle back into her harness, but in doing so she was faced with a still more disagreeable fate: her belief that she always deserved something better than that which she possessed was her engine, and without it she would surely grind to a halt. The thought of what might happen if she did filled her head with such noise that the sound of other perils was lost. She put Mr Lancing's tape into the machine and switched it on. He had placed his mouth too close to the microphone, and when she put on her headphones she could hear his breath grating against her ears. She fixed her eyes on the screen and began to type.

At twenty past five Francine switched off the tape and started gathering her things. Mr Lancing's letter dangled unfinished on the screen, but considering the effort she had gone to in making the gesture at all she felt it couldn't be expected of her then to put herself out by staying late. Lorraine sat stolidly at her desk, as if she had no intention of going home. When she saw Francine rise from her chair, she looked at her watch. The telephone rang just as Francine was putting on her coat and she stiffened with impatience.

'Miss Snaith? There's a Stephen Sparks waiting for you in reception.'

'For me?' said Francine, not understanding.

'That's what the gentleman says.'

Francine put the phone down, her heart pounding with

pleasure and fear. What was he doing here? As she stood the moment grew around her, glowing with significance. In it, the flavour of excitement, untasted for so long, deliciously returned. She had known he would come! There *had* been something between them at the party – all this time he must have been trying to find a way of seeing her alone! If only she hadn't started things with Ralph, who knew what might have happened? The brutal thought that Ralph himself might have sent Stephen to talk to her stamped a sudden, heavy foot on her blossoming hopes. Would he have dared? The idea was disagreeable, and she took immediate action against it by ejecting it from her thoughts.

'Bye,' said Lorraine, without looking up.

'See you tomorrow,' said Francine, picking up her bag and sweeping past her.

She saw him as soon as she came through the glass doors; or at least, his demeanour informed her that it must be him, for she barely recognized his appearance. He was sitting on one of the large leather sofas at the end of the foyer, reading a newspaper. In his casual clothes he looked leisurely and incongruous against the hushed, industrious marble of the hall, his rustling pages loud above the tapping of heels and the low purr of telephones. His concrete presence, after the night-time memory she had nurtured of him, surprised her with its unfamiliarity. He leaned back into the sofa, smiling at something he was reading. Far from threatening his confidence, his separateness made it monolithic, and Francine felt suddenly rather afraid of him. She crossed the hall and stood in front of him.

'What are you doing here?' she said finally, when he didn't look up. Now that she had said something she felt better, and she readied a smile for his attention.

'Aha!'

He leaped from his seat and to her surprise kissed her

cheek. His skin was soft and slightly perfumed, like a woman's. For a moment she could feel more than see him and her nerves instantly burned with consciousness. The force of his physical proximity seemed to envelop her in its currents, like heat.

'How did you find me?' she said, drawing back. She tried to stop herself from staring at him – he was so good looking, like somebody from a magazine! – but there was something beleaguering in the mobility of his face, his flickering smile, the enthusiasm of his limbs pressing against his clothes, which made it hard to unstick her eyes.

'Not difficult.' He shook his head and made a tutting noise through his teeth. With a pang Francine wondered if he was laughing at her. 'Ralph told me. Weeks ago, I'll admit, but how could I forget Lancing & Louche? *Louche!*' He cackled. 'Anyway, I was in the area, so I thought I'd drop in. Time for a drink?'

'I suppose so,' said Francine with studied reluctance, resolved to play him at his own game. She looked at her watch. 'Where shall we go?'

'Leave that to me,' said Stephen, taking her arm and leading her towards the large glass doors. 'I know a place.'

Francine felt an almost suffocating admiration at her throat as she permitted herself to be led. She remembered then that Stephen had been like that at the party, at once pinching and caressing, and the memory reassured her. He was so forceful, so completely in control of things; he made her feel alive! Her tainted circumstances, momentarily forgotten, came back to her blacker than ever. Why couldn't Ralph be like that? Why had she chosen him, when Stephen had been there too? He liked her, it was obvious that he did. If only she had waited! She vaguely remembered waiting, in the days after the party, for Stephen to call, her disappointment, her bewilderment, when he didn't.

'So how are you, Francine?' he said as they walked, arms still linked, out into the street. He glanced at her. 'As lovely as ever, I see.'

'Oh, I'm all right,' said Francine wistfully.

'Good.' He steered her down a narrow turning into a small alley. 'That's good. Here we are.'

They had arrived at a small bar which, as Francine hadn't known it was there, appeared intriguing. Stephen held open the door and she walked in ahead of him and down a flight of wooden steps, into a large cellar with barrels against the walls and tables with candles. Despite the early hour it was already crowded and echoing with laughter and conversation.

'This is nice,' said Francine.

'Stick with me, honey,' he said in a comic voice. 'I know this town – I've been thrown out of most of it.' He laughed, as if he were joking. 'Go and sit down. I'll get us something to drink.'

He wandered towards the bar while she sat down at an empty table. She watched him as he ordered, saying something to the barman which made him smile. He was wearing a suede jacket which looked expensive. Moments later he came to the table with a bottle and two glasses.

'Thought you'd prefer white,' he said, setting the bottle down on the table.

'I do,' said Francine, thinking triumphantly of the bitter ink Ralph had made her drink. Stephen inspected her with amused, brazen eyes, and as she felt his examination she realized that she hadn't assessed her appearance in front of a mirror before she'd left the office. She looked back at him boldly to deflect him. Meeting his gaze, its unexpected penetration almost caused her physically to lurch, as if he had suddenly pressed himself against her. The warm tentacles of his proximity curled about her skin. For the first time in her life, she felt as if it didn't matter what she looked like. His mouth, which moved constantly in a perpetual curve, seemed instead to be tasting her, feeding from her face.

'So who are Lancing and Louche?' he said, filling her glass. 'They live up to their names, I hope.'

'They're my bosses,' said Francine, sipping delicately. 'They're really boring.'

'No skirmishes behind the filing cabinets, then?'

Francine giggled. 'Not really.'

'I bet you're a bit of distraction, though, aren't you? Running around the office in your – your *very* short skirt, if I may say. I see major deals falling through as you bring them their coffee, Francine.'

Francine giggled again. She felt her skin begin to blush beneath his words, as if they were hands. The sensation surprised her with its unpleasantness, and she tried once more to bathe in his attention. It was just as she had hoped it would be! Looking at his careless face seconds later, she felt a more distinct twinge of discomfort. She hadn't felt that way at all when she'd first met him, had felt a glow, in fact, which had lasted for days afterward, and it dimly struck her that something had happened to her. A ridiculous ache for Ralph grew tight across her chest, and she picked up her glass and emptied it with one bitter swallow.

'Steady on,' laughed Stephen. 'I won't be able to carry a big girl like you all the way home.'

'I can look after myself,' said Francine, irked by his physical assessment of her

'I'm sure you can.'

A brittle edge to his voice sundered their atmosphere and stranded them in silence. Stephen looked about him, suddenly indifferent to her presence, and when an attractive girl walked by Francine was astounded to see his eyes follow her quite openly, as if attached by invisible threads to her flanks. His gaze came back to her and his face assumed an expression of amusement, as if he could see what she was thinking. In that moment she suddenly hated him, hated him almost as much as she hated Ralph. Their connection with each other made a circuit for her anger and it flowed effectively between them in her thoughts.

'How do you know Ralph?' she said sharply, desperate to regain his attention but unable to think of anything else to talk about. The wine was beginning to creep numbly through her veins.

'What? Oh, Ralph. We were at school together.'

Francine knew that already, but Stephen didn't seem to think it odd that she should say she didn't.

'What was he like?'

'At school?' Stephen barked with laughter. 'He was a prat, if you really want to know. A right little goody two-shoes.'

She felt a vague plummeting of disappointment, but the thought that Stephen might say more bad things about Ralph – things she could repeat to him later if the necessity arose – encouraged her back to interrogation.

'Why were you friends with him, then?'

'Well, I wasn't, not to begin with. But then we had a sort of – arranged marriage.'

'What do you mean?' She wondered why Stephen could never say anything in a normal way.

'Oh God, it was so long ago now.' He waited, as if he had changed his mind, but when she didn't speak either he continued. 'Well, I got into a spot of trouble, as it were, and as a punishment they made me look after Ralph.' He laughed. 'Not much of a compliment to him, I suppose.'

'What sort of trouble?'

'You're a nosy little thing, aren't you? Well, it was just a bit of, um, high spirits. Public school, you know, hothouses of impropriety. Actually, it wasn't really my fault. We all got caught by one of the masters, but they pinned the whole thing on me.'

'Caught doing what?'

'Don't ask.' He laughed delightedly.

'I want to know,' said Francine irritably.

'Well, we were – how can I put it?' He laughed again. 'We were engaged in an *initiation ritual*, I suppose. It happened to most of the new boys, sort of to break them in. It was all pretty harmless, just sticking their heads in the bog or something.'

'Oh.'

'Except it all got a bit silly and the poor chap ended up strung up by his ankles with his face in the pan. No wonder he's such a miserable bastard. Scarred him for life, probably.'

'It was Ralph!' said Francine triumphantly.

'Clever girl.' Stephen refilled their glasses. 'So there you have it. That's how we got lumbered with each other. Quite touching.'

'Didn't he have any other friends, then?'

'Not really. Scholarship boy. His parents didn't pay for him to go to the school,' he explained when he saw that Francine didn't understand. 'And all of us nascent little snobs looked down our noses at him because he emanated from a council house. He was having rather a rough time of it. Shameful, really.'

As the words reached her ears with a muffled thud, Francine understood that she was witnessing the sudden, utter reversal of everything she had thought to be true. She sat in silence, her thoughts erased.

'His father came to the school once to see him. Looked like a bloody tramp.' He shook his head. 'Then he died. They found him in some god-awful hotel room up in the north, rotting away. Horrible. I never met the mother, she was gone a long time ago. Cancer, apparently.' He drank swiftly from his glass. 'Poor chap's a bit of a sad case.'

As quickly as she could accommodate each blow, another rained down on her, and as the images grew in her head she felt their contamination. She imagined his house, drawing vaguely on the topography of her old town to depict a bleak box wreathed in grubby washing, and then thought of Ralph's father, a filthy tramp, lying in a hotel room. She had been cheated! How could he have lied to her, with his books and his educated voice and his pathetic exhibitions! How dared he make *her* feel inferior, as if there were something wrong with *her*, when he was just a common kid from a council house, the sort of person she had been taught never even to associate with! 'Might as well get another,' said Stephen, cheerful again suddenly as he emptied the last of the bottle into her glass.

And she had actually thought that he was *posh*, like Stephen – Stephen's father was a lord, Ralph had told her – but he was just a pathetic nobody, a – what had Stephen called him? – a 'sad case' for whom people like Stephen felt sorry.

'Yes, let's,' she said. She waited while he went to the bar, her mind churning up new outrages with every passing second. 'So how did he get into university, then?' she asked when he got back.

'Ralph? Because he's clever, of course. You don't get into university for being rich, you idiot.'

'I was only asking,' said Francine bitterly. An urge to keep his alliance sweetened her tone. 'I was just interested, that's all. He never told me any of the things you just told me.'

'Oh, he didn't, did he?' Stephen's smile broadened. 'Well, perhaps he doesn't like to talk about it. It's not all that surprising, is it?'

'No,' said Francine. Seeing that Stephen was defending Ralph, she dropped her eyes, drawing his attention to her own victimized feelings. 'It's just that I feel as if he's lied to me.'

'How's that?'

'Well, he pretended that he was – you know—' Francine writhed her hands in distress and saw a look of comprehension dawn across Stephen's face.

'Thought you'd landed something out of the top drawer, eh?' He laughed loudly, throwing back his head. 'You little bitch! If the old dingbat had known *that* would make you jump ship, he'd have told you himself!' He laughed again, wiping hilarious tears from his eyes.

'What's that supposed to mean?' said Francine furiously.

'Oh, calm down, Francine,' said Stephen. 'You're a nice girl. Just go easy on Ralph. He deserves better.'

'What, like you?' she spat.

'Oh, I'm no bargain, I know. God knows why he puts up with me.' He sat back in his chair, crossing his legs, and then all at once impaled her with hard, frightening eyes. 'I should have had you myself, saved him the trouble.'

'So why didn't you?' she threw back.

'Couldn't be bothered.' He shrugged. 'For Christ's sake, what does it matter?'

'It's what I wanted anyway.'

'Did you now?' He laughed.

'I still want it.' Francine felt wild with drink and daring. She thought of Ralph, of the loathsome thing that was inside her. 'What's wrong? Don't tell me you're scared!'

'There is the small matter of *Ralph*.'

'I don't care about Ralph,' smiled Francine. Exhilaration sharpened her, and she felt keenly, deliciously herself. 'Anyway, he doesn't need to know.'

'You're not such a nice girl, are you?' Stephen sat back in his seat, amused, and shook his head. 'Sorry, Francine, can't do it, not again. I wouldn't get a wink of sleep. Although I have to say, we're made for each other.'

'Why not? Just tell me why not?'

'Ralph would kill me.'

'I told you, he won't find out.'

'Of course he will. You'll tell him. You won't be able to resist it. I've been here before, believe me.' She looked at him, not understanding, and he laughed. 'So he didn't tell you that, either? My, he has been discreet.'

'Tell me what?'

'Oh, just a little past naughtiness. It was a long time ago.'

He fiddled shamefacedly with a beer mat, and Francine suddenly saw it.

'With his girlfriend?' she said deliriously. 'With – what was she called – with Belinda?'

'Clever girl.' He smiled. 'I fucked the love of Ralph's life and he still goes to the pub with me. That's friendship for you.'

'Does he know?' said Francine, victorious with information.

'I told you, of course he does. First sign of a quarrel and out it came, whack over the head. And that was the end of that.'

'What was she like?'

'Ah, lovely,' said Stephen wistfully. 'But she was a bitch to Ralph. And so are you.'

'Ralph and I are finished,' said Francine. 'I finished it last night.'

'So you've finally freed the poor creature from your clutches?' Stephen laughed. 'About time too. Was he pleased?'

'So there's nothing to stop us.'

Through a fog of drunkenness she heard the shrill music of her voice. Stephen drew back slightly at the sound. She tried to soften herself, smiling and leaning towards him.

'Look,' he sighed, picking up his glass. 'You're a beautiful girl, Francine, but at the moment I need you like I need –

look, I don't want to get involved, OK? It's too late for all that. So just drop it.' He looked at the wine bottle. 'This is empty. We might as well go.'

He stood up and began putting on his jacket. When Francine got to her feet the room whirled, listing like a flailing ship. Her thoughts spun with it, indecipherable, but through them she felt something hard and compelling, a wire drawn tight along which she appeared to be strung. Stephen draped her coat around her shoulders and she gripped his hand as he led her through the crowded tables and up the stairs.

'I'll find you a cab,' he said when they were outside. 'Come on.'

The night had grown black and the air was piercing, agonizing. As they set off towards the busy street Francine felt the drag of failure, and the penetrating cold shrank in seconds the heady dilation of the recent hours. She felt packed again with all the lumpy, ugly furniture of anxiety which had come in the past few weeks to clutter spaces which had once been bright and empty, and trapped amongst it a searing, hopeless consciousness of the fact that things were going wrong visited her. In that moment, as Stephen walked ahead, a violent flame of resistance coursed through her and consumed it all. She would not let this happen to her! Why, when every glance in the mirror told her, when every look and gesture confirmed it, when she knew – had been told time and time again! – that she could have anything she wanted, why then was nothing as she wanted it to be? How had she come to these doomed and darkened passages, so far from the world she knew; what had happened to her magic, the arts she had practised for as long as she could remember, the spells which she had known would one day conjure success? A wave of drunkenness washed over her, and she stood still as the alley blurred in her eyes. Everything seemed all at once rather muddled. A jumble of images churned and then settled thickly on her surface. For a moment all of her was gathered and a forgotten doubt began to revive and struggle in her, beating its wings. She was sick, sick of herself.

'Come on, Francine,' said Stephen, waiting for her up ahead. He turned and walked back towards her. 'You're a bit tanked up, did you know that? Decidedly squiffy, as my dear old mother would say.'

Francine watched his mouth moving. Who was he, standing there making fun of her, talking about his mother, when he should be begging to touch her? They all wanted her – they all said it, that she was the most beautiful, the most desirable, that they would do anything for her. She hated them all, all of them! And most of all she hated Ralph, who had ruined everything and made it disgusting! Stephen was close to her now. She felt a pressure across her shoulders and realized that his arm was around her.

'Come on,' she whispered, turning and pressing herself against him. She felt him recoil slightly and she pressed harder.

'Jesus,' he said, laughing and putting his arms around her. 'What are you doing?'

Her face was almost level with his and she lunged forward, trying to insinuate her tongue into his mouth.

'Christ, Francine!'

He twisted his head to avoid her as a group of people came loudly out of the bar and along the street. One or two of the women giggled as they passed and a man shouted something.

'Who cares?' said Francine. 'Ignore them.'

'You're drunk,' said Stephen. His tone was milder now, and he ran a hand up and down her back. 'Come on, stop it.'

'Take me!' she shouted. Her voice echoed along the empty alley.

'*What?*'

Stephen began to laugh, but she planted herself against his

open mouth and suddenly he started to kiss her violently, grabbing her hair with his fist and pulling back her head. He tugged her blouse free of her skirt with his other hand and she had a dull consciousness of pain as his teeth bit into her lips.

'Is this what you want?' he said viciously in her ear, turning her and forcing her against a wall. Her head banged on the cold brick. She struggled against him with surprise but his body was a cage, pinning her where she stood.

'Stop it!' she said, writhing against his grip as terror penetrated her drunkenness. His breath gusted warmly in her face. 'Get off!'

As quickly as it had started the tumult stopped. The pressure of his weight fell from her, and seconds later, feeling the cold gather at her clothes, she realized he had gone. The sound of fading footsteps drifted to her ears and she turned her head to watch his dark back grow smaller as he disappeared. As if feeling her eyes, he raised his arm in a salute without turning around.

'Bye, Francine!' he called.

The sound of his laughter bounded back down the alley towards her and vanished. She heard the silence of the small street in the darkness, and beyond it the sound of cars passing, going somewhere far away. The wall at her back was cold and continuous. She tucked her blouse back into her skirt, drew her coat around her, and began to walk as elegantly as she was able towards the road.

Sixteen

Ralph left the Tube station and turned up Camden High Street towards home. The days were getting longer now – he could suddenly feel it, the almost imperceptibly slow arm wrestle, the gradual gain of light over dark – and the sky was still bright with the memory of sun as he walked towards the Lock. He passed the launderette and then the funeral parlour, behind whose tinted windows pale ruched curtains were lavishly bunched above a thick pink lawn of carpet, suffocating as a girl's bedroom. Inside, a middle-aged woman stood proprietorially at the glass, peering anxiously up and down the pavement like a waiter looking for customers at the door of an empty restaurant. He walked on, surprised to feel his lips stretching with a grin.

Tentatively, running nervous fingers over his feelings, prodding his situation again with a scientist's circumspection, he could admit that things hadn't been so bad today. Yesterday he had felt cast out, irretrievable, doomed to patrol the border of what he could endure, and it had come as a surprise to him to wake the next morning and realize that something, if only a day, now lay between him and his catastrophe. His sense of his own survival gave way as he walked to more expansive thoughts, a feeling of having been aroused from some long dormancy, the revivification which he recognized was the residue of pain. His life echoed now, empty, filled only with the potential for beginning it again. The idea lent some enchantment to the darkening street lit gold by a putative halo of street lamps, the friendly, sleeping faces of shops, the shy eyes of passers-by violet in the dusk, even the beating of his heels and the puff of his own breath! His body seemed suddenly rather miraculous to him, the ambulant parcel of himself: he was contained, all of him, in this machine bent only on doing his bidding, this vehicle in which he could travel wherever he chose. He wondered why he had never thought of his sufficiency before, for it liberated him to consider it, drew his muscles tight and ready beneath his skin. Remembering times when he had felt as if he were dragging his punctured form about after him, or were lying opened on a table with the world performing his dissection, he resolved to think of it more often.

He reached the Lock and walked briskly over, exchanging smiles with a man coming the other way. The man looked at his watch as he passed, and before Ralph could defend himself against it the thought had flown into his head that Francine must have left the office by now, and that from this moment he didn't know where she was. He felt a pain in his chest, a bristling of nerves beneath his skin while she moved darkly across his thoughts, the light in her belly bobbing as she walked. All day he had been rehearsing arguments against such moments, but when it came to using them he suddenly found himself unable to remember how they worked: he groped for their analgesic while misery grated back and forth at his heart like a saw. He strained to be home, directing his legs to go faster, imagining the rooms of his flat, his possessions homesick for him, his fridge offering itself to his hungry fingers. He saw himself watching television later, warm and alone, laughing at something funny, the telephone ringing perhaps. What was she doing now? Where was she going, with his stolen property? There in the street he shrugged, irritated, and let a sigh escape his lips. He had to stop indulging himself like that. It would spoil him, like a child, inflame his emotions. The baby had seemed so separate that night – so distinct that he had thought he could just break it off and keep it! – but now that it had receded back into the tangled ropes of her body, an inextricable, futile thing, he knew that he must sever himself or be dragged stomach down after it. He remembered his flashes of hallucination, saw again the terrible images he had harboured of harming her, until his head ached with them. He reached his turning and heard his heels clop loudly like hoofs in the sudden quiet of the small street. What would it have been like? Who would it have become? He had thought *that* before, hundreds of times already in only a couple of days. Of course, it was always himself he saw, never her; himself going through life again, except knowing the road now, with all that had been wrong put right. It dogged him like a little ghost, and he wondered if it always would, would walk beside him through all its ethereal ages. He checked himself again, walking faster now with the naked trees flying by him in a rush. If such a thing could live, it would only be as the product of his own invention. It was nothing, less than nothing, a loveless clot of bad blood, just something he had done, like other things, not a miracle but a mistake. It had the consistency of an idea, and he could refute it. He could choose, really, not to care about it at all, switch off feelings like lights in a house. He would have a bath and then cook dinner. He saw himself reading the paper while he ate.

Approaching his flat in the failing light a sudden prophetic fear passed over him, as if something were about to happen, and in the next moment he saw a figure standing outside his front door. He couldn't see her eyes but he knew from the erectness of her head that she had seen him. He slowed his steps while his thoughts, busy with the provision of sedatives, instead struggled to manufacture panic. What was she doing here? He was close enough now to see her face, and felt himself so simultaneously drawn and repelled that he stopped altogether, wondering if he could find another avenue which might carry him through what at that moment seemed impossible to bear.

'Don't worry,' she called out, seeing him halt. 'I only want to get my things.'

Her words were lobbed awkwardly towards him, and hearing them he knew that she had selected them before he had even arrived. He wondered what else she planned to say to him, and the thought made him want to grip her shoulders and shake her until it all fell clattering out of her mouth to the pavement.

'Oh.' He walked carefully past her to the door and took out his keys. His hands were trembling. 'Come in, then.'

In the stronger light of the hall he risked a glance at her as she came in behind him. Seeing her face he felt as if he had never been away from her, as if he had woken from a forgetful sleep and felt the memory of her drop like a weight through his empty spaces. It was a moment before he realized that she looked awful, quite unrecognizable, and it was in his mouth to ask her what was wrong before remembering that this was how things always began between them.

'I'll just let you get on with it, shall I?' he said, opening the inner door to his flat.

She didn't answer, but he saw with despair from the slight shrug of her shoulders that she still wanted to talk to him, to prise reactions from him like teeth. The gesture reminded him of his relation to her, her strange significance which was so surprisingly easy to forget when she was there before him. The pregnancy seemed not to be a part of her physical presence – if only he could see into her, look through her walls just once as if they were made of glass! – although now, noticing her curious deterioration, he wondered if this were its manifestation: something gnawing malignly at her insides, the proud extension of his own self, feeding, growing, planning its escape. Her face was deflated, the skin collapsed like a tent on the narrow ridges of her bones, and the hollows of her eyes were painted with shadows. He reminded himself that their poetry was a delusion, a limerick which he must not hear, and he turned away from her and walked into the sitting-room. Moments later he heard her in the bathroom, opening cabinets. He sat on the sofa, rigid with the tension of her presence. In a few minutes she would be gone. He desperately wanted a drink, but he knew he would not sustain his detachment if he made one. He would offer her one too, and she would jam her foot through the crack of his kindness and force herself in. He closed his eyes for a minute and when he opened them again she was there, standing in the doorway.

'That was quick,' he said stupidly, rubbing his eyes.

'There wasn't much.'

She watched him as a thick silence spread over the room. He looked down, unable to bear her gaze, while a polite impulse to make conversation fought in his chest.

'So that's it, then!' he burst out finally, meeting her eyes.

'Oh, I'll be gone soon,' she said acerbically, for once understanding him at the very moment in which he wished to be most opaque. 'I just wanted to tell you something I think you should know.'

'And what's that?'

He caught the split second of her hesitation, and knew suddenly that he had been wrong, that she hadn't even thought of what she was going to say until that moment.

'I'm going to keep the baby,' she said, throwing his gaze back at him defiantly. 'I've decided.'

Ralph found that he could not take his eyes from her,

although a fierce desire to pound his own head with his fists had gripped him. He felt the tide of confusion begin to rise again, the great gorge of their debris swilling on its surface, and he held his breath.

'Well?' she said. 'Don't you have anything to say?'

'No,' he said. His voice was a whimper and he put his head in his hands.

'Why not? You have to say *something*. I've said I'm going to keep the baby, and you—'

'What baby?' He heard the shout come from him, and then the slam of his hand on the coffee table. The room capsized in an angry blur. 'It's not a bloody baby, for God's sake! It's not a baby!' He wondered what sounds would fall from his lips if he ceased to restrain them with words, what grunts and howls and strange language. He felt an eruption at his eyes, his face growing messy. 'I don't *love* you, do you understand? I – I barely know you, I don't actually know who you are!' A drop of mirthless laughter spilled from his mouth. 'Please leave me alone. Do you hear? Leave me *alone*.'

He hadn't been looking at her but he sensed her suddenly come at him, and then felt the dark flaps of her coat baffling around his head. He realized to his astonishment that she was hitting him with her fists and he put out his arms to protect himself.

'How dare you?' she panted, drawing back. 'How dare you speak to me like that? I know about you!' Her voice hauled itself higher on a new rope of initiative. 'I know all about you!'

'What do you know?' he spat back, laughing. 'You don't know anything about me at all!'

'Yes I do!' she said triumphantly, folding her arms. 'I know what you are – you're a fake!' She waited, watching him, and when he didn't do anything she said it again. 'You're a fake!

You act all superior and high and mighty, but you're not, are you? Oh, I've found out everything!'

'What on earth are you talking about?' said Ralph.

He felt all at once calm again. He wondered if she had actually lost her mind, but then realized that he was merely seeing more clearly into it: its accumulation of junk, its piles of magazines from whose covers trapped, vacant beauties stared, its reels of bad films, its numbing hours of television; all these broken, abandoned versions of reality strangling her soil, clogging her consciousness. She lived beneath a dictatorship of nonsense; she imitated that which itself was only an imitation, and try as he might to search for her in this hall of mirrors, he would find time and again only comical, distorted reflections of himself. The worst of it was that, despite everything, he saw she had been capable of dragging him down with her; for every soft, silly thing she threw at him concealed a sharp rock of implication, the fact that he himself had chosen her.

'*What on earth are you talking about?*' Her voice sung with affected mimickry. 'Oh, very realistic. Is that what they taught you at your posh school, then?'

'I suppose so,' said Ralph gaily, suddenly finding the whole exchange hilarious.

'It's not how your parents talked, though, is it?'

'I shouldn't have thought so,' he replied, pausing with surprise. 'I don't really remember. Look, is that what this is all about? I hardly think it matters how my parents spoke.'

'You lied to me!' she shouted. Her fingers stiffened into fists and her face, hanging above him, was a lamp of anger. He saw that she was incensed, quite genuinely, and realized that she had expected him to be ashamed. 'All this time you've been looking down your nose at me, acting like I'm not good enough, and it's *me* who should feel sorry for *you*!'

'Why's that?' said Ralph. He felt peculiarly unmoved, and it surprised him to notice that his heart was thudding.

'Everyone feels sorry for you!' She waited, watching him until he met her eye before she delivered her meaning. 'Your father was a disgusting tramp and you came from a council house, and even your precious Stephen was only friends with you because he was forced to be!'

Something dropped through his centre like a pebble thrown down a well, a long, silent fall. He felt its faint impact down in the pit of himself.

'That's not true.' He sat back firmly on the sofa and folded his hands.

'Oh, yes it is! He told me so.' Her face was excited now. 'He told me it was his punishment, to be friends with you!'

'What *do* you mean?'

'He got into trouble,' said Francine victoriously. 'And the *master*' – she used the word carefully, and Ralph suddenly knew beyond doubt that she was telling the truth, that somehow Stephen had really told her these things – 'the master said that instead of being expelled he had to be friends with you, because nobody else wanted to. He said he wished he'd been expelled,' she finished matter-of-factly.

Ralph opened his mouth but found himself disarmed. The litany of Francine's voice assaulted him, hammering against his thoughts and then slotting in amongst them, into spaces he had not really known were there but which now he saw fitted them perfectly. He saw the matrix of truth, touched its cold, steely walls, and knew himself captured.

'He told me other things too, all sorts of interesting things about you. He took me out last night to a wine bar and we got drunk and talked about everything. I told him how bad you were to me and he said it wasn't surprising, considering your background, and I should just feel sorry for you, like he does. He says you're jealous of him because of Belinda, because she liked him more than she liked you. She was all over him, he said.' He heard her laugh. 'And you still go to the pub with him! It's pathetic, it really is. Just pathe—'

Ralph saw himself spring to his feet and put his hands about her throat, but it was only the warm shock of his skin meeting hers that told him it was real, that he was now committing an impossibility, a physical rebellion which demanded to occupy seconds and space and would change everything. Her neck was surprisingly thick, resilient with cords. He squeezed with his hands, frightened by the sudden silence and then amazed by it, and as he looked into her startled eyes his heart flew to his fingertips and for the first time he felt locked with her in an unutterable intimacy. For a moment she was still, long, glorious seconds of quiet in which he looked at the petrified face in his hands and knew himself completely, but then she struggled, clawing at him with rigid fingers, and he let her go. To his surprise she didn't recoil from him but stayed motionless where she was, the panting sound of her breath the only trace of what had happened. He waited for an aftermath, for something to flow into the vacuum of what he had done, but the room seemed just then to stand still with the evidence of his crime, and hers, the impossibility of retraction. He prayed for her to do something simple, cry perhaps, something which would retrieve them from this desolation where they were too far to be heard or rescued. Finally, she lifted a hand and touched her throat with her fingers, and he saw there the imprints of his own in a ghastly tattoo. His palms burned.

'I'm sorry about that,' he said, astonished at the familiar sound of his own voice, its politeness. 'I don't know what happened.'

To his surprise he saw her lips unfurl in a curious half-smile, and as her eyes grew excited again he realized that he hadn't changed anything at all, merely delayed the progress of a strange campaign by which he had long been surrounded.

'He did it to me too!' she said, the wing of a shriek flitting across her voice. For a moment he didn't understand her, but then his shame came back to him with redoubled force, dragging with it all the things she had said, the sound of her voice, the chasm into which he had for a moment frozen his fall. 'He pushed me against a wall and did it to me right there in the street! I asked him to!'

A cry crowded fluttering in his mouth and he let it escape, hearing its soft progress through silence. With a painful grinding of joints he finally felt himself turn away from everything he knew, from the ugly, familiar place where he had always been, and it was as if something else, a clear and frightening range of vertiginous truths, had been there, just behind him, all along. He saw the sweep of it in seconds, exhilarated and despairing, and felt a rush of knowledge pass through him. He had done wrong, a terrible, intractable wrong reached by a steep stairway of mistakes and failures, from whose top he could view all the things he should have done and realize only how far he was from them. His helplessness could not absolve him: he had failed to defend what was his as it floated alone in its troubled sea, had abandoned where he should have protected, had cast away his fragile creation and left it to cower at the drip of wine-toxic blood, the rooting jabs of a stranger, the unfriendly air in which he himself was betrayed and reviled.

'Poor thing,' he muttered, hardly knowing what he said. 'Poor little thing.'

'Oh, don't feel sorry for me!'

Their eyes met. Ralph endured the final, fatal collision of their differences and felt laughter jump in his throat. He saw Francine pick up her bag and he gasped, putting out a hand to stop her.

'Don't you touch me!' she shrieked, skipping from the compass of his arm.

'Please don't go, not yet.'

He fixed her with his eyes, trying to fill them with some as yet unspoken promise, some prize which might lure her back to him. For a moment he held her, but then the knowledge of his own emptiness leaked from him and her eyes grew bored and looked away. She turned and left the room with his voice still ringing in her absence as if it had been the signal of her liberation, and seconds later he heard her shut the door.

'Is that you?'

Ralph's voice was barely more than a whisper. Stephen's phone had rung for a long time, hundreds of rings, each one pounding like a hammer in his heart. Then finally there had been the click of someone picking it up, and now just the sound of breathing.

'Is that you?'

'Who's this?' barked Stephen suddenly. 'Speak up whoever you are or bugger off.'

'It's me. Ralph.'

'It's Ralphie! It's my old friend Ralph,' said Stephen, shouting as if to a room full of people. Ralph could hear static in the background and beyond that, nothing. Stephen was drunk, or stoned, or both, he could tell from his voice. 'This is a bit of a late night for you, old chap, isn't it? Rebelling at last?'

Ralph felt himself break again, a strange sensation of inner collapse, something giving beneath him like a rotten bridge and then the blurred velocity of falling. He had felt it several times in the hours since Francine had left.

'Still there?' Stephen tapped comically at the receiver.

'Yes.'

'What's up?'

Ralph waited, but nothing came. Now that he was here, claiming what was owed to him, his injury seemed fluid and ungraspable, impossible to lift from the mire which surrounded it and hold dripping above his head.

'You've – *wronged* me,' he said finally, and then instantly regretted it.

'I what? Speak up. Can't hear you.'

'You've wronged me.'

Stephen was silent for so long that Ralph felt himself begin to disappear. He heard a dry cough in the receiver, a clearing of the throat.

'Look, what's this all about? Are you pissed or something?'

'No.'

'You've gone a bit nuts, then, if you don't mind my saying so.'

'You've wronged me.'

'Yes, so you keep saying. Can't help you, I'm afraid.'

Ralph tried to speak and felt a terrible constriction at his throat. He thought of Francine's face above his hands, the face of a doll, her eyes empty as marbles.

'She told me,' he said, his voice strangled. 'Everything you said to her, she told me. I know everything.'

'Ah, *I* see,' said Stephen. His laugh rattled in Ralph's ear. 'Well, I wouldn't take it to heart if I were you. We were both a bit pissed, that's all.' He laughed again. 'My God, she was—'

'You told her things about me,' interrupted Ralph. The sound of his own voice excited him.

'Did I? Can't say I remember.'

'Private things. You told her private things.'

'Oh, for Christ's sake!'

He muttered something else which Ralph couldn't hear. He sounded distracted, as if he wanted to be off the telephone.

'All my life,' began Ralph; but then he stopped, unable to say something so portentous.

'What was that?'

'I said, all my life you've fucked me up.' He strained over the words, finding them hard and unnatural. 'All my life.'

'Nothing to do with me. Fucked yourself up. Pathetic bastard, that's your problem. Nobody forced you.'

Tears sprang to Ralph's eyes and he put a hand to his forehead.

'You've taken things from me!' he said desperately.

'Look, you only ever had one thing worth taking. She wasn't yours anyway. As for the other one, she wasn't worth the trouble it would have taken to shag her. Those are the facts. Now, why don't you just toddle off to bed and get off my bloody case?'

'She's pregnant!' burst out Ralph.

Stephen paused for a long time.

'Not by me, she's not,' he said finally. 'Anyway, you're well shot of her.'

Ralph felt himself smelted down to his hot, thudding heart, saw the room around him and dissolved into its walls, evaporated in its corners.

'And you,' he said.

'What?'

'I'm well shot of you.'

Ralph could hear the measure of his breathing, up and down.

'Oh. All right, then.'

'I don't want to see you again.'

'Righty-ho.'

'Do you understand?'

'Yes, yes, I think you've made yourself quite clear. Goodbye.'

The line went abruptly dead and Ralph replaced the

receiver. The silence around him was towering, enormous. He lay back on the sofa, stretching himself out so that he lay flat. Birmingham, Lancaster, Crewe. He closed his eyes and waited.

Seventeen

It was better than she'd expected, especially after the long, unnerving walk through a vast catacomb of cavernous, neon-lit corridors in which she had distinctly heard the dungeon sound of dripping, its echo ghostly behind her footsteps. On the way she had come across two or three berobed old women stranded in wheelchairs like spectral, crippled sentries at isolated outposts. She had followed signs to the clinic, pinned intermittently on walls down which green limous streaks ran like eccentric beards, and had finally arrived after what seemed like miles at a newer and more hospitable door made of wood and chrome. She pushed it and entered a hushed and carpeted enclave where telephones quietly chirped and potted plants proudly proclaimed the tiny region's luxurious independence. Its immediate resemblance to offices in which she had worked, or even the agency where she used to go to collect her cheques and receive news of her next assignment, at first soothed and then disturbed her. She instantly warmed to the superiority of her treatment, but remembering the collapsed and crumpled faces of the corridor's abandoned residents, their lumpy, useless forms rooted like unattended overflowing bins in concrete wastelands, she wondered at the severity of her own condition that it should elicit such reverence.

'What name is it, dear?'

She turned and saw a woman standing near her with a clipboard in her hand. She was wearing a white uniform, with a stiff white veil of the same material covering her head. For a moment she thought nervously that the woman was a nun, for the soft, coaching tone of her voice and her ready, pliant face seemed to anticipate tearful confessions.

'Francine Snaith.'

Francine moved closer to the woman as she said it, in an attempt at discretion. The woman had a plastic rectangle pinned to her breast with 'Nurse Rogers' written on it. She could now see the entire waiting-room from where she stood. Other stout, white figures moved soundlessly around a neat row of chairs on which six or seven young girls sat like novices. At one end of the room was a large glass window, behind which a man sat. The telephone rang and he answered it.

'How are you feeling, Francine?' said the nurse.

'I'm fine.'

'Any sickness?'

'No.'

'Good girl,' she said, nodding and writing something on her clipboard. 'Why don't you just pop over and have a word with John behind the window there, and then you can sit down with the other girls.'

Francine crossed the waiting-room. All of the girls looked up in unison as she passed and she glanced back at them. Their pale, worn faces were eager with recognition, as if urging some sense of community upon her, and she looked away. She stood at the glass and waited while John spoke on the telephone.

'Right,' he said, nodding. 'OK, that's fine.'

He was young, with dark ruffled hair and a lean face, and when he sensed Francine standing there he looked up, smiling, and raised a patient finger. She saw that he was handsome, and she felt a wrench of frustration at the disagreeable fact of her presence there, the undisguisable nature of its shame.

'Sorry about that,' he said cheerfully, putting down the telephone.

'It's OK,' said Francine softly.

'Name?'

'Francine.'

'Francine, Francine,' he muttered, looking down at a typed list. 'Francine Snaith, 110 Mill Lane, Kilburn, London. That you?'

'Yes.' She smiled.

'Well, Francine, we're running a bit late this morning, but you should be called in about half an hour. All right?'

'That's fine.'

Francine leaned on the counter, closer to the glass, and he looked up. An expression of surprise flitted across his face and he looked back down at his page.

'Let's see. Right, how will you be getting back to Kilburn?'

She hesitated, unprepared for his question and flattered by the concern it implied.

'I don't really know.' She wondered if he would offer to take her home himself.

'Oh. Well, we normally recommend that patients take a taxi home afterwards rather than public transport. Could you give me the name of the person who's coming to collect you?'

Francine was silent. A wave of nausea mounted in her stomach and hovered trembling.

'Nobody.'

He didn't say anything for a moment, his pen poised.

'What about your boyfriend?' he said finally, without looking up.

'I don't have one.'

'What about this name you gave to your doctor? Ralph Loman, is he not your boyfriend?'

'No.'

'Is there a friend you could call?'

'No.'

He raised his head slowly and looked directly into her eyes. His gaze was evaluating, calculating not her assets but her lack of them. She knew that he felt sorry for her. The small office in which he sat was bright and ordered. He raised a hand to his chin and she saw the mocking glitter of a wedding band on his finger.

'Nobody at all?' he said.

'No,' she said, hating him.

Janice had been meant to come, but that morning, when Francine had opened the door to her darkened bedroom, Janice had called out from beneath a mound of covers that she didn't feel like it. Her voice had been irritable, and the room had smelt thick and sour. The night before, the woman who owned the boutique where Janice worked had come to the flat and demanded to speak to her. Francine had heard her shouting behind the closed sitting-room door, her voice interspersed with Janice's indecipherable murmurs.

'You're lucky I've decided not to take this any further!' she had said several times, while Francine sat alone in the kitchen. Finally the door had flown open and the woman had marched past her without saying anything. When she had left, Francine had gone into the sitting-room. Janice was sitting on the sofa, smoking a cigarette.

'What's happened?'

'Silly cow gave me the sack,' said Janice, sucking in smoke. 'Silly bitch.'

Francine asked her why, but she wouldn't say.

'Doesn't matter,' she said. Her face was ugly, abandoned by expression like a room after a party. 'I'm not worried. I've got other sources.'

'I wish I did,' said Francine.

Her job at Lancing & Louche had finished a week ago. Lynne had been odd about it, her voice unfriendly on the telephone. When Francine went to the agency to collect her money the receptionist said that Lynne was in a meeting and gave her the cheque herself. She had called once or twice after that, but the receptionist had told her that there wasn't anything for her, and when Lynne finally called it was to say that she was very sorry but they were going to have to take her off their books.

'Do you?' said Janice, suddenly giving her a cool, appraising look; a look which reminded Francine of the looks men usually gave her. Janice looked at her for a long time. It made her nervous. 'I might be able to help you out,' she said finally, sending a long finger of smoke towards her.

'You'd better sit down,' said John. His manner was disengaged. 'One of the nurses will let you know when they're ready.'

Francine turned and saw that the other girls' eyes were still on her. Their gaze was unembarrassed, knowing. There was an empty chair at the end of their row, but she walked past it and sat on one opposite. Eventually their eyes dropped to their laps, except those of a girl with long red hair who sat directly across from Francine. She was staring at a point above Francine's head. She looked young, like a child. Francine saw that her face was filled with immediate terror, as if someone was about to attack her. She looked away abruptly, skirting along the row until her eyes fixed on a very fat girl slumped in a chair to her left. The girl's face was vast and pasty, the bumps of her features resembling the deformities of vegetables, sly potato eyes, a lumpy tuber nose. She sat miserably with her legs apart, her thighs melting over the sides of the chair like warm cheese. Francine stared at her, trying to imagine the coupling which had brought her here, the kisses on her doughy breasts. The thought repelled her.

She wondered how someone could have chosen that girl, selected her from others, and felt her own mysteries crumble and spoil.

'Miss Franklin?' called a nurse, coming into the waiting area.

The young red-haired girl shot to her feet and Francine was disconcerted to see that large, childish tears were rolling down her cheeks. An older woman whom Francine hadn't noticed stood up beside her and gently put an arm around her shoulders, whispering something in her ear. Her hair was red too, streaked with grey, and she realized to her amazement that the woman must be her mother. A gorge of jealousy rose to her mouth.

'Come on, love,' said the nurse softly, taking her by the hand. 'Don't worry, you'll be fine.'

The girl strained like an animal, resisting her hand, and for the first time Francine felt a bolt of fear fly through her. She gripped her bag, seeing herself quite clearly running from the room, her feet echoing down the empty corridors, out into the car park past impervious porters and sleeping ambulances, melting into the busy pavement along which waiting traffic throbbed. The singularity of her imprisonment erected its swift bars around her and she struggled against them as her thoughts reasoned her back into the room like diplomats. There was no escape from that which ticked like a bomb inside her, that which her enemies had implanted and she was entrusting those around her to remove. She calmed herself with thoughts of the purge which would free her, the gratifying image of Ralph, Stephen, the hungry blockage in her belly, the confusing maelstrom of her past, all of it sucked mechanically from her, leaving her new and gleaming, a vacuum to be filled with delightful, unknown things. She had been told it wouldn't hurt. It didn't matter anyway. Her body felt heavy and used, sluggish with nausea and mistakes. She almost looked forward to its cleansing. Afterwards she would begin again.

A nurse walked past her, her uniform efficient and trust-worthy. It wasn't that bad here, after all. She had wanted a private clinic, of course, but she hadn't had the money and she couldn't have asked Ralph. It would have spoiled her plan of telephoning him afterwards to tell him what she had done. She thought of telling him she had gone to a private clinic and making him pay her back. It was the least he could do. She needed money. Anxiety closed around her as she thought of the rent, counting weeks with a beating heart. She hardly had enough to last her until the weekend. She had to get another job. Lynne wouldn't give her a reference, she'd said as much. Personnel had lodged a complaint. Francine was too unrelia-ble these days, and she had her own reputation to consider. There was something else, Janice's offer, waiting darkly like a stranger at the door. It made her uncomfortable and she shied from it dimly. She would think about it later. As she shrank from it, it caught her in its ropes and reeled her back, insinuating itself, not discouraged by her firm rejection. Her thoughts were relenting to its persuasions. What else did she have? It might take her weeks to find a job, and then another week's delay until she was paid. It would only be for a while, a temporary thing, just until she sorted herself out. It was easy, Janice said it was. It wasn't how you would think. You didn't have to do anything if you didn't want to. She knew people, she said, people who would really appreciate Francine. She had laughed at how shocked she was.

'How else do you think I could afford this?' she had said, raising her glass to Francine and gesturing at the room.

The door to the waiting-room opened and a man in a bomber jacket came in. He stopped, looking around.

'Over 'ere, Ian,' said the fat girl.

He grinned, and Francine watched him hesitantly cross the

room, his hands stuffed in his pockets. The other girls shifted up the row to make room for him and he sat down, putting his arm around the fat girl's shoulders.

'All right?' he said, his face close to hers.

'Yeah,' she said, patting his knee.

The girls were watching them with silent interest.

'Couldn't get off earlier. Barry didn't turn up for his shift till ten past. Bugger was out on the piss last night.'

'Was he?' The girl laughed, her mouth forcing up mountains of flesh on her cheeks. 'That's typical, that is.'

'Miss Snaith?' The nurse arrived again with her clipboard. 'Is Miss Snaith here?'

Francine froze for a minute and then stood up.

'Right, dear, come along with me.'

She led Francine through a swinging door at the other end of the room. Beyond it was a long white ward with military rows of beds along its walls. In one of them, the young girl lay immobile, her red hair streaming like blood across the pillows. Her mother sat beside her, reading a book.

'I didn't know I'd have to go to bed,' said Francine, panic beginning to struggle in her again at the sight of the ward.

'Oh, it's not for long,' said the nurse. 'We've just got to give you a tiny injection, and afterwards you'll want time to wake up. Just slip your clothes off for me now behind this curtain. There's a robe hanging beside the bed.'

She manoeuvred Francine into a cubicle and then drew a flowered curtain briskly around her. Francine took off her jacket. She had only been in hospital once before, for her appendix, when she was a child. She remembered her mother stroking her forehead, her father nervous at the foot of the bed, jumping out of the doctor's way. A sharp consciousness of her loneliness pricked her, and then she felt something else, something heavier. She wished Janice had come, saw her huddled beneath the bedclothes, her voice angry. The thought of not liking Janice made her panic. She needed her. She had said they would do it together. Quickly she took off the rest of her clothes and was surprised by the sight of her body in the white light. It looked mottled and bumpy with gooseflesh, and the purple tunnels of her veins seemed alarmingly close to the skin. She saw the spread of her hips, the pouch of her stomach, and realized that she had put on weight.

'Knock, knock!' said the nurse brightly, fiddling with the curtain. 'Can I come in?'

'Yes,' said Francine, putting on the white cotton robe. It came down to her knees and fastened at the back. It looked like something a prisoner might wear, or a patient in a mental hospital.

'All right? Just pop yourself on the bed.'

The nurse waited until Francine had clumsily mounted the bed and then sat down beside her. She was middle-aged, her face a creased history of smiles.

'Am I right in thinking you haven't anyone coming to collect you?' she said, leaning forward confidentially.

'Yes.'

'The father couldn't come?'

For a moment Francine couldn't think of who she was talking about, and then realized it was Ralph.

'He doesn't know I'm here.'

The words crystallized something in her, a sudden crust forming around her tenderness and then covering it completely. She felt herself harden and glimpsed a person she could be.

'I see.' The nurse was impassive, looking at her clipboard. 'And what arrangements have you made for getting home?'

'I'll take the bus.'

'We usually recommend a taxi for afterwards, dear, just in case you're not feeling too well. I can arrange one for you if you like.'

'I don't have enough money.'

The nurse turned a face full of sympathy towards her and Francine met her eyes, repelling the humiliation she offered. She looked surprised and drew her eyebrows together in an irritated, despairing point.

'Right, well it's up to you, of course. We did send you these details, and it's up to you if you ignore our advice. It's your decision.' She stood up. 'The doctor will be with you in a minute.'

The ceiling was rushing over her, its long, luminous tubes speeding and then flashing past as if she were flying. A pair of doors appeared ahead and she narrowed her eyes as the trolley shot towards their grim, closed lips with uncontainable velocity. They flew open just in time, like a fairground ride, and her limp body, warm beneath its blanket, swept through.

'There in a minute, love,' said a man's voice above her.

She wanted it never to end, their fantastical journey, the trundling excitement of motion, the trolley to which she was strapped and secured, tiny now, her thoughts a bowl of bliss. She might stay here for ever, injected and looked after, rushed from place to place in her snug bed by green-clad men with kind faces. She closed her eyes, her body melting with the vibration of wheels, and when the vibration stopped she opened them again. She was in a room where everything was still. A crowd of people stood above her, their faces a ring of masked moons.

'All right, Francine,' said a woman's voice. She couldn't tell which face it was that spoke. 'We're just going to put you to sleep now.'

Someone clasped her fingers. One of the faces leaned towards her, a man's face, his eyes large and frightening as an owl's above his mask.

'Ralph?'

'Don't struggle now, Francine. We're just putting something in your hand.'

She felt a pressure on the back of her hand and seconds later pain filtered through the warm mist of her body. A dark tide of fear lapped at her and suddenly she was alone at its shore. She was alone. Where had everybody gone?

'Francine?'

Everything would be all right. It would only be temporary, just for a while. There was nothing to worry about. Her cheeks were wet. Was she crying? Why was she crying?

'Can you count to ten for us, Francine? See if you can count.'

Something unfurled, beat against her lazy walls. A flash of terror mired. Too late.

'Francine? Come on, one, two—'

'One . . . two . . .'

Ralph's face, a bitter taste on the tongue of the ravenous dark.

Eighteen

Ralph left the Tube station and turned towards home, swinging his jacket over his shoulder so that it hung from the peg of his finger down his back. The evening was as light and warm as an afternoon, holiday weather, and the joyful consciousness of summer burst in on him suddenly like a revelling crowd and swept him up in its ebullience. He had experienced several such explosions of silent happiness lately, without ever growing accustomed to the mute flash of their radiance. He would feel each glittering bloom with wonder, fearing that it would be the last; but they were delicate, responsive things, and could be triggered merely by a thought or the lightest survey of his circumstances. He would only have to look at his desk, for example, the sleek telephone crouching in service, the console dignified as a butler, the friendly scatter of pens or the brimming boat of his tray, to feel warm with good fortune; and a broader glance at the pensive, lovely faces of his colleagues – Mark, Richard, and Angela, whose desks formed a firm, efficient platform with his own – their mouths sweet and unconscious with concentration but ready to erupt into laughter at the slightest shared hilarity, would almost stupefy him with pleasure.

His briefcase was heavy in his hand, but he swung its pendulum back and forth in ungrudging appreciation of its weightiness. He had brought some work home with him from the office, although he wouldn't have time to do very much before the party. He liked to have it with him, in any case, to feel the daily accretion of his importance, the newly dense portion of his responsibility. When he had first started his job, he had felt such disbelief in the evenings away from it that he had begun to bring his briefcase home merely as proof to stay the dreamlike recession of his days. By the time his position fitted him, so comfortably that he could hardly remember its first stiffness, he had realized that working at home immersed him more deeply in the themes of the office, meaning that his grasp of them the next day was rather better than that of Mark and the others, and he made the furtive, regular execution of it a policy. He had been singled out for praise once or twice and felt his appetite for success increase.

The sun began its downward cant over the High Street and he forced briskness upon himself as he moved through the golden haze of its benediction, not wanting to be the grateful witness of beauty but its rightful and slightly indifferent recipient. He would walk to the party later. It was at Angela's house – not far from where he lived, he had been gratified to discover, her sophisticated proximity sanctioning his own choice of the area anew – and quite a few people from the office had said they would be there. There would be other people too, of course, people he didn't know. He waited for the habitual tremor of anxiety at the thought of their unfamiliarity, their slick, bored faces before him, but it didn't come. Instead, he saw himself saying that he worked in television, with Angela actually, and watched their expressions flower with admiration and envy, or perhaps relax in a more companionable recognition as aloofness was dispelled. He wondered if he would ever tire of it, this fantastical self he could produce from his pocket like a jewel to murmurs of appreciation. It still amazed him to think of how completely, how magically, he had been transformed, plucked from his ignominy by a strong celestial hand, removed from everything he now realized he had hated and given what he now realized he had longed for, as if it was a gift!

He had been lucky, of course, but what astonished him now was to remember how little he had cared about it at the time. He had seen the job advertised in a newspaper and had forlornly applied, his sense of the need to change himself dutiful and fatigued. Swept through each stage of the process, a fateful, almost comical languor had gradually come over him. He had thought of nothing, had formulated no dizzy or concrete hopes, but a strange intuition had tugged him on as if by an invisible thread until he knew that this chance was to be his, that it was being pressed upon him as if by ordination. He had not been surprised when he got the job, and its marvellous result had only dawned on him later, rising up from the darkness of his suppressions and urging him towards belief. What did surprise him was how quickly it had replaced everything that had gone before it. Within days of his succession, the banishment of his past was so complete that he hardly knew himself. He was once more in his bright infancy, the howling spectres of experience purged. Fearfully inspecting his nascent self, he saw that all his cords were cut, and for a while his severance terrified him. Nothing that had made him remained. Once familiar faces became fragments of nightmares, old feelings the faintest of memories for which he could not now find words. He was still wary of his darkness, wondering if one day he might turn a corner or open a door and topple again into its swirling chasm. Occasionally he had felt a frantic, amnesiac urge to summon up purposefully the things which he knew, rather than felt, had once mattered, but as he dug, poised for sorrow, at the withered tentacles of his roots, he could find no life in them. Even there, the fleshy, sturdy stubs of his new existence already held him. The joy of it came to him tentatively, but eventually he accepted its truth. He lived and breathed independently.

He crossed the lock, his swift steps bringing him abruptly up over the blind of its rise behind someone walking ahead of him along the pavement. He had been going too quickly, jogging more or less, and he reined himself back to avert a collision. For a moment the figure was only vaguely in his sights as he adjusted his speed to accommodate it, but then something came to him too late in a terrible flash, a recognition of a present danger, and in the next minute he saw her. Her ambulant back reared up before his eyes, the metallic sheet of hair swaying above a tall and angular form, her purposeful, predatory stride. Panic bolted from him as if at a gunshot. The girl slowed, sensing him behind her. Any second now she would turn around. A tumult of old fears roared like trains through the junction of his thoughts, and he swerved abruptly off the pavement and on to the side of the road, still walking, unable to stop, as if he were caught in the web of a magnetic field. A speeding car passed within inches of him. In the instant before the angry shriek of its horn he closed his eyes and when it came he felt his legs grow numb beneath him. At the periphery of his vision he saw her head snap round and in that moment an invisible path opened up for him across the road. He flung himself towards it with a thudding, thankful heart, his senses wild and alert. Her eyes burned at his back. He reached the other side, panting, and drove on up the pavement with his head clamped straight in a rigid vice of will. He mustn't look back, he mustn't. He sensed her moving parallel with him across the road like a shadow. His turning was up ahead, only a minute's walk away. A second later something broke and he couldn't stop himself from glancing over his shoulder. She was walking fast, her face trained on him like the barrel of a gun. He was almost there now. His feet pounded the pavement like flagging horses. He heard a shout from behind and when he looked around she was cutting across the road towards him. She glittered like a blade in the melting air. He began to run.

Also by Rachel Cusk

ff

Saving Agnes

Agnes Day – sub-editor, suburbanite, failure extraordinaire – is unwell. Terminally middle-class, incurably romantic and chronically confused by life's most basic interactions, Agnes discovers disconcerting gaps in her general understanding of the world, making recovery unlikely. Life and love go on without her, but with a little façade, she can pass herself off as a success. Beneath the fiction, however, the burden of truth becomes harder to bear.

'Sceptical, ironic, beautifully resonant prose . . . a splendid novel.' *Guardian*

'She is a writer with a poet's eye for convincing detail, and touches on the raw emotions of life in a way that is affecting and true.' *Sunday Telegraph*

'Told with irony and insight and some surreally beautiful imagery. At times it made me laugh out loud.' Shena Mackay

ff

The Country Life

Stella Benson sets off for Hilltop, a tiny Sussex village where she has taken the role of au pair for the Maddens' irascible son Martin. Her hopes for this larger-than-life family may be high, but her station among them is undeniably low. What could possibly have driven her to leave her home, job and life in London for such rural ignominy? Why has she severed all contact with her parents? Why is she so reluctant to talk about her past? *The Country Life* is a rich and subtle novel about embarrassment, awkwardness and being alone; about families, or the lack of them; and about love in some peculiar guises.

'Funny and poignant . . . a pleasure to read.' *Sunday Telegraph*

'Like the novels of Evelyn Waugh or Stella Gibbons, *The Country Life* has a moral core, meticulously disguised by comedy. Cusk is a highly interesting, original writer and more unusually she is a joy to read.' Helen Dunmore, *The Times*

'This book is a delight . . . *The Country Life* is remarkable for two things; its humour and its menace . . . Its mixture of P.G. Wodehouse, *Cold Comfort Farm* and Jane Austen is a pleasure to read.' Tibor Fischer, *Sunday Express*